MAHU MEN

Mysterious and Erotic Stories

NEIL S. PLAKCY

mlrpress

MLR Press Authors

Featuring a roll call of some of the best writers of gay erotica and mysteries today!

M. Jules Aedin	Drewey Wayne Gunn
Maura Anderson	Samantha Kane
Victor J. Banis	Kiernan Kelly
Jeanne Barrack	J.L. Langley
Laura Baumbach	Josh Lanyon
Alex Beecroft	Clare London
Sarah Black	William Maltese
Ally Blue	Gary Martine
J.P. Bowie	Z.A. Maxfield
Michael Breyette	Patric Michael
P..A. Brown	Jet Mykles
Brenda Bryce	Willa Okati
Jade Buchanan	L. Picaro
James Buchanan	Neil Plakcy
Charlie Cochrane	Jordan Castillo Price
Gary Cramer	Luisa Prieto
Kirby Crow	Rick R. Reed
Dick D.	A.M. Riley
Ethan Day	George Seaton
Jason Edding	Jardonn Smith
Angela Fiddler	Caro Soles
Dakota Flint	JoAnne Soper-Cook
S.J. Frost	Richard Stevenson
Kimberly Gardner	Clare Thompson
Storm Grant	Lex Valentine
Amber Green	Stevie Woods
LB Gregg	

Check out titles, both available and forthcoming, at
www.mlrpress.com

MAHU MEN

Mysterious and Erotic Stories

NEIL S. PLAKCY

mlrpress

Copyright 2010 by Neil Plakcy

Published by
MLR Press, LLC
3052 Gaines Waterport Rd.
Albion, NY 14411

Visit ManLoveRomance Press, LLC on the Internet:
www.mlrpress.com

Cover Art by Deana Jamroz
Editing by Kris Jacen
Printed in the United States of America.

ISBN# 978-1-60820-129-7

First Edition 2010

To Marc, as always — You are my true companion.

Kimo has been helped along the way by many people, including Angela Faith Brown, Anthony Bidulka, Chris Kling, Cindy Chow, Dan Jaffe, Deborah Turrell Atkinson, Eliot Hess and Lois Whitman, Fred Searcy, Greg Herren, Jim Born, Jim Hall, Joe DeMarco, Joe Pittman, John Dufresne, John Spero, Les Standiford, Mike Jastrzebski, Neil Crabtree, Pat Brown, PJ Nunn, Shane Allison, Stacy Alesi, Steve Berman, Steve Greenberg, Richard Curtis, Jay Quinn, Vicki Hendricks, Ware Cornell, and Wayne Gunn.

Some of these stories have been previously published:

"Kelly Green" and "The Price of Salt" have been available through the Amazon Shorts Program. "The Sun God and the Boy He Loved" is also available through Amazon, under the title "All The Beautiful Boys."

"Christmas in Honolulu" took second place in a "Bad Santa" contest at *Mysterical-E*, and then was reprinted in *By The Chimney With Care*.

"Island Ball" was originally printed in *Fast Balls*.

The title of the story "The Price of Salt" is a small homage to Patricia Highsmith, who wrote a lesbian novel by that name.

I first began writing about Honolulu homicide detective Kimo Kanapa'aka in 1992, after my first visit to Hawai'i. His first appearance, in very different form, was in a failed book called *Death in Waikīkī* — a generic title for what was shaping up to be a generic book, about a beach boy private eye who was a former cop.

Part of the credit for Kimo's transformation into the man featured in these stories goes to James W. Hall, who was my MFA thesis advisor at Florida International University. I'd already graduated from FIU and was attending a workshop in Seaside, Florida, where Jim read 40 pages of *Death in Waikīkī*. When we sat down together to go over his comments, his first question was "How much of this have you written?"

When I told him I'd written about 200 pages, his face fell. That's never a good sign. "Why did Kimo leave the police force?" he asked.

I was stumped. I'd made Kimo a former cop just because I thought a lot of private eyes had that background, and I had only the vaguest idea of why he'd left—an inability to work with authority. Jim told me that wasn't good enough.

Disappointed, I went back home and shelved the project. It wasn't until a few years later, as I was going through my own coming out process, that I started thinking about a book in which a cop just experimenting with being gay found a body outside a gay bar, and that forced him to confront his sexuality.

I realized that my cop could be Kimo, my Hawaiian private eye—but that I'd first have to write the book in which Kimo went through the controversy that arose after he found that body, and had to admit where he'd been.

By the time I finished the revised *Death in Waikīkī*, Kimo told me that the character I'd created wasn't the kind of guy who'd quit in the face of a challenge, and that as far as he was concerned, he was staying on the force.

There was something about Kimo that continued to fascinate me, even after I'd finished the book. I wanted to know what happened to him. But I wasn't willing to commit to writing another novel when there was no guarantee that the first book would be published. So I started writing short stories about him.

I'd written three or four by the time I began working with a literary agent, who thought that the book's title should be changed to something less generic. He suggested *Mahu*, a derogatory term for gay in Hawaiian, because it was an interesting and unique word, and I went along with him. Since then I've had a lot of opportunity to research that term, and I hope that by using it in my titles I'm helping to take the sting out of it and reclaim the power behind it.

Once *Mahu* was represented, I thought it was sure to be published, and that my job was to write the next book, so that a publisher would see that Kimo was the kind of guy who could carry a mystery series. At the time, the big news out of Hawai'i was the movement to legalize gay marriage, so I decided that would be the centerpiece of my new plot.

That book began its life with the title *Noho Mahu*. In the Hawaiian language, the term for marriage has both male and female versions. *Noho kāne* means to marry a man; *noho wahine* means to marry a woman. So I coined my own phrase, *noho māhū*. Eventually, though, I decided that was a little too obscure for a title, and I switched to *Mahu Marriage*.

By 2002, both books were still unpublished, but it was looking like Haworth Press might buy *Mahu*, and I was energized to revisit Kimo and his world. Because of a quirk in the calendar for the college where I worked, I had nearly five weeks off at Christmas, between final exam week and the holidays, so I thought I'd write another Kimo story.

I liked the idea that Kimo's first assignment at his new department would be an undercover operation, where he'd revisit his surfing past on the North Shore. He wouldn't be able to tell anyone that he'd returned to the force, though, to enable him to penetrate the surfer world there, and that put him in the interesting position of having to lie to friends and family, just as he'd begun telling the truth about his life.

It was such an interesting idea, though, that it grew from a short story into a novel. Along the way, I began to understand more about what makes a story idea versus a novel idea. In a story, the action is confined to the characters involved in the plot—the victim, the suspects, and a bit of Kimo himself. In a novel, the plot begins to expand to involve Kimo's family and friends, and the action grows too complicated for the short story format.

So I was stuck with a third novel, *Mahu Surfer*, one which had to come between the two I'd written. Fortunately, the short time frame between *Mahu* and *Mahu Surfer* (about two weeks), and the location on the North Shore, meant that there wasn't much I had to do with the third book to make sure that everything fit.

There isn't much room for Kimo's sexual experimentation in the novels; they are primarily mysteries. So I began writing erotica about Kimo, too. I think that sex is an important part of Kimo's growth as a character and as a gay man, and I enjoyed the chance to show him in a variety of different situations.

I kept on writing these stories, publishing them in a variety of places, as *Mahu* and *Mahu Surfer* came out. I started thinking about a collection of these stories around the time that Alyson Books published the third book in the series, renamed *Mahu Fire* (because my editor didn't think *Mahu Marriage* was a dangerous enough title for a mystery. I had a feeling that was because he'd never been married.)

The first of the stories begins shortly after the events of *Mahu Surfer*, when Kimo has returned to Honolulu to full–time work as a homicide detective in Honolulu's District One, which encompasses downtown Honolulu and a few of its suburbs. Because of his position as the department's only openly gay detective, he occasionally gets the chance to range outside those boundaries.

These early stories take him through about four or five months when he's just beginning to get comfortable with his sexuality—encounters with the general public, as well as some sexual experimentation. Shortly after "The Cane Fields," in which Kimo investigates the disappearance of a man who has been living with his life partner, he gets the chance for a partner of his own, in *Mahu Fire*.

"The Sun God and the Boy He Loved" is the first story after Kimo and Mike meet. It grew out of a few days at the Key West Literary Seminar in 1997, which that year focused on "Literature in the Age of AIDS." It was a fascinating event, and I heard one lecture about gay elements in Greek myth, particularly in the story of Apollo and Hyacinthus, a beautiful boy he loved who was killed by a discus thrown by Apollo.

What an interesting metaphor, I thought, for a character who has been infected with the HIV virus by a lover. I used the names Paul and Hy for the characters—and Paul drives a van for a company called Sun Tours.

Kimo and Mike are still together for the action of "The Whole Ten Million." But Kimo is so well–known in the gay community that it's tough for Mike, who prefers to remain closeted. Since this is the first meaningful relationship for both of them, they have intimacy issues, too, and they break up after dating for about six months.

The break up sends Kimo into a spiral of sexual activity—as represented in the erotica here. During the year that follows, Kimo experiments with different kinds of sex, and solves a bunch of mysteries. The last story here, "Mahu Men" takes place a few months before the novel *Mahu Vice*, where Mike and Kimo are able to try again for a happy ending.

There are a few more stories between "Mahu Men" and *Mahu Vice*, as well as some that take place after that novel, including one that explains what happened to Jimmy Ah Wong, the teenaged boy with the blond Mohawk who makes his first appearance in *Mahu*. But they'll have to wait for another collection—along with more stories I hope to write about Kimo, as he and Mike, and the friends and family who surround and support them, continue their journey in the Aloha State.

I've tried to be correct when it comes to the use of two pieces of punctuation in Hawaiian—the okina and the kahako. The okina is a backwards apostrophe, read as a glottal stop (a pause between two vowels.) The macron is a line over vowels which indicates more stress.

The word māhū, for example, is properly written with a kahako over the ā and the ū. In the book titles, though, I don't use them, because my original publishers felt it would make the books harder to find through computerized searches. It's my understanding that the word would be pronounced maaah–huuu in that way. Kimo's last name, Kanapaʻaka, has an okina in it, indicating a pause between those two a's, rather than eliding them together.

I have tried my best to ensure that I've spelled Hawaiian words and names correctly, and apologize for any unintentional errors. I've learned a great deal about Hawaiʻi through writing these books, and hope to keep doing so for a long time.

I Know What You Did

Dark clouds were massing over Tantalus as I responded to the discovery of a murder victim at the Vybe, a gay club on University Avenue in the Moʻiliʻili neighborhood of Honolulu, near the Mānoa campus of the University of Hawaiʻi. But it was sunny on the H1 highway, and I wasn't worried that rain would damage the crime scene. Our island is composed of microclimates, and if you don't like the weather where you are, just drive a few minutes away. It will change.

What does not change is that people commit murders. I am a homicide detective, and that means there will always be a job for me. A few months before, after six years on the force, I came out of the closet, the first openly gay police detective in Honolulu. I'd been to the Vybe before, for the Sunday afternoon tea dance. My friend Gunter liked the Vybe's outdoor patio area, which had a good dance floor, a couple of bars and a stage. If I hadn't been on duty, I might have been at the club myself, dancing and having a good time.

When I pulled up across from the club, I spoke to the first cop on the scene, a middle-aged Chinese guy named Frank Sit. We shook hands, and then he nodded toward the corpse. "911 got an anonymous call, reporting a man injured in the parking lot here."

Sit had already cordoned off the immediate area around the body, and called for backup to help us conduct a search. "Looks like a bashing," he said. "Poor guy was coming out of the bar, and somebody came along and started whaling on him."

I kneeled down to examine the body. He was a *haole*, or white male, in his early thirties, lying face down on the ground. He had been beaten extensively around the head and upper body. Head wounds are often big bleeders, and this case was no exception. Blood had pooled around the man's head, running in a single stream down toward the curb. His skull had been fractured, but there was no brain matter exposed, a small favor for which I was grateful.

I took a couple of pictures with my digital camera, memorializing the scene and the way the body had been found. Then I stepped aside to let the medical examiner's guys do their work.

Four uniforms showed up to help search the immediate area for the weapon. "Look for any kind of blunt object, or anything that looks like blood drippings. We can get the crime scene techs to spray with luminol if we can't find anything else."

They walked off, and I looked toward the small crowd of men in short shorts and tank tops who clustered just beyond the crime scene tape, speaking in low tones to each other. Most of them were in their early twenties, probably students at UH.

It was just after six, and the tropical sun was turning the sky orange as it began its descent over Sand Island and the Ke'ehi Lagoon. The air was heavy with humidity, exhaust from the highway, and the faint scent of plumeria blossoms coming from a discarded lei on the ground nearby.

"My name is Kimo Kanapa'aka, and I'm a homicide detective," I said, to the crowd at large. "I assure you I'm going to do everything possible to find out what happened here this evening." I pulled out my pad and pen. "Any of you know the victim?"

A muscular guy in his late thirties, with a brush cut and combat boots, said, "I danced with him but I never got his name."

A slim Japanese guy said, "His name was Jimmy. He was here every Sunday."

I worked my way through the crowd, one by one. No one could recall any incidents involving the victim, no one claimed to know him well, and nobody remembered seeing him leave. The crowd had been sparse at the tea dance, and the rest of the businesses in the area were closed on Sunday evening, so no one had seen anything outside.

By then, the medical examiner was finished with the body, and I pulled on a pair of plastic gloves and knelt down. I carefully turned the body over. The victim was wearing a silver chain with a St. Christopher's medal on it, and a couple of silver rings. One of them was in the shape of a snake, wrapping around his right index finger. I found his wallet in his front pocket and extracted it.

There was $18 still in it, along with his identification: James Fremantle, 31, a Waikīkī resident. So his assault wasn't a robbery, which lent more credence to the idea of a gay bashing. Since I had come out, I'd started paying closer attention to crimes against gay men and lesbians, and I'd noted that gay bashings were on the rise—just a few days before, a couple of teenagers from Aiea had been caught in Waikīkī, punching a gay man who they said had made advances toward them, and that was by no means an isolated incident.

I stood up and told the ME's team that they could take the body away. Then I walked inside the Vybe. It was decorated in Pan–Asian neon, all paper umbrellas, earthenware ashtrays embossed with ideographs, and electric signs like those in Tokyo's Ginza.

The bartender, a blonde woman with a bouffant, told me Fremantle was a regular, and that afternoon she had served him a couple of Cosmopolitans. Her name was Peg, and she'd been working at the tea dance since opening. Fremantle wasn't one of the first to arrive, but she knew he'd been there at least two hours.

Within about fifteen minutes, I'd spoken to anyone who had anything to contribute, and I walked back outside. Sit called me over; he had found a bloody baseball bat in a dumpster down the alley from the club.

The bat was brand–new, and though I couldn't see any fingerprints, there were several smudges in the blood consistent with a perpetrator who used plastic gloves. "Something here doesn't seem right," I said to Frank. "The new bat, the gloves. That sounds like premeditation."

"Bashing's an impulse crime, in my experience," he said.

"Mine, too." Usually a bunch of guys got liquored up and went out looking for trouble. Sometimes they found prostitutes, and sometimes they got into traffic accidents or other minor scrapes. And sometimes they found some innocent gay guy, by himself or with a friend, and they used their fists and whatever debris they found handy. Buying a new baseball bat and a pair of gloves didn't fit.

I spread some newspapers on the floor of my truck and gingerly placed the bat there. The last thing you want to do with something that's wet and bloody is put it into a plastic bag and seal it up, particularly in a hot, humid climate like ours. You do that, and very soon you get bacterial growth that wipes out any DNA evidence.

Then Sit and I walked the parking lot, looking at the position of the building, the cars, the street light. "At this point, I don't want to assume that Fremantle was the victim," I said. "We don't know if the killer targeted him, or he was just at the wrong place at the wrong time."

I looked around. "If Fremantle *was* a target, then the killer needed a place he could stay out of sight, but with a good view to who came out of the club."

The Vybe fronted on University, with an alley on one side. Across the alley was the back door of a photocopy place where no one would notice you, and yet you'd have a clear line of sight. Sit and I searched the immediate area around the back door, finding a couple of fresh Juicy Fruit gum wrappers, which I placed in an evidence bag.

It was dark by then. I pulled out my cell phone and got Fremantle's number from directory assistance. When I called, I discovered he had a roommate, who said he'd be home for the next hour.

Waikīkī is gay headquarters for Honolulu and the island of Oʻahu. Most of the gay bars are there, and the hotels and stores cater to gay tourists. I lived there, along with lots of other gay men, particularly those who have been in the islands only a few years, and who work in some kind of service industry. Waiters, store clerks, personal trainers and hotel employees live two, three or four to an apartment in the towers and rundown low–rises between Ala Moana and the Ala Wai canal. More affluent or educated gay people, such as businessmen, teachers and so on, tend to live a little farther out in the suburbs, but they still come to Waikīkī for a social life.

Fremantle had lived in a high rise on Kalākaua, about two blocks from its intersection with Ala Moana. From my days as a detective in Waikīkī, I knew that the area was busy, noisy, and moderately unsafe. There were drug deals regularly at the convenience store, and the tricky confluence of streets made for a lot of minor traffic accidents. I had trouble finding a parking spot and ended up walking four blocks.

When he answered the door, Fremantle's roommate wore only a pair of white Calvin Klein briefs. He was a queeny boy in his early twenties, with pouffed up blonde hair that came to a stylized point above his forehead. He was waifishly thin, but his arms and legs were muscular.

"You're the gay cop!" he said, when he saw me. "Oh, darling, I'm so excited." Before I could react, he leaned forward and kissed me on the lips. His breath tasted sweet and somehow familiar. "Oh, now I can say I kissed the gay cop!" He danced backwards a little, leading me into a living room furnished with Salvation Army castoffs. Dirty clothes littered the tattered sofa, and were strewn over the no–color carpet and a couple of dubious–looking chairs. A big old TV squatted in one corner, one of the talk show hosts encouraging some poor soul to bare his problems.

The boy, whose name was Larry Wollinsky, sprawled on the sofa, knocking a jumble of shorts and T–shirts to the floor. "Come sit by me," he said, patting a place on the sofa next to him. "I'm just crushed by all this, you know."

I sat in an armchair across from him, and he pouted. "Tell me about James Fremantle," I said. "Was he your lover?"

Larry laughed. "Jimmy? My God, no. Although," he leaned forward, "there was this one time, after a volleyball game at Queen's Surf, when we were both so horny. I mean, you know what that's like, you just have to do something about it. But no, we were just roommates."

Queen's Surf was the gay beach; I'd been there myself a few times, but had not yet joined in a volleyball game. "Not friends?"

"Not really. Jimmy was kind of a loser. He didn't have a lot of friends."

I learned that Jimmy Fremantle was from Nebraska, employed in store merchandising, what I'd be tempted to call window dressing. He'd worked his way west doing that: Lincoln, then Denver, then San Francisco. He'd come to Honolulu about two years before, working first as a clerk at Liberty House, then moving up to merchandising again once the chain was bought out by Macy's. Wollinsky gave me Fremantle's boss's name and the store phone number.

"So he kept to himself?" I asked. "You said before he didn't have many friends."

"Not for want of trying," Larry said. "You've got to give the boy credit, though. He was out there all the time. He caught every strip night at every club. He'd be at Fusion one night, then Trixx, then the Rod and Reel Club, then Windows, then Michelangelo." He leaned forward like he was confiding a secret to me. "He even started country and western line dancing. I mean, really!"

"Can you tell me some other people he knew?"

He gave me a couple of names and phone numbers. "I swear, it's not safe to go out anywhere without a police escort." He leaned back on the sofa and casually moved his three–piece set from one side to the other through his Calvins. "How about you, detective? Would you like to escort me to a club some night?"

I ignored the overture. "You have any problems with him?" I asked. "Any reason why you might want to see him dead?"

Wollinsky shook his head. "Like I said, I wasn't exactly his best friend, but I didn't hate him."

"Know anybody who did?"

"I'm sure people got annoyed with him—he was an annoying kind of guy."

"Where were you this afternoon?"

"Here. Asleep. A boy's got to get his beauty rest, you know."

"I appreciate your help," I said, standing up. "If we need any more information, an officer will be in touch with you."

Larry Wollinsky stood up and trailed me to the door. "At least he had his fifteen minutes in the spotlight."

"You mean getting killed?"

"No, silly, being on TV. He was on *The Shirley Ku Show* last week."

I turned around and nodded him back toward the sofa. "Tell me about *The Shirley Ku Show*."

"Only if you sit next to me."

I sat. He looked at me and I scooted over a bit, so my left leg was next to his right one, close enough that I could feel heat rising from it. His skin was as smooth as a baby's. "Talk," I said.

Shirley Ku was a Chinese–American woman with a trash talk show in the middle of the afternoon on KVOL, the island–based station my older brother Lui manages.

"You never know what she's going to do," Larry said. "I'm like a total Shirley Ku addict. I work nights, I'm a dancer, so I watch her every day. Jimmy was sick one week, a cold or something, and he was home with me, watching. They announce ideas they have for future shows, and they ask you to write in if you want to be on. One day she said they were going to do a show on "I know what you did." They wanted people who had secrets about other people to come on and tell them. On TV. Can you believe it?"

I believed it, and I had a sinking feeling that I knew what was coming. Larry shifted next to me, resting one pale hand on my thigh. Through the khaki I felt my skin tingle.

Gently, I lifted his hand off. "What did Jimmy know?"

"There's this guy he used to work with at Liberty House," Larry said. "The guy was like, totally homophobic. He used to make jokes about fags, Jimmy said. He was mean." His gaze drifted for a minute. "Poor Jimmy. I guess nobody was really as nice to him as he deserved."

I spoke gently. "What did Jimmy know about him?"

"Jimmy was at the store late one night, changing a display, and he went back to a storeroom to get something. He saw this guy, Vince, giving a blow job to another guy." He smiled. "Vince quit the next day and Jimmy didn't know what happened to him. But just before he caught that cold, he saw Vince working at a store somewhere."

I shifted my leg from Larry's. "And that's what he did? He went on this Shirley Ku show and said he'd seen Vince giving this guy a blow job?"

Larry nodded. "But it was more than that. They'd tricked Vince into coming on the show, too, and they kept him in a soundproof booth while Jimmy told his story. Then they brought Vince out, and when they told him what happened, he looked like his world had fallen apart."

I knew what that felt like; I'd been outed in the press while investigating a murder case. I sympathized with Vince, but at the same time I could see a motive for murder forming.

"You know where I can reach Vince?"

Larry shook his head. "But *The Shirley Ku Show*, I'm sure they know where to find him."

I stood up, and Larry stood with me. "You think Vince killed him?"

"I'm going to find out." I stopped at a framed picture of Jimmy and Larry. They both looked happy. "Can I borrow this? I might need to show Jimmy's face around."

"Sure." He picked it up and handed it to me, and then walked me to the door. "Jimmy was just my roommate. Like I said, we weren't really friends. But I miss him already."

"You'll find another roommate." I took his hand in both of mine. "Think good thoughts about Jimmy."

Since I was already in Waikīkī and it was the end of my shift, I called in a brief report and went home. The next afternoon when I got to my desk I found the autopsy report on Jimmy Fremantle. He was dead by the second or third blow to his head. The rest had just been insurance. It was sounding like somebody had a real beef with him.

I called Fremantle's boss, and the couple of friends whose names Larry Wollinsky had given me. No one knew anyone who had a grudge against Jimmy, or any reason to dislike him. I started to get a picture of Jimmy and the lonely life he must have led.

A production assistant on *The Shirley Ku Show* told me that the show was about to go on, for its daily four p.m. live broadcast. "But I can get you in with Shirley at five, when she comes off," he said. The studio was just a couple of blocks down from headquarters on South Beretania and it was a gorgeous fall afternoon, sunny and crisp, so I walked over there.

I showed my badge at the door and was allowed to slip into the back of the audience, where I caught the last half hour of *The Shirley Ku Show*. The guests were caregivers who had sex with their elderly patients. The audience laughed loudest when an elderly lady commented on the size of her beefy male nurse's member. She was a frail little thing with white hair pulled up like Pebbles and tied with a pink bow. "I been around the block a few times, and let me tell you, he's got a big one," she said. I was afraid for a minute that Shirley was going to ask him to prove it.

The other two patients were both elderly men cared for by young, attractive women. One said she had to use a vacuum pump to help her patient perform, and the other said she sat on her patient's face so that he could lick her. The audience roared and Shirley Ku made a few funny comments.

Shirley was a tiny woman, barely five feet tall, with a thousand–megawatt smile. There was a small step that the camera never showed that helped her get up onto the barstool where she sat, her legs demurely crossed, while her guests revealed their innermost secrets.

When the show was over, the retirees, middle–aged women and teenagers in the audience filed out and I went backstage. A grip pointed me down the hall to a door that had Shirley Ku's picture in the center of a big red star.

She was sitting at a counter taking off her makeup when I walked in. Just beyond her was what I could only call a shrine to Connie Chung— a life–sized cutout, and dozens of candid and posed photos of the former network newswoman. "You like Connie?" Shirley asked when she saw where I was looking. "Shirley Ku is her biggest fan. Someday, Shirley is going to be a big star, just like Connie."

"I wanted to talk to you about a show you did recently," I said. "It was called *I know what you did*."

"Good show. What about it?"

I explained that Jimmy Fremantle had been killed, and that I wanted to know more about his appearance. "It may be related to his death."

Shirley looked stunned. "We had four guests on that day. A mother confronted her teenaged daughter about having sex. A clerk at a lingerie store downtown identified a man who admitted to shoplifting lace panties there. Jimmy Fremantle was the third guest. The last was a woman who revealed that her sister had an abortion when she was a teenager." She continued taking off her makeup. "The sister is married to Councilman Yamanaka," she continued. "You know, the one who makes such a fuss about Christian values."

She looked back at me. "Great ratings for that one. And you know something, the next day Councilman Yamanaka resigned from the anti–abortion group he chaired and it fell apart." She stood up and walked to a Japanese screen painted with a silver egret standing amidst green reeds. At the edge she stopped and said, "So you see, Shirley Ku does some good things, too."

She stepped behind the screen and began changing her clothes. "Tell me about Jimmy Fremantle," I said.

"I guess you know the basic story," she said from behind the screen. "We brought the other guy in saying someone had a secret crush on him." She stuck her head around the screen. "I think that was a little true." She disappeared again. "We kept him in a soundproof room while the audience heard Jimmy's story. We got hold of his personnel record from Liberty House, which showed he quit the day after Jimmy saw him. Then we brought him out."

She emerged from behind the screen wearing a sleeveless white blouse and a pair of pink shorts. "He wasn't happy, but he didn't go crazy either. He admitted he'd done it— you know, had sex with that other guy in the storage room. He said, "So I did it. So what?" And then we cut to commercial. We came back to Councilman Yamanaka's sister–in–law."

"Do you have a last name and an address for Vince?" I asked.

"My assistant will get it for you. I'm sure we had him sign a waiver before he went on the air." She paused. "Anything else?"

"How about a copy of the tape? I'd like to see it for myself."

"You never saw it? How'd you know to ask about it?"

"Fremantle's roommate, Larry Wollinsky. He told me about it."

"Wollinsky? He was Jimmy Fremantle's roommate?" She looked like she was ready to spit.

"You know him?"

"He submits ideas for the show every week. Dozens. Stupid ideas. He's a drag queen, you know? He does Edith Piaf. Who wants to see Edith Piaf in Hawai'i? He's not even very good. We finally had him audition for one of our makeup tips shows. He was terrible!"

I thanked her, and she found her assistant, who copied the episode onto a DVD and gave me an address for Vince Gaudenzi in Mo'ili'ili. "I think he works at that big bookstore in the Ward Warehouse," she said. "You might be able to catch him there."

"Thanks." I walked back to headquarters and retrieved my truck from the garage. I drove over to the Ward Warehouse, fighting the rush hour snarl, and found Vince Gaudenzi behind the bookstore's information counter. I showed him my badge and asked if there was somewhere private we could talk.

He wasn't a very imposing figure. Mousy brown hair, a thin mustache and traces of five o'clock shadow. He didn't look like he got to the gym much, though it was hard to tell through his baggy clothes.

He found someone to cover for him and led me outside, to a stone table and bench overlooking the highway. I'd stopped at the candy store in the mall first and bought a pack of Juicy Fruit gum. I offered him a stick before I took one for myself. "No, thanks," he said. He opened his mouth wide and showed me a set of silver braces. "I can't chew gum. It gets caught."

I told him about Jimmy Fremantle, watching his face as I did. If he was faking, he did a good job. "How'd you feel about him getting you on *The Shirley Ku Show*?" I asked. "That piss you off?"

"At first," he said, nodding. "Then I thought, you know, I might as well just get over it and get on with my life." He looked at me. "I read about you in the paper. You know what it's like. I mean, it's no use denying it any more, is it?"

"Guess not." I asked him where he had been on Sunday afternoon.

"At the Rod and Reel Club," he said. "The bartender, Fred, he knows me. And there's a guy, I went home with him, oh, around four o'clock. His name's Gunter."

"Tall guy? Blonde hair shaved down to a stubble?"

"You know him?"

I'd first met Gunter myself at the Rod and Reel Club. "How long were you with Gunter?"

He thought for a minute. "I got to the club around three, I think, and I saw Gunter. I don't know, something kind of attracted us to each other. We kept cruising around the bar, looking, and finally he came up to me and whispered in my ear."

I knew that routine; that was how Gunter and I had first connected.

"Like I said, I think we went back to his place around four. We went to bed, then we dozed off for a while. I left him to go home just as it was getting dark, around seven, I think. Gunter can tell you that."

That pretty much cleared Vince for the time of the murder, as long as Gunter agreed with his time line. "I'll talk to him."

I picked up some takeout chicken, and drove back to the station, considering. From what I'd seen, I didn't think Vince Gaudenzi had killed Jimmy Fremantle. He didn't seem to be holding a grudge, he didn't look strong enough to wield a baseball bat, and he couldn't chew gum. But if he didn't do it, that left me back at square one.

I ate as I played the recording of *The Shirley Ku Show*. The segment came off pretty much the way it had been described to me. Vince didn't seem angry, just confused. I knew how he felt.

When my shift ended, I checked myself out in the mirror in the men's locker room. I combed my hair, tucked in my aloha shirt, did a quick spit–shine on my leather deck shoes, and drove home. I parked and walked down Kuhio Avenue toward the Rod and Reel Club. If Gunter was running true to form, he'd be there, having just finished his security shift at a fancy condo tower.

Sure enough, he was sitting at the bar, making conversation with Fred. I came up behind him and ran my hand over the fuzzy stubble on the top of his head. It seemed a little longer than usual. "Letting your hair down, Gunter?" I sat next to him, smiled at Fred and said, "I'll take a Longboard Lager, if you please."

"Well, well, well, Detective Kimo," Gunter said. "What brings you to this fine establishment this evening?"

Fred pulled my beer from the cooler with a couple of theatrical moves and handed it to me. I tilted it in Gunter's direction and said, "You." I took a sip.

"I'm flattered." Gunter turned to Fred and said, "Maybe this'll be an early night after all."

"Tell me about Vince Gaudenzi," I said. "You know him?"

He looked a little startled. "Vince? You mean yesterday's Vince? What's the matter? He was over twenty–one, wasn't he?"

"I didn't ask his age. How long were you with him?"

He told me the story. He'd slept late, after a busy Saturday night, and ended up at the Rod and Reel around two. He estimated he was there around an hour before Vince walked in.

"You know how Gunter's standards go down after the first hour," Fred said, wiping down the bar in front of us.

Gunter pursed his lips and blew Fred a kiss. "Love you, baby." He told me he and Vince had made out for a while at the bar, and then they'd gone back to Gunter's place. He started to give me explicit details but I stopped him.

"How long were you together?"

"A couple of hours. We had a mini–sleepover. He left just as it was getting dark. I could barely rouse myself to come back here." Gunter suddenly put it together—I wasn't just his friend asking about a guy, I was a cop. "He's all right, isn't he? He's kind of a doll. I wouldn't mind seeing him again."

I told Gunter about Jimmy Fremantle. He didn't know him, but knew about Vince's guest appearance on *The Shirley Ku Show*.

"So that means Vince didn't do it, right?" he asked. "Because he was with me."

"I guess that's what it means."

Gunter ordered himself another green apple martini, and another beer for me. "So how are things?" he asked. "The boys down at the station treating you all right?"

He had a lot of charm, and he was a good listener. We talked for a few hours, and eventually he leaned over and kissed me, and I kissed him back. He put his hand on my crotch, and I reached up under his shirt to feel his hard chest, and then we faded into one of the darker corners of the Rod and Reel Club.

I didn't want to go home with him, though. After we'd made out for a long time, I pulled away. "I like you, Gunter," I said. "And if I went off with you tonight I wouldn't be able to hang out with you any more. And I'd miss that."

"You're a sweet boy," Gunter said. "But just so you know, we can have sex sometimes and still be friends."

"I'll take your word on that."

We walked together for a couple of blocks under starry skies and neon signs, then parted with a long, intense kiss. As I walked the last blocks to my apartment, I thought about kissing. I had kissed two men in two days, and walked away from both of them. Only something was nagging me about one of those kisses. Maybe if I hadn't had that third beer I'd have thought of it then.

I slept until dawn and then rolled out of bed and into my board shorts. I grabbed my surfboard and walked down to Kuhio Beach Park just as the sun was peeking over the Ko'olau Mountains. I wasn't really awake, just focusing enough of my conscious mind on the waves so that I didn't fall. I swam, and surfed, and sat on my board treading water, while my mind woke up. And when it did, I knew what I had to do at the station that afternoon.

I removed the picture of Jimmy Fremantle and Larry Wollinsky from its frame, and sent the frame downstairs for fingerprint analysis. I found out Wollinsky had an old conviction for petty larceny, stealing a bunch of wigs from a discount store, and requested his prints. Then I spent the rest of the afternoon going to every place that sold baseball bats.

The prints on the Juicy Fruit wrappers and the picture frame matched the file prints for Wollinsky, and I had a photo ID from the clerk who sold him the baseball bat. I presented it all to my boss.

Lieutenant Sampson is a good guy. He hired me after all my troubles in Waikīkī, when I'd thought my police career was over. Though I'd only worked for him for a few months, I'd come to trust his judgment. "Why?" he asked.

"I think he was jealous," I said. "He tried dozens of times to get on *The Shirley Ku Show*, and then his roommate got on the first time he tried. He figured we'd either accept it as a gay bashing or pin it on Vince Gaudenzi."

"When do you want to pick him up?"

"I've got an idea about that. The department can use some good publicity, right? And I know Shirley Ku would love to film us arresting Wollinsky."

Lieutenant Sampson was behind me. We bumped it up the ranks, and got the final okay just after ten o'clock that night.

I called Larry to make sure he'd be home, and he sounded eager to see me. We arranged to meet Shirley Ku and her crew at Larry Wollinsky's apartment. I hoped, as I knocked on his door, that he would be wearing more than his Calvins for his chance at fame on *The Shirley Ku Show*, but I wasn't prepared for who opened the door.

It was Edith Piaf, down to the artistic mole applied to the left cheek and the jaunty black beret. Wollinsky looked at the cameras and immediately launched into Piaf's signature song, "*Non, je ne regrette rien.*"

I waited until he'd finished, and said, "Larry Wollinsky, I know what you did."

It all started with a POG.

POG is the nickname for a pineapple–orange–guava juice drink, and you get one any time you fly between islands. I was returning to Honolulu from the Big Island after a police training class, and I had to hurry to make the last flight back. I didn't get a chance to visit the men's room at the Kailua–Kona airport, and as soon as I drank that POG I had to pee like a racehorse.

I didn't even slow down long enough to bolt the door behind me, just kicked it closed as I unzipped my pants. I stood, and peed, and man, it felt good. I was finishing when the door to the tiny bathroom opened and the male flight attendant, Keoni, slipped in. I shouldn't have been surprised. My picture had just been in *Honolulu Weekly* in a feature on gay professionals around the island, and Keoni had made it clear he knew who I was when he served me the POG.

He was a cute guy, and I admit I'd entertained a brief fantasy as he handed me the POG and our gaze met. I'm thirty–two, and he was about five or six years younger, but we had the same slim build. He was a few inches shorter than me, about five–nine, and we both had dark hair, tanned skin and hairless forearms. The little porno movie played in my head for just a minute, and then he moved on, and I drank the POG, and suddenly all I could think about was getting to the lavatory and emptying my bladder.

Keoni had other things on his mind. There wasn't much room in the tiny lavatory, but he kneeled in front of me, pushing me against the back wall, and I balanced myself, one hand against the counter and the other against the side wall.

My dick wasn't hard, and there were a few drops of urine still dribbling out, but Keoni didn't seem to mind. He took me in his mouth as he unbuckled my belt and opened my pants, dropping them to my knees, then reached up through the leg of my boxers (tropical fish in neon colors, not nearly as embarrassing as some in my drawer) and fondled the underside of my balls.

It was like he flipped a switch, and my dick responded, inflating to its full six inches. I'm a cop, after all; I don't lie, even about the length of my dick. His finger kept working me, stroking the sensitive area between my ass and balls, as he sucked and licked, and all too quickly I felt shudders rising.

But he pulled back, and I didn't come. I was still hard, my mouth was dry, and my groin was roiling, but I didn't come. Keoni said nothing, but his index finger found my asshole and started wiggling, and a minute or two later his mouth was back on my dick. He deep–throated me, then pulled back to lick me like I was an ice cream cone. The tip of his tongue penetrated my piss slit and goose bumps rose on my arms.

I felt the pressure build—but so did Keoni, and he backed off. Three times he brought me to the point of explosion and backed off. By the fourth time, though, I was ready to beg. I couldn't tell how much time had passed, but I was sure there was somebody else with a full bladder waiting outside the lavatory, and my arms had grown so weak I was having trouble keeping my balance—and I NEEDED TO COME.

Keoni knew that, too, without my having to do anything more than utter a few inarticulate moans and whimpers, though I tried my best to be quiet and keep what we were doing in there a secret from anyone standing outside. As the pressure built inside my groin for the fourth time, Keoni didn't let up, and it felt like every nerve ending in my body became electrified as my cum exploded down his throat.

I don't get as much sex as you might admit for a reasonably good–looking guy with a dick, an ass and a pair of handcuffs. Maybe it's the long hours I work, or the fact that most of the guys I come in contact with are in the process of committing a crime or being arrested, but it had been a while since a cute guy's mouth had come anywhere near my circumcised dick. So I was reeling and had to sit down on the toilet—fortunately after having the presence of mind to flip the lid.

Keoni stood up. "I need your help," he said.

"You could have just asked," I asked, after catching my breath. "You didn't have to blow me first."

"I did that because I wanted to. Can you stay in your seat after we land, until the rest of the passengers get off?"

I started to laugh. "Don't tell me you're going to blow every one of them?"

He gave me an evil look—which made me like him even more. "Sure," I said.

"Lock the door after I leave. Stay here for a minute and then come out."

He opened the door and stepped out. "I'm sorry, there's a problem with this lavatory," I heard him say, as I reached over and locked the door behind him. "Can you please use the one at the rear of the plane?"

By the time I'd flushed the toilet—I had peed, after all—closed up my pants and washed my hands, there was no one waiting outside, and no one even seemed to notice that I'd come out of a lavatory that was supposedly broken. A sunburned tourist was ready to jump in as soon as I got out, as if he'd never heard Keoni make his announcement.

I waited in my seat until the rest of the passengers had left. I followed an elderly couple in matching aloha shirts, and Keoni fell into step behind me as we exited the jetway. "I have a stalker," he said. "I need you to help me get rid of him."

"Let me guess. You gave him one of those world–class blow jobs and he keeps coming back for more."

"Something like that. Listen, I need to clock out. Can you wait for me at the front of the terminal?"

I agreed, and after a few minutes, Keoni arrived. "If you can give me a lift to Waikīkī, I'll explain the problem," he said.

He waited until we were out of the terminal to say, "I don't usually give blow jobs on the plane. I wouldn't want you to get the wrong idea. But I do occasionally slip a napkin with my phone number on it to a cute guy. That's what I did with Jerry, and he called me as soon as he got off the plane."

We crossed the street to the short–term parking lot, where I'd left my car for the day. "We met outside Lappert's Ice Cream in the interisland terminal," Keoni continued. "I took him into a back corridor I know, and blew him. I figured that would be it, but he called me the next day. He found out my schedule from the airline, and he looked me up on the Internet and found out where I live, and a whole bunch of other stuff about me."

"It was a hell of a blow job. I can see why he'd want another one."

"You help me get rid of Jerry, I'll give you all the blow jobs you want," Keoni said. "As long as you don't turn into another stalker."

"Stalking's not my style. What do you know about Jerry?"

He gave me Jerry's phone number, and a general description. After I dropped Keoni off at his apartment, a low–rise building in a rundown area of Waikīkī, I stuck my Bluetooth on my ear and called Jerry on my cell phone. "Hey, my name's Kimo," I said. Fortunately, Kimo's a pretty common name in the islands; it's the way the early missionaries translated the name James when they were converting the Bible into Hawaiian. "Keoni told me you've got a big dick and you like blow jobs."

Keoni actually hadn't said anything about the size of Jerry's dick, but I've never met a gay man yet who wasn't flattered by the compliment. "Keoni's a great guy," Jerry said. "Nobody gives a blow job like he does."

"That's because you haven't gotten one from me yet. You want to give it a try?"

At the time, I didn't have any plan to go down on Jerry; I was just trying to get him to meet me. "Sure," he said. "Where can we meet?"

The Rod and Reel Club has a couple of rooms in the back, and if you slip Fred a ten–dollar bill (or if you're a regular customer, like me) he'll give you a key for one of them. It's not like the baths;

you can't sit there with the door open and your dick waving in the wind like a rainbow flag. But if you meet somebody at the bar and you just can't wait to get to his motel room—or, more likely, if he lives with his mother in some distant suburb—you can stroll down the hall, slip inside, and close the door behind you.

You can't leave used condoms on the floor, and you can't howl like a wolf when you come, but pretty much anything else goes. I told Jerry to meet me at the Rod and Reel, and to head down the hall and knock three times on the third door. "Give me a half hour to get there," I said.

I parked back at my apartment building and walked over to the bar, only a few blocks away—very convenient when I'm either thirsty or horny. And despite the world–class blow job from Keoni, my accumulated sexual drought had left me still on the horny side. I was leaning against the wall, with my badge pinned to my shirt and a pair of handcuffs in my hand, when Jerry knocked.

I opened the door, let him see only my face, and ushered him inside. He was a good–looking guy, with a chiseled face and slicked–back hair that reminded me of a young Arnold Schwarzenegger. He was just a little on the stocky side, but that happens to be how I like my men—with some meat on their bones.

He was wearing flip flops, a tank top and compression shorts, and his hard–on stretched against the nylon fabric. I moved behind him and locked the door. That's when he turned and saw the badge.

"What the fuck?" His hard–on quickly deflated.

"Keoni says you've been bothering him," I said. "That true?"

"Dude, you gotta understand. I never had a blow job like that before."

"How long ago did you meet him?"

He frowned. "About a month ago, I guess. I went over to the Big Island for a couple of days, and I was flying back when he slipped me his phone number."

"How often have you seen him since then?"

The room was small, with a single bed jammed up against one wall, and a rubber sheet stretched over it. There was a drain in the center of the concrete floor, and a flip top trash can with the word "Mahalo," thank you in Hawaiian, on the flap. I motioned him to the bed, and I leaned back against the door.

"The first week, I saw him every day when he got off work. I knew when his last flight arrived, and I used to hang around at the airport waiting for him."

"And he gave you a blow job every day?"

He nodded. "Then he started avoiding me. I guess I got a little obsessive."

"You know that's stalking, don't you?" He nodded. "And you know that's wrong?"

"But dude, he does stuff no guy has ever done for me."

"I know. He blew me in the lavatory on my flight."

"So you know."

"Yeah." And suddenly, I understood how I could get Jerry to stop bothering Keoni. "And now that I know, I bet I can do it myself, and teach other guys to do it to me. I don't have to keep going back to Keoni."

I grabbed the single pillow from the bed, threw it to the floor, and got down on my knees in front of Jerry. I jerked his compression shorts down, causing him to jump a little. His limp dick sprung free, and I reached up under his balls the way Keoni had done to me. In a moment, his dick came to life.

It was thicker than mine, and a little shorter, but it tasted just fine to me. I tried to remember everything Keoni had done to me. I began by licking his dick from the root up to the tip, like a lollipop. Rotating my head, I got the whole thing glistening with my saliva. I wrapped my hand around the bottom of his dick and started slowly jacking him, while nibbling and sucking at the top of his dick.

Jerry seemed to like it, and I willed myself to go slowly, and pay attention to his reaction. I deep–throated him a couple of times, relaxing my gag reflex enough to go down so far his pubic hairs tickled my nostrils, then pulled back and licked him a few more times.

My nose was filled with the rich, earthy, locker–room smell of a dick in heat. I stroked the area behind his balls as I took each one of his goose eggs in my mouth. He groaned. As I licked and sucked, I listened for those little signs that he was losing control— quickened breathing, slight moaning, a stiffening in the loins.

As soon as I felt his body responding, I pulled off.

"Dude, don't stop," he panted.

I ran my index finger along the inside of his thigh, and he shivered. After a minute, when the moment of ejaculation had passed, I went back down on him. My own dick had begun straining for release, but I knew that as soon as I started touching myself, I'd forget all about monitoring Jerry's excitement level. So I left my dick stuffed awkwardly into my pants, and focused on Jerry—on his solid, beefy thighs, his hairy, low–hanging balls, and his fat, juicy dick. Twice more I brought him nearly to the verge, then pulled back.

He was starting to whimper, begging me, trying to hold my head in place over his dick. At that point, I abandoned my strategy. I fumbled with my pants and gave my dick the open air it had been craving. With my right hand, I pulled some saliva and precum from Jerry and used it to lubricate myself.

Then, I began furiously jacking myself while sucking him strong and fast. It didn't take long for us both to erupt. Jerry's whole body shook as the semen coursed out of his dick and down my throat. Mine spurted up like an eruption from Mauna Loa, spilling onto the concrete floor.

"Dude, that was awesome," he said, when we'd both caught our breath. I struggled up from the floor and sat next to him on the bed, both of us slumped against the wall.

"But not as good as Keoni?"

"Keoni never got himself off at the same time. That was major hot, watching you jack off while you were sucking me."

About a month later, I checked in with Keoni. I thought I was about due for another one of his special treatments, and I wanted to see if Jerry had stopped bothering him. "Yeah," he said. "He called me once, a couple of weeks ago, and we got together. But he promised not to stalk me, and he's been good."

We made plans to meet. I wanted to ask him about a couple of techniques. I'd been getting a lot of practice lately, and I knew there were a couple of things I needed to improve. I was laying back on my bed, naked, thinking of seeing Keoni, and stroking myself lightly, when my cell phone rang. I looked at the display, and then answered.

"Jerry, you've got to stop calling me every day," I said.

By the time I arrived at the Honolulu Arts College, the haole in the Santa hat was dead. Two bullets to the heart will do that to you. In addition to the red hat with its white pompom, he wore a pair of board shorts, sandals, and a T–shirt that read "Jesus Loves You Best." An island–style Santa, one who looked ready to deliver the roof–rack full of presents atop his Jeep. He didn't have the white hair or full beard, though he did have a little soul patch on his chin.

The patrol officer who'd responded to the initial call, Jimmy Chang, finished his radio call and walked over to me. "Hey, Kimo, howzit?"

"Hey, brah, they got you moving up in the world." We were indeed up, in the mountainside suburb of Mānoa, which looks down on Honolulu like a rich sister. I had driven past the University of Hawai'i, then taken Mānoa Road farther up to the HAC campus, where a couple of academic buildings clustered around an open green. A Norfolk Island pine had been decked with strings of lights, and a banner hung from one building read "Mele Kalikimaka."

Jimmy recapped the situation for me. The body had been found outside Reese Hall, the building sporting the banner, which housed faculty and administrative offices. Two other buildings held classrooms filled with computers, scanners, all manner of hardware and software used in teaching students about web design and animation.

Since it was the twenty-second of December, the only people I saw on the campus were the police and a young Chinese girl whom Jimmy introduced as Susie Lo. She was petite and chunky, with black hair that hung like a curtain over half her face.

"What brought you up to campus when everything's closed?" I asked her, as we walked over to a cluster of wrought–iron benches painted white. A crumple of wrapping paper blew past us in the light breeze.

"Today's officially the last day of school," she said. "Most classes are finished, but my English teacher said if I dropped my paper off before four he wouldn't take off points for being late."

I looked at my watch. It was about half–past four; the 911 call had come in at 3:45. "Cutting it a little close, weren't you?"

"I had to work lunch at my parents' restaurant. He was in his office, so I gave him the paper, and then I came downstairs. As I was walking out the building, I heard these two noises, like firecrackers. Then I saw that man."

She looked like she was ready to cry, so I patted her shoulder. "It's okay," I said. "Take it as slow as you need."

"That's all I know. I called 911 right away."

"Did you look at his face?" I knew the body had been found face up.

She nodded. "But I don't know who he is."

Susie Lo told me the student body was small and she was pretty sure she knew everybody by sight. Nor was the dead man a faculty member or a member of the staff, as far as she knew. "But a lot of adjuncts come up here to teach a course or two. He could be one of those."

I got Susie's address and phone number, and let her go. By then, the crime scene techs had checked out the area, and the medical examiner's guys were ready to take the body away. I snapped a couple of pictures, scribbled some notes, and let them go.

In the hour we'd been there, no one had come or gone. There were still a dozen cars in the parking lot, though, so I knew somebody had to be around. I went into Reese Hall and started knocking on doors. The ground floor administrative offices were clustered around a central atrium —admissions, registration, student services. There was only one person in each office, and none of them had heard the shots, or recognized the dead man.

I climbed a circular ramp to the second floor, where I found four office suites: Computer Applications, Sciences, Fine Arts, and Humanities. The doors to the first three were locked, but Humanities was propped open, and I walked in, calling out a hello.

A tall, lanky man in his early sixties stuck his head out of an office door. "School's closed. You'll have to come back after New Year's." He wore a T–shirt, jeans, and sandals, and had a red and green plastic lei around his neck.

"I'm a detective," I said, showing him my badge. "Can I ask you a few questions?"

He shrugged. "Not sure how good my answers will be, but you can ask," he said, stepping back into his office so I could follow.

I saw Susie Lo's paper in a plastic tray affixed to his door as I walked in. A placard on the desk, nearly buried by debris, said the man's name was Ted Kiely. A big picture window on the far wall looked downhill toward Honolulu, the ocean a blue strip on the far horizon. Bookshelves lined both side walls, stacked haphazardly with books thin and thick. Papers flowed over piles on the floor and the desk.

I told him about the body that had been found outside, and asked if he'd heard anything.

He shook his head. "We had a little party here earlier this afternoon. I had too much to drink and didn't feel up to driving home, so I took a nap while I was waiting for late papers."

"May I show you a picture of the man we found?" He nodded, then caught his breath as he looked at the screen of my digital camera.

"I know him, but I'm not sure of his name. He's a book buyer." He turned to his desk drawer and started fishing around. "I have his card here somewhere."

"What do you mean by book buyer?" I asked, as he bent his shaggy white–haired head over the drawer.

"The textbook reps send us dozens of books every year, trying to convince us to select them for our courses. Book buyers come around and buy them from us for a few bucks, then resell them to wholesalers—which eventually sell them to stores that cater to students, or to used book stores, or web sites."

He looked up. "Here are the cards. There are four buyers who come around regularly—but clearly your victim isn't Luisa Santa Maria or Nguyen Giap. Your man is either Jerry Epworth or Rich Figueroa."

Kiely handed me the two cards.

"May I keep these?"

"Certainly. The one who is alive will come by again at the beginning of the year with another card, and the one who isn't…" he shrugged.

"Can you tell me anything about him?" I asked. "Beyond the fact that he was a book buyer?"

"We don't get into personal discussion. And I couldn't have a conversation with him about the books—they were just inventory to him."

"You said there was a party earlier?"

"One of the aforementioned textbook reps," he said, "brought us pizza and beer, by way of a Christmas party. We ate and drank in the faculty lounge. When I got sleepy and retired back here, there were still a few people left, but I'm sure they're gone by now."

I got the details he could provide—names of those who had attended the party, along with their home addresses and phone numbers. "Conveniently, I have the department directory here somewhere." After shuffling through papers for a while, he found it. "Take it. I'll have the secretary run me a new one in January." He also found the card for the textbook rep who'd thrown the party, a man named Miller Stevenson, which he said I could keep as well.

I thanked Kiely and stood to leave. "Sad, isn't it?" he asked. "Just before the holidays." He paused and began looking through his books. "Reminds me of a quotation. I'm sure I've got it here somewhere."

I looked at my watch. "Wish I could stay to hear that, sir. Unfortunately, I've got a lot of people to call. Thanks for your help."

The headquarters for the Honolulu Police Department was in full holiday mode by the time I got back to my desk. Little white lights in the palm trees outside, an inflatable Santa in board shorts and flower lei, miniature Christmas trees on a number of desks and tables. There was a radio going somewhere in the background, Jimmy Buffett's version of "Mele Kalikimaka" playing. Man, I hate that song.

And I really hate a murder at Christmas time. It's hard enough to talk to the next of kin the rest of the year—but to know you've ruined their holidays, now and probably for years to come—that's worse.

Fortunately, Rich Figueroa answered his phone quickly, verifying that he was indeed very alive. Just to be sure, I asked what color hair he had. "Black. Why?"

I explained about the murder. "Our victim's hair was dirty blonde. Just wanted to make sure I was still on the right track."

"Jerry Epworth has hair that color," Figueroa said.

"You know him?"

"Just to say hello. Sometimes our paths cross on a campus somewhere." He filled me in on some more of the details of the book buying business. "Jerry carrying any cash?" he asked.

"No wallet, no cash or ID."

"I usually carry a couple hundred bucks cash with me all the time," Figueroa said. "You run across a professor with books to sell, he's not going to take American Express."

I wrote *Motive = Robbery?* on the pad in front of me, and thanked Figueroa for his time.

Epworth's card only had his name, the words "Book Buyer" and a cell phone number. The number rang once and voice mail picked up. I left a message, asking anyone who retrieved the message to call me at the station, and hung up.

I pulled up the address Epworth had used on his driver's license. There was no phone number listed there, though, so I had to drive out. But hell, I was on duty 'til midnight.

First, though, I started calling Ted Kiely's colleagues. One by one, they confirmed what he had said. There had been a party, sponsored by Miller Stevenson, and most of the department had left the building by two p.m. Kiely had a reputation as a cat napper; no one was surprised that he'd hung around, especially as he often accepted late papers, and no one knew of anything that connected Jerry Epworth—if indeed that's who our dead man was—to Kiely or anyone else in the department, other than the occasional commercial transaction.

Around eight o'clock, after I couldn't delay any longer, I drove to Epworth's address in Pearl City, on the same bay as Pearl Harbor. It was a nondescript apartment building, three stories and a little patch of grass out front guarded by a single tall palm tree. No one had bothered to decorate for the holidays, though a few homes in the area were lit up with lights and dioramas of Santa, sleigh and elves.

I could never relate to the traditional Santa Claus when I was a kid. I didn't know from snow and reindeer and coats with fur collars. My image was an island Santa, a big fat jolly guy like the ones who rent surfboards out on Waikīkī. My Santa wore rubber slippers and drove a team of dolphins. My Christmas carols all featured slack–key guitar and island melodies, and when I went to the mainland for college and saw the Santa the rest of the country knew, he seemed like a foreign creature.

The door to the building lobby was unlocked, and on the mailbox for apartment 3–D I saw the name Stevenson, with "Epworth" scrawled next to it in pencil. I climbed the stairs and knocked.

The man who answered the door was haole, in his early thirties, wearing a T–shirt that read "So many books, so little time." He had tousled brown hair, and he looked like he'd had a bad day. I showed him my badge, introduced myself, and asked his name.

"Miller Stevenson."

It took a minute for my brain to connect the dots. "The textbook rep?"

He nodded. "What's this about?"

"May I come in?"

"Sure." He stepped back to let me into the Zen–like living room—an Eames chair, a braided rug, a flat–panel TV on a Scandinavian teak stand. The simplicity was marred, though, by the books—books on shelves, books spilling out of boxes, books covering the coffee table and piled in teetering stacks along one wall. A Santa hat similar to the one Jerry Epworth had been wearing was tossed on the dining room table, next to a backpack, a laptop computer, and a pile of red and green plastic leis.

"Do you recognize this man?" I asked, showing him the screen of my digital camera once he had closed the door behind me.

His face paled, and he swallowed hard. "It's—Jerry. Jerry Epworth. My roommate."

"Why don't we sit down," I said gently, motioning him to the sofa. I sat across from him.

"What happened?" Stevenson asked.

I explained how Epworth's body had been found. "When was the last time you saw him?"

"This morning. He wanted to get an early start, catching professors before they left for the holidays. He hoped that some people who wouldn't normally deal with him might need money for last minute Christmas shopping."

"Did he usually carry a lot of cash with him?"

Stevenson nodded. "At least two or three hundred. He said he was going to hit the ATM on his way in."

I gradually drew information out of him. Epworth's plan had been to spend the day at the University of Hawai'i, traveling from one office building to the next. He dragged around a rolling suitcase, stashing the books he bought inside, periodically dropping them at his car. I got the make and model of Epworth's car and made a note ask patrol to see if it was still in the parking lot at HAC.

I looked around. "These books all Jerry's?"

"The ones along the wall are texts, ones Jerry was going to wholesale just before school starts in January. Everything else is either from my publisher or my own collection."

We talked some more about the book business—that lots of people had reason to believe Jerry would be carrying cash, that his unassuming demeanor made him a target for crooks. He had been robbed once, leaving UH after dark one day, but after that he'd been more careful.

"How about the two of you?" I asked. "You getting along?"

He shrugged. "As well as usual."

I had the feeling that Epworth and Stevenson were more than just roommates, but I'm lousy at recognizing who's gay and who's not. So I chose not to ask anything more. Besides, it looked like a robbery gone bad, in which case what Jerry and Miller got up to on their off time was nobody's business.

I got whatever information Stevenson had about Epworth's next of kin, and left, after telling him that I was sorry for his loss. Roommate or boyfriend, they had still had a relationship, and now it was gone.

The next day I subpoenaed Epworth's bank records and found he had indeed taken $400 out of an ATM that morning. Epworth's car was towed to the police lot, and an evidence tech and I looked it over. There were only a few books in the trunk, so it was likely he'd still had most of that cash by four o'clock in the afternoon.

I caught another homicide late that day, and worked right up until Christmas Eve, when I finished my shift at midnight. It was too late to drive to my parents' house in St. Louis Heights, and yet I was too worked up to head for home. So I found my way to the Rod and Reel Club.

The celebration was well under way by the time I arrived. Shirtless muscle boys wearing too–tight shorts, plastic leis entwined with mistletoe, and little else, danced to a pounding beat on the patio. I made my way in to the bar, where I found Gunter engaged in conversation with Fred.

I kissed Gunter and wished him a Merry Christmas, then ordered a Longboard Lager. "What, no cute boy ready to unwrap under your tree tomorrow morning?" I asked.

"The night is still young," Gunter said. "And so am I." He leaned over. "I've got my eye on that honey in the corner—the one in the Santa hat."

I looked over at where he was pointing, and it took me a moment in the dim light to recognize Miller Stevenson. So my gaydar had been working, after all. And knowing that, I wondered if the case really had been more than just a robbery. "I'd stay away from him if I were you. His last boyfriend ended up dead."

"I wish you'd stop bringing your work home with you. You have a way of wilting a boy's hard–on."

"Gunter, you say the sweetest things."

"So what was it?" he asked, leaning in close to me. "A little S & M gone too far? Some auto–eroticism, perhaps?"

"Nothing so sexy. Robbery."

"I thought there was something tormented–looking about him," Gunter said. "Stupid me, I always find that sort of thing sexy."

I looked over at Miller Stevenson. He did look tormented. "Maybe I should offer him a little comfort and joy," I said.

"Comfort and interrogation, more likely." A pair of sweaty muscle boys entered from the dance floor, and one of them caught Gunter's eye and smiled. "You go ahead," he said, nudging me. "I think I've found a new present to unwrap."

I carried my beer over to where Stevenson sat, leaning against the wall at the end of the bar. "Howzit," I said.

"I thought I recognized you. You're the gay cop."

"So you could have told me Jerry was more than your roommate."

"It's a habit. You know how it is. What I do in my bedroom is my business."

"In a murder case, sometimes your business becomes police business."

"So what, I was supposed to tell you everything about him? That he could be a whiny little shit?" Stevenson asked. From the slight slur to his words, I could tell the beer he was holding wasn't his first.

I nodded. "Pretty much. Anything you tell me stays in confidence, you know, unless it's relevant."

"I don't know what I can tell you. We dated for about six months, and then his lease ran out and he moved in with me."

"Did you set him up as a book buyer?"

He nodded. "Not that he was grateful, you understand. I mean, Christ, the prick never even finished college, and he thought he should be rich, just because he had a sweet little ass and he could suck dick like a Hoover."

I took a draw from my beer, giving Miller a chance to think. "He treated you like his sugar daddy?"

"You bet. I bought him that car. And the laptop he carried around with him."

"He didn't appreciate it, did he?"

"As if."

"I'll bet you bought him a gun, too, to protect himself in case someone tried to rob him again."

"I bought everything. The only thing Jerry ever bought was dope, booze and poppers."

I racked my brain. It was late, and I struggled to remember the details of the autopsy, which had arrived just before I left the office. The medical examiner had indicated the bullets that killed Jerry Epworth had come from a 9 millimeter.

"A Glock's good for that purpose," I said. "Small, lightweight. But it packs a wallop."

"Yeah, that's what the guy at the gun shop said. He told Jerry he ought to go out to the range, get comfortable with it. But as usual, he couldn't be bothered."

"But you knew how to handle it. You're that kind of guy. The one who keeps track of all the pieces."

He nodded. "Yeah, that's me, all right." He drained the last of his beer.

"What did you do with the gun?"

"Threw it in the ocean. Off Queen's Surf. That's where we met, you know." He didn't seem to be paying attention to what he'd said—he just kept trying to get another beer from Fred.

"Why did you do it?"

"He was pressuring me to order books and hand them over to him," he said, turning back to me. "He was tired of going around to the professors. Some of them are rude to the book buyers. A couple even have these decals on the door, that they don't sell books." He gave a half laugh. "My publisher makes those up, and I send them out. That really pissed Jerry off."

"Did you know he was going to be up at HAC?"

He nodded. "He knew I was hosting that party, that I was bringing books up to give to all the faculty. He caught me as I was leaving Reese Hall, wanted me to give him all the books I hadn't passed out. We argued."

"How'd the gun figure into it?"

"He was such an idiot. He kept the gun in a pouch on the outside of his backpack. I just finally had enough, you know? I couldn't take any more. So I reached down, grabbed the gun, and shot him. He had the dumbest look on his face."

He looked down, remembered that his beer was empty, and went to raise his hand to Fred for another. "I think you're done," I said. "Come on down to the station with me, Santa. I don't think you'll be making it back to the North Pole this year."

There was no cute guy waiting under my tree for me to unwrap when I finally made it back home as the sun was rising on another Honolulu Christmas. But sometimes, solving a case is just as good.

A maid at the Honolulu Regent Hotel discovered the body around one in the afternoon. When I arrived on the scene a little while later, Lidia Portuondo, the uniformed officer who had responded to the 911 call, was in the hallway outside the room speaking soothingly in Spanish to a petite Filipina in a crisp pink uniform.

"This is Detective Kanapaʻaka," she said to the maid. "Can you tell him what you told me?"

The maid shook her head and burst into tears. "There's not much to tell, Kimo," Lidia said to me. "She was making her rounds a little while ago, cleaning the rooms. She knocked, and didn't get an answer, so she opened the door with her passkey. She saw the body, screamed, then after she caught her breath she called 911. She's been out here in the hall ever since."

"Thanks, Lidia. Ask her if any of the other guests are in their rooms."

Lidia murmured something in low Spanish. "No, only four rooms on this floor were occupied last night," she told me, after listening to the maid. "The other three rooms have already checked out."

"No witnesses." I shook my head. "If you've got her statement, she can go."

Before I entered the room, I looked up and down the hall. The Honolulu Regent was a Japanese–owned luxury hotel which had opened downtown just a few months before, to great fanfare. We were on the twentieth floor, and a tall window at the far end of the hall framed a view of the Aloha Tower. A bank of elevators were at the other end; the floor had only a dozen rooms, each of them with a view of the ocean or the cityscape.

The hotel placed a premium on privacy. Unfortunately, that meant the murderer could stroll through the elegant lobby unmolested, ride the elevator to the half–empty floor, and enter the victim's room unnoticed.

The maid had left the door ajar; I used my pen to push it fully open. It was an elegant room, with floor–to–ceiling windows facing Punchbowl Crater and the Cemetery of the Pacific. A love seat rested just inside the door; immediately beyond it a round mahogany table and two chairs sat on a circle of parquet. At the far end of the room, a king–sized bed lay in disarray. The body of a dead man rested atop the sheets, his severed head lolling at a gruesome angle beside him. I could see why the maid had screamed.

Before I stepped inside, I surveyed the room. There was no sign of a struggle other than in the rumpling of the sheets. The drawers of the bureau were intact, and a laptop computer and cell phone sat on the table. I began making notes, taking pictures and sketching the layout of the room and the position of the body. A tremendous amount of blood had spattered everywhere, even on the walls.

The crime scene tech arrived just as I was preparing to enter the room, Doc Takayama behind him. Doc is the medical examiner for Honolulu City and County, and he comes out himself for the high–profile victims and interesting cases. He was the youngest graduate of the medical school at the University of Hawai'i and chose pathology because his youth made it hard for him to instill confidence in patients.

At thirty–two, he looked barely old enough to drink. "Morning, Kimo," he said. "Have an ID yet on this gentleman?"

"Hotel records say the room was rented to a Muhammad Idris, a diplomat from Indonesia." The fifty–something man on the bed was short, with black hair and skin the color of teak. Chances were good he was the diplomat in question.

Two techs from Doc's office followed him in, and we all got to work. Following a trail of drips from the bed, I discovered an ornate sword in the bathroom shower stall, covered in blood. A blood–spattered jumpsuit, of the type worn by cleaning people, had been stuffed into the bathroom trash can.

I found Idris's passport in his briefcase and verified his identity, while Doc did a preliminary examination of the body. Robbery was not a motive; a gold Rolex and a gold rope bracelet rested on the nightstand next to the bed, and there was close to a hundred dollars in U.S. currency in Idris's wallet.

I put in a call to the honorary consul's office to notify him of Idris's death, and made an appointment to speak with the consul later that afternoon. Then, based on the department's protocol for incidents involving foreign diplomats, I called the local office of the FBI as well. A receptionist took down my information and said that an agent would be in touch if appropriate.

Most of the paperwork in Idris's briefcase related to the importation of U.S. food products to Indonesia, not a subject I knew or cared much about. I did find something a little unusual stashed under the paperwork, a bag from the 80% Straight store at the Eaton Hotel, which contained lube, condoms and a cock ring. A receipt indicated the items had been bought a week before. Not quite what I would have expected from a diplomat from a heavily Muslim country. I knew that in the past gay Muslims in Indonesia had been terrorized, beaten up and even castrated.

Doc stripped off his rubber gloves just as I was pondering this issue. "Time of death was approximately twelve hours ago," he said. "No defensive wounds, so he was probably either sedated or suffocated before he was beheaded. The cuts in the flesh around the neck are consistent with the sword we found in the bathroom."

"You know anything about that sword?"

"Beheading is a ritual killing," Doc said. "Since our victim is Indonesian, and the *keris* is an Indonesian sword, my educated guess is the bathroom sword's a keris."

There were no visible prints on the sword or the jumpsuit, indicating the very careful killer had used rubber gloves, but I packed it all up for further analysis. Doc and his techs took the body away, and the crime scene tech finished taking his samples and photos, so I headed back to the station, with instructions that the room should not be disturbed until I gave permission.

As I drove back to police headquarters I wondered about the gay paraphernalia I'd found in Idris's room. Had he been murdered because he was gay? As far as I recalled, homosexual acts were criminal in his homeland. The ritual nature of the killing seemed to indicate a cultural motive; I'd have to ask the consul for advice.

Back at the office, I laid the case out for Lieutenant Sampson, then got on line to see what I could discover about Muhammad Idris. There wasn't much; he had spoken at a trade conference in Tokyo two years before, so I found he was 53, held a master's degree in public planning and policy from the University of Indonesia, and had been an under minister in the Department of Trade for ten years. As an English major myself, I couldn't make heads or tails out of the paper he had presented at the conference.

I was puzzling over tariffs and trade concessions when my phone rang. The FBI was interested in Muhammad Idris, after all, and an agent who identified himself as Francisco Salinas asked if we could meet to discuss the case. One of the two Starbucks on Bishop Street was around the corner from his office, and I agreed to be there in half an hour.

Salinas was easy to spot— a tall, dark–haired haole with a military–short hair cut and navy suit and white shirt. We shook hands at the barista line, then took our cappuccinos to a blond wood table in the back corner. "What do you know about Idris so far?" he asked, taking a sip of his coffee.

"Not too much." I laid out what I'd learned from the conference web site. "Obviously, you know something more. Is that something you can share?"

Salinas pulled a manila folder out of his briefcase. "Idris is a PEP," he said. "We've had our eye on him for a while."

"What exactly is a PEP?"

"A Politically Exposed Person. Someone from a foreign country who has the potential to move illicit cash or financial instruments around," he said. "The concept originated with the

Swiss over twenty-five years ago, when they instituted enhanced due diligence when dealing with senior foreign politicians and their families."

"People like Marcos and Duvalier."

"Exactly. Although Idris was not on their level, it looks like he may have moved close to two million dollars out of Indonesia to offshore bank accounts."

"How can a low–level guy like Idris get access to so much cash?"

"Idris's job was to purchase large quantities of food from foreign sources, under government contracts, then resell it to local wholesalers. You've seen the headlines—Russia buys a billion dollars of wheat from the U.S., and so on."

I drank some coffee. "Go on."

"He arranged to buy products here in Hawai'i and paid significantly over the going rate. We think that difference was siphoned into his offshore accounts."

"You have proof of this?" I asked, nodding toward his folder.

"Not completely. It's Indonesian money, not U.S., and it's small potatoes for us. But we've been collecting data."

"You think this operation of his put him at risk for murder?"

Salinas shrugged. "My grandmother had an expression. 'You lie down with dogs, you wake up with fleas.' It's possible somebody got wind of our investigation and killed Idris to cover his tracks."

"You know anything about Idris's personal life?"

"Wife and two kids back in Jakarta. They've never come to the U.S."

"Any indication he might have been gay?"

Salinas nodded. "I got a call a little while ago from a buddy of mine at the State Department. Seems Mr. Idris applied for asylum three days ago, due to his well–founded fear that he would be persecuted and perhaps killed if his homosexuality were to become known in Indonesia."

"Three days? Is that enough time for his government to find out, and arrange to have him killed?"

"If they cared. It's one thing to get caught with your pants down, so to speak. But I think it's a stretch to assume somebody in Jakarta got wind of his asylum bid and sent a hired killer all the way to Honolulu."

"Stranger things have happened. But you're right, it does seem a little far–fetched." I thought for a minute. "Idris have any local contacts?"

"I put together what I could for you," Salinas said, handing me the folder. "There isn't much, but it should get you started."

Salinas was being too helpful, and that made me suspicious. "And what do you get out of this?"

"I get to close a case." He drained the last of his coffee. "You have any idea how many of these I'm investigating? You need a Ph.D. in Economics just to follow the money trails. Since 9/11, we're cracking down on any foreign currency transactions that can be considered suspicious. We're swamped. Every PEP has family, friends, and associates. Just following one money trail can take hundreds of hours. I guarantee you, you're doing me the favor by taking this one off my desk."

He stood up. "Good to meet you, detective. Let me know the outcome of your investigation."

"Will do." I stayed at the coffee shop for a while longer, nursing the last dregs of my cappuccino and reading about Idris and his financial dealings. He had set up letters of credit to pay shell corporations for commodities at prices Salinas's notes indicated were inflated. The Indonesian government paid the money on signing, not on delivery, so often no merchandise was ever delivered.

The letters of credit had all been arranged through The Hong Kong Bank of Trade, an offshore bank with offices just a few blocks away. I decided I'd pay the account officer a visit.

The bank's offices were on the twenty-fourth floor of a luxury office building with a view of Honolulu Harbor. I showed my ID to the receptionist and asked to speak with Edward Nordahl.

Nordahl's hawk nose put him just the wrong side of gorgeously handsome, but the rest of the package was there—white–blonde hair, prominent cheekbones, broad shoulders and a trim waist. My gaydar has been improving in the year since I came out, and it told me Nordahl was batting for my team. Maybe it was the stylish cut of his Italian suit, the crispness of his white starched shirt, or the way his gaze rested a little too long on me.

I introduced myself, and he led me back to his office, which had a stunning view of Waikīkī Beach and Diamond Head. "I understand you handled some transactions for Mr. Muhammad Idris, a trade minister from Indonesia," I said, as I sat in a teak armchair across from Nordahl's desk.

"That's correct. I facilitated the letters of credit for various purchases by the Indonesian government."

"What does that mean, exactly? I'm not much of a finance expert."

"A letter of credit is a document issued by a bank that guarantees the payment of a customer's draft." Nordahl's smile was sexual, in contrast to his words. "It substitutes the bank's credit for the customer's credit. Mr. Idris would negotiate a purchase, and then come to us for the letter of credit. We'd pay his vendor, and the government of Indonesia would reimburse us."

I shifted uncomfortably in the teak chair. We weren't at the Rod and Reel Club; we were talking about a murder. There was something weird about the sexual tension he radiated. "Why would somebody do that? Why not just invoice the government directly?"

"Ah, now you're asking for a semester–long course in economics," he said, leaning back in his chair. "The letter of credit is a guarantee that your bill will be paid. If the government, for some reason, defaults, then the bank pays. Many vendors are hesitant to deal directly with third–world countries—unstable political situations, currency fluctuations, lack of familiarity with the necessary paperwork."

"You provide the insurance that the bill will get paid," I said, nodding. "And charge a fee for the service, of course."

"Of course. May I ask you what this is all about?"

"Mr. Idris was murdered last night." Nordahl's mouth dropped open and his eyebrows raised. "I'm trying to understand what brought him to Hawai'i."

"I'm shocked, to say the least. I didn't know Mr. Idris well, but I can't imagine why someone would murder him. He was very… innocuous."

"Did you ever have any indication that Mr. Idris was gay?"

Nordahl looked at me. I imagined he was considering how much he could or should tell me. I knew the feeling; even though my coming–out story had been splashed across the headlines, I still found myself in situations where I had a choice between outing myself or remaining closeted. I hoped Nordahl would realize that I could keep his secrets, if they didn't impinge on my investigation, and that he'd feel comfortable confiding in me. That is, if he didn't try to jump my bones first.

"I read about you in the paper," he said finally. "I admire you for your honesty. Some of us, however, work in environments where that kind of honesty isn't possible."

"I understand. Anything you tell me will remain confidential, unless it has a direct bearing on Mr. Idris's murder."

"Muhammad was deeply closeted." I noticed the shift from last to first name. "Being gay isn't just frowned on in Indonesia. It's a death sentence."

"That must have been very difficult for him."

Nordahl nodded. "He said sometimes he found it hard to breathe when he was in Jakarta. Here, he could be himself."

"Did you two have a personal relationship?"

"Just as friends." Nordahl held up his hands. "It took him a long time to come out to me, and then I was a sort of mentor to him. Explaining about gay bars, places he could trust and places he couldn't. That kind of thing."

"Did he go to places he shouldn't trust?"

Nordahl shrugged. "I don't know, but that's always a possibility, isn't it? When you're so deep in the closet, you get desperate for sex, and sometimes you do things you shouldn't." I wondered if he was speaking from his own experience. I knew that had happened to me. Losing control had put me in dangerous situations in the past. "Could he have picked up a piece of rough trade?"

Rough trade was a term used for a kind of male prostitute, specifically the type that could just as easily beat you up as give you a blow job. Some men thrived on the danger inherent in such guys. "Was that where his interests were?"

"I don't know. We didn't get that specific." He shuddered. "The poor guy. Was he robbed? He had a Rolex and some nice gold jewelry. I always told him not to wear that when he went out."

I shook my head. "Robbery doesn't seem to be involved. Was he ever worried that someone from Indonesia might find out about him?"

"All the time. But once he opened up, he couldn't stop. You know how it is. That taste of freedom can be so intoxicating." He looked at me again, and I could feel his gaze like lasers on me.

I stood up, and handed him my card. "If you think of anything that could help, please call me," I said. "I may get back to you, if I come up with some more financial questions."

"Certainly. I want to do anything I can to help." His handshake was warm and firm, with eye contact. I did my best to smile back, but leaving his office I couldn't help feeling like I'd escaped from a crocodile's jaws.

A deeply closeted crook, embezzling millions from a country where his sexuality was against the law. It was no wonder someone had killed Muhammad Idris.

The possibility also existed that Edward Nordahl had been closer to Idris than he let on. I'd have to look through the paperwork Francisco Salinas had given me, and I'd have to learn a lot more about Idris before I was ready to come to any conclusions.

From the bank, I headed a few blocks away to the offices of the honorary consul, who was not Indonesian, as I expected, but instead a California surfer dude named Jamie Wills. His company manufactured electrical circuit boards in factories outside Jakarta, he told me, and he'd accepted the honorary consul position as a way to facilitate trade.

"Did you know Mohammed Idris?"

"I met him a few times, but I can't say I knew him well," Wills said. "Quiet kind of dude, kept to himself mostly."

"Do you know anything about the purchasing he was doing here? Who he bought from, what he bought?"

"Can't say I do. My field's high—tech; Idris was in agriculture."

I had one last question. "How about Indonesian weapons. Know anything about those?"

"You mean the keris?"

I nodded.

"Well, there I can help you. Come on, let me show you my collection."

I followed him out of his office and down the hall. He opened a side door and led me into a small room lined with display cases. "The keris is the traditional weapon of Indonesia, the Philippines and the Malay peninsula," he said. "Each area has its own traditions, but it's basically a double—edged dagger. I won't bore you with all the technical terms, but there are a number of features which make it unique. Mostly it's here, at the hilt." He pointed. "The asymmetrical triangle at the end of the hilt is characteristic. The blade itself comes in over a hundred different shapes."

I turned on my digital camera and showed him a shot of the sword. "I assume this is a keris."

He nodded. He took the camera from me, fiddling with the dials to enlarge and zoom in on the picture. "I can't be a hundred percent sure, but this looks modern, probably made in the U.S."

"Here?"

"Not in Hawai'i. There are a couple of swordsmiths on the mainland who either reproduce ancient weapons or design their own. If you come back to my office I can give you some websites to look at."

As we walked, Wills said, "If you're not picky, you can search for a couple of minutes, type in your credit card, pick your shipping option and, voila, you've got yourself a keris."

He opened a couple of web pages in quick succession, and cut and pasted the URLs into an email, which he addressed to me. I shook his hand and said, "You've been very helpful, Mr. Wills. I really appreciate your time."

"Glad to be of help. These are beautiful pieces of armament, and I hate to see them misused."

Back at headquarters, I got online again, this time using the URLs Wills had sent to look for information about the keris and how easy it was to order one. He was right; a few clicks, and you could have yourself a ritual murder weapon.

I matched the keris from Idris's room to a picture on a website for a company in Sausalito, just outside San Francisco. I called the number on the site, and reached the swordsmith's wife, who handled sales.

She had shipped a weapon like the one I described to Honolulu, she said, but not in the last few days. She'd sold it almost a month before. "We're always willing to cooperate with law enforcement, detective," she said. "However, you understand I need to be sure of who I'm dealing with." She asked me to fax her a formal request for information, on department letterhead, with a verifiable department number she could fax back to.

I prepared the fax and sent it, then sat back in my chair. Was this a ritual murder, or just supposed to look like one? Some rabid Muslim with a hair up his ass about gay people could have assassinated Idris, using the keris for ritual effect. Or some home-grown crook could have chosen the weapon as a red herring.

In either case, the crime had turned into one of premeditation, since the weapon had been purchased a month before. The fax came through a few minutes later; the credit card was registered to an Ernest Nicholson, and sent to an address in Kaka'ako, a residential district just outside downtown. Nicholson, however, was not listed, and a call to the credit card company told me that the card had been cancelled over three weeks before, after a report of unauthorized use.

A quick records search indicated that the owner of the condo where the sword had been shipped was a corporation called Hawaiian Coast Salt, which had paid $750,000 cash—no mortgage was recorded.

That name sounded familiar, so I looked back over the records Francisco Salinas had provided me. The biggest purchases Idris had made were from Hawaiian Coast Salt, but I couldn't find a listing for them in the Honolulu phone book. Nothing on line, either.

I started calling food wholesalers, asking for information. No one had ever heard of a company by that name, but they were all willing to sell me the same commodity Idris had bought, red salt. It was a pale orange specialty product whose unique color came from the addition of volcanic clay. It was pricy, and I wondered why Indonesia needed so much of such an expensive condiment.

I called Edward Nordahl, but he couldn't tell me anything about the company. "You must have bank information," I said.

"I'm sorry, but that information is confidential. I can't reveal it to you without a court order. It's bank policy."

A buddy over in Customs told me they had no records of a shipper called Hawaiian Coast Salt, and no records of any large shipments of salt to Indonesia, either. It was all ground Salinas had covered, but I kept going over the data, hoping to find something he'd missed.

A judge wouldn't give me a subpoena for information on Hawaiian Coast Salt without some connection to Idris's murder, and I wouldn't have that unless I could prove that the keris shipped to the condo the company owned was the same one used to kill Idris. Since the weapons were historically accurate, there was no marking to differentiate this keris from any other one made by the same swordsmith.

I clocked out at the end of my shift and headed home to Waikīkī. There was still time to surf a few waves at Kuhio Beach Park, down the street from my apartment. But as I passed the Ala Wai Yacht Harbor and saw the street sign for Hobron Lane, I made a quick detour to 80% Straight, the store where the bag I found with Idris's body had come from.

It was just after five, and the neighborhood was crowded with tourists and business people from the offices at Eaton Square. A year ago, I wouldn't have gone to a store like 80% Straight, too afraid that someone might see me there, or even see me going in.

I stopped just outside the store. How did a guy like Muhammad Idris go in, then? He was closeted, fearing for his life if the repressive regime in Indonesia knew about him. The receipt had been dated a week ago, days before his asylum bid. There was no way I could see him going into the store, no less buying condoms and a cock ring. Someone must have bought them for him.

I turned around and went back to headquarters, where I hunted down photos on the Internet of both Muhammad Idris and Edward Nordahl, and printed them out on Lieutenant Sampson's color laser printer. Then it was back to 80% Straight.

I knew Ronnie, the store manager, and he knew me. Not that I was such a great customer; you get your picture in the bar rags, and other gay men notice, and remember. "Eh, Kimo, howzit?" he asked as I walked in.

He was a skinny haole with multiple piercings and a purple streak in his blonde hair. We made small talk for a few minutes, and then I pulled out my pictures. "You ever seen either of these guys in here?"

He studied Muhammad Idris, and shook his head. But he pointed to Edward Nordahl and said, "Him, I remember."

"How come?"

"Asshole was in here about a week ago, buying shit. I remember when he was checking out, he had a small size cock ring, and I kind of looked at him, like, dude, I know this is not for you."

I laughed. "Come on, Ronnie, you've got that good of an eye?"

"Duh, yeah," he said. "But he looked at me and smirked. Said it was for this Asian guy he knew, and then he made this nasty crack about Asian guys and small dicks. Shit, man, my boyfriend's Chinese and he's hung like a horse. I just shook my head and rang him up."

He reached under the counter and brought out a shrink–wrapped DVD. "Hey, we got this new release in, I thought of you," he said, handing it to me. It was called *Surf's Up*, and the cover shot was a beefy haole with a huge dick, leaning naked against a surfboard. "Go ahead, on the house. I think you'll like it."

With Ronnie's keen eye, he could probably spot the immediate reaction I had to the cover shot. "Thanks, brah. I appreciate it. And thanks for the photo ID."

"No problem. Always eager to help out a man in uniform."

"Guess I'll have to wear mine in here one day, then."

"You do, you'll cause a riot. Just give me some notice, man. I can draw a crowd for that."

I knew I was blushing by then, so it was time for me to leave.

On the drive home, I stashed the DVD under the seat so I could concentrate on Ronnie's ID. Edward Nordahl had bought the paraphernalia for Muhammad Idris. That didn't prove anything, but it did open a door.

The next morning, I swung past Honolulu Hale, our city hall, on my way to work. The massive stone building, with its ornate chandeliers, houses the corporate records office, where I searched for information on Hawaiian Coast Salt. No luck, though; no incorporation papers, no "doing business as" notices. You needed a business license to open a bank account in a company name, so that meant that Hawaiian Coast Salt was banking offshore, in one of those cash havens Francisco Salinas had mentioned.

As I drove back to the station, I wondered who else would be affected by Idris's decision to ask for asylum. His wife and kids. His office. His banking contact in Honolulu – Edward Nordahl. Suppose Nordahl had been playing Idris all along, assuming that the Indonesian would always go back to his wife in Jakarta. One day Muhammad says to Ed, "Honey, I'm not leaving you again." What does Nordahl do then? Buy a keris and chop his lover's head off? And if he did, how could I prove it?

I needed to talk to Nordahl again. I called his office, but his secretary said he wasn't in, and she hadn't heard from him. I picked up the white pages, and his number was listed—in Kaka'ako. The same address where Ernest Nicholson had received delivery of the murder weapon. I noted the similar initials – EN.

Nordahl didn't answer his phone, but he'd changed his message before he left. He was going out of town for a while, he said, but leave him a message and he'd get back to you.

The only way off an island is either by boat or plane. I gambled that if Nordahl was running scared, the easiest way to escape was by plane. I printed a dozen copies of Nordahl's picture, then ran for my truck and drove to Honolulu International. On the way, I tried to think like Nordahl. He'd planned enough to order the murder weapon weeks before he needed it; he'd used rubber gloves and an industrial jumpsuit. I thought he'd have an emergency exit plan, too, just hadn't thought he needed it until I pegged both him and Idris as gay.

So that meant he had a hidey hole set up somewhere in a place that didn't extradite. Which led me to believe he was heading for the international wing of the airport. From my truck, I called for backup, and after I parked in the airport garage I met up with a dozen uniforms and security guards in front of the TSA scanners.

I handed out the photos and gave them all a quick description, then started prowling the gates, looking for tall, blonde and handsome. Nordahl had majored in Far East studies in college, I knew, and I was pretty sure I remembered he spoke some Chinese. So I focused on flights to Hong Kong, Beijing and Shanghai. JAL had a flight to Hong Kong that was about to begin boarding, so I ran to that gate. And sure enough, Nordahl was waiting in line for his row to be called.

I radioed for backup, and kept an eye on him until two uniforms arrived. "Mr. Nordahl, we need to have a talk," I said, walking over to him.

"He thought we could be together," he said, looking at me. "That I loved him, that he would move into the apartment he bought me and we'd live happily ever after. Silly little man, really."

"Come with me, and you can tell me all about it," I said, pulling a pair of handcuffs from my belt.

As a homicide detective in Honolulu, I spend my working time solving mysteries. When I get a little personal time, I like to surf, but when a mystery presents itself, even a small one, it's hard to resist. When you add in that I'm a sucker for a big dick (no pun intended), I couldn't help wondering why the sexy guy walking toward me on the beach looked so miserable.

I'd just finished surfing a set and was relaxing on the sand at Kuhio Beach Park when I saw him, about ten feet away from me. He was a big fat boy, in his early twenties, at least six–three or six–four. Roughly two hundred seventy five pounds poured into a red nylon bikini. I first noticed him from the back, eying the way the fabric stretched unsuccessfully to cover the big round globes of his ass; at least an inch of crack peered above the elastic band.

He turned around, and as he got closer to me I could see he had a whomping big dick stuffed into that tight bikini, and that he dressed to the left. He was carrying a towel as well as a cell phone on a string around his wrist. The edges of his mouth drooped and his big brown eyes squinted in the sun. Unlike the other beachgoers around us, who were smiling and laughing and enjoying the gorgeous day, he looked miserable.

I'm a soft touch. Something about a sexy guy with a big dick and a sad face really turns me on—and sets my detective instincts going.

I stood up, dusting the sand off my board shorts, and walked toward him. As I got closer, I noticed the blonde hair on his pecs and upper arms, and a forest of darker blonde curls peeking out above that ample dick, at rest now but clearly outlined against the thin, red fabric. Jesus, I thought, who let this guy out of the house in such a skimpy suit?

"Hey," I said. "You looking for a place? 'Cause you can come sit by me." I nodded toward my towel.

A smile broke across his big face, stretching from one dimpled cheek to the other. He checked me out—though he tried to hide it, he wasn't very suave. I guess he liked what he saw; I had to be at least ten years older than he was, but I was shirtless, showing off my pecs, my biceps and the six–pack abs I work to maintain.

I wasn't nearly as showy as he was; my dick was secured inside my board shorts, though I had a feeling if I didn't sit down quickly I'd have to perform a discreet adjustment.

"That would be great." He followed me to my square of sand, like an obedient Saint Bernard, and laid his towel down next to mine.

I found out, in quick order, that his name was Tom, he was in college in Oregon, and that he'd come to Hawai'i with a couple of friends—because the room was cheaper when you split it four ways, he said.

"I'm Kimo," I said, sticking out my hand. "Where are your friends now?"

"Getting lucky at happy hour," he said, with a frown. "They're all really good–looking, and they didn't want me around when they're trying to pick up guys." His mouth dropped open, like he'd just realized he'd outed himself.

"It's okay," I said, reaching over to touch his shoulder. "I'm gay, too." I looked down my lashes, trying to be shy. "It's why I went over to talk to you."

Because I was looking down, that big dick of his was right in my line of sight, and I swear, I've never seen one spring to life so fast. The fat, fleshy head jumped right over his waistband, and in embarrassment he stuffed it back into his bikini.

"They sent you out in that suit?" I asked. "Your friends?"

"They call me a whale when they think I can't hear," he said miserably. "But without them I wouldn't have any friends at all."

"My older brother's about your size. The last time he was out here surfing with me he left a pair of board shorts at my apartment. It's only a couple of blocks away—you want to come over with me and try them on? Otherwise I might have to arrest you for public indecency."

I looked down at his crotch and there was a little wet spot, pre–cum oozing out of his piss–slit and into the shiny red fabric. He looked down himself and gulped a couple of times. I was afraid he was going to cry. "You're a cop?"

"Homicide detective. But don't worry, I won't turn you in to Vice—as long as I can get you out of that bikini."

I reached over and took his hand. "Come on," I said, standing up. I wrapped his towel, fortunately a super–sized one, around his waist, hoisted my board, and we walked back up the beach together. He asked me about being a gay cop, and then we talked about his college, and a few minutes later we were at my apartment.

"The first thing we have to do," I said, once the door was closed behind us, "is get you out of this suit." I untied the towel and let it drop to the floor, then slipped my hands around his waist, under the waistband of the suit, and pulled it down. As I did, his big dick flopped out. If anything, it was fatter than I had imagined when I saw it pressing against the thin red fabric.

It wasn't quite hard, but it stiffened when I dropped to my knees and started licking it. His body shuddered as I wrapped my hands around those big globes of his ass and started moving his dick in and out of my mouth. It was too big for me to swallow comfortably, but he didn't mind—it was only a minute or two before he started panting and whimpering, and I pulled my mouth off just as he shot a load all over my chest.

"Sorry," he said, in a small voice.

"Never apologize for coming," I said, standing up.

"But it's all over your chest!"

I wrapped my arms around his waist and pulled him close to me, rubbing my chest against his as I leaned up and kissed him. "Oh, gee, now it's all over you, too," I said, when I finally leaned back. "Guess we both have to take showers."

My bathroom has a combination tub and shower, plenty big enough for Tom and me—provided we stayed close to each other. I turned the water on spray and then faced him, my hard dick rubbing against his thigh, which was lightly dusted with the same blond hair that freckled his chest.

We kissed again, and he grabbed my dick and started jerking it. "Slow down, cowboy," I said, taking hold of his wrist. "Nobody's in a hurry here, right?"

He grinned sheepishly. I took a bar of soap and began lathering him up, beginning with his shoulders, then his pecs, paying close attention to his nipples, which stood up like little toy soldiers by the time I was done with them. I spent a long time on the big expanse of his belly, running my hands up and down the smooth acres of flesh, then around and around in circles.

By this time he was hard again, though there wasn't much difference in size from soft to hard. I avoided the pubic area, working first down one leg, then the other, squatting down to massage each thigh and calf with lavender-scented soap. Every now and then he'd gulp a little, or sigh, and I kept up a steady patter, complimenting the softness of his flesh, the strength of his tendons, the sheer wonderful size of him.

I was turned on by how much of him there was. I didn't quite know why; many guys, Tom's roommates included, probably saw his fat as unattractive. But I've been with skinny guys who have nothing you can hold on to, dicks the size of pencils, lips that make you feel like you're kissing hard plastic.

I've been with guys I felt I could break if I wasn't careful, and I was reveling in Tom's size, even as I turned him around and began soaping the backs of his legs and that wonderful big ass. I greased up a finger with lather and pried apart his ass cheeks to find his puckered hole. Tom hiccupped a little.

"You like that?" I asked. "You like me to play with your ass?"

He sighed in response. I took that as a yes. I stood up, lathered my dick back into a rock-hard state, and then pressed myself up against his back. I reached around him for his tits, and fingered them while my dick struggled to make its way through his mountains of flesh and into his ass.

It was a tough go, I have to admit. I was fucking his ass cheeks more than his hole, but it still felt damn good to me. I thought about getting a condom but because I couldn't get into him I didn't think I needed one. Just being pressed up against him, his skin sliding against mine, was enough to get me off.

We rinsed and then stepped out of the tub. Tom immediately wanted to cover himself up with a towel, but I wouldn't let him. "Where's that phone of yours?" I asked. "We've got to send some photos to your so-called friends."

His eyes lit up. I kneeled down in front of him, pulled his fat dick straight out toward my face, and said, "Take this picture."

He leaned down and snapped. I stood up and then lay down on the bed, face up, with my legs pulled up to my shoulders. "Come over here. Spread my ass cheeks and stick your dick there. Then take a picture."

I loved the feeling of my legs resting on his shoulders, the way he was so big and so close to me. I was hard again, and thought I might come just from being near him.

"Oh, man," he said, when he'd snapped the shot and sent it. "Those guys are gonna cream."

He stood up and showed me the pictures. They were hot. I rolled over and said, "Come on, sit by me on the bed," making a place for him next to me.

"I should get dressed," he said, looking around the room. "You said I could borrow a pair of your brother's shorts?"

"Later. You're not getting away from me so easily. Come here, you big sexy thing."

He sat next to me, and his body language said he wasn't happy. I stretched out next to him and said, "Would you do something for me?"

"What?"

"Lie on top of me."

"I can't. I'll crush you."

"I'm not made of glass, brah. You won't crush me."

He faced me, swung one massive leg over me and balanced on the bed. Then, very carefully, he lowered himself onto me. But he was still supporting himself with his hands; there was almost no pressure on me. I took his head in my hands and brought his lips down to mine. He relaxed as we kissed, and I felt all his weight settle on top of me.

I had to stop kissing him to take some shallow breaths, but I didn't mind. It felt good, having all that weight on me. I felt safe and secure under him, and as a cop, I don't get that feeling very often.

His dick was rock hard, pressing against my stomach, and so I said, "Rub it. Rub that big dick against me."

He did, tentatively at first, but then he started getting into it. He leaned down and kissed me again, harder this time, and my stiff dick was rubbing against his as our tongues dueled, and I could only breathe through my nose so I wasn't getting that much oxygen to my brain. I think I experienced that heightened sense of orgasm that guys get when they try to strangle themselves while jerking off, because man, was that a powerful sensation. Every nerve ending in my body tensed and then released as the cum shot out of my dick, and at the same time I felt him come, too. He was still there on top of me for a minute, and then he rolled off.

"I never thought I could come like that," he said, panting. "That was awesome."

I could barely speak. "Me, too," I croaked.

"Jerking off in the bathroom is never going to be the same again."

I finally got my breath back. "Man, you have the dick of death. There must be enough size queens in Oregon so you never have to jerk off again."

"You think?"

"I know."

His phone rang. He looked at the display. "It's them."

"Go ahead, answer it."

He did. "With this guy I met at the beach. Yeah, that's him in the picture." He listened. "You didn't, huh? That's too bad."

He looked to me and whispered, "None of them got lucky."

"Aw, what a shame."

"Right now?" he said into the phone. "We're just fooling around. I might hang here for a while." Suddenly he laughed. "What do you mean, you never knew my dick was that big? I've been living with you guys for three months."

He listened some more, then looked over at me. "Go on, if you want to," I said. "You've worn me out."

"All right," he said back into the phone. "I'm just going to borrow some shorts. That bikini is way too skimpy."

He stood up. "Well, if you say so," he said, after a minute. "All right. I'll be back to the hotel in a few minutes." He hung up. "They want to see me in the bikini again. I know the three of them have fooled around together. I guess I'm finally going to get to join in."

"Go for it," I said, waving at him from the bed.

He leaned down over me and kissed me, hard, his tongue roaming around my lips like a predatory animal. "You are awesome," he said, and then, after squeezing back into that skimpy red bikini, he was gone.

And so the case of the miserable guy with the big dick was solved. Not one I'll write up for the police department, though. I'm not sure this is what the tourist office means when they ask us locals to extend the spirit of aloha to our visitors. But hey, it works for me.

Online, Nobody Knows You're A Dog

When I arrived at the House of Lo, a Chinese restaurant just off University Avenue in Mānoa, Jimmy Chang was having a hard time keeping a middle-aged Chinese woman away from the body of a young woman in the back parking lot. It was just after two in the morning, and I was cranky about being on the night shift to start with. Pulling up at the scene, I could see it was going to be a tough call.

A patrol car with reinforcements was right behind me, so Jimmy turned the hysterical woman over to them and came to talk to me. "The deceased is Susie Lo, a waitress here at her family restaurant."

The parking lot started to get busy, as the crime scene techs arrived, followed by the guys from the medical examiner's office. "That name sounds familiar to me."

"She was the one who found the body of that guy up by Honolulu Arts College at Christmas."

"Good memory."

He shifted uneasily from foot to foot.

"And?"

"I might have gone out with her once or twice."

I took his arm and walked him over toward University Avenue, where we could stand under a street light away from the rest of the crowd. "Might have, Jimmy?"

He shrugged. "She wasn't really a witness. I came here for dinner once and she was my waitress. We started to talk, and we hit it off."

"How long did you date her?"

"I wouldn't call it dating. We went out once, dinner and a movie, then I think we had coffee once up by her school. That was it."

"We'll get back to that. Tell me how you got here."

"911 call from a couple of UH students who were cutting through the parking lot on their way to a club. They found Susie—I mean the deceased. I got here a couple of minutes later."

He motioned over the two UH students who had found the body. The girl was freaking out, shivering and shaking, and the boy had his arm around her shoulders. From the tentative way his hand rested on her, I figured it was only a first or second date. They hadn't seen anyone else in the parking lot, or running past them as they approached. I got their names and numbers and let them go.

Jimmy's squad car was parked at the edge of the lot, its lights still strobing the night with blue light. He walked me back to the body, and the crime scene techs stepped away as I knelt down to look at her. Susie Lo was petite and chunky, with long black hair. I remembered how it had hung like a curtain over half her face.

"Those her parents over there?"

Jimmy nodded. A female officer was comforting Mrs. Lo, who was alternating between crying hysterically and screaming in Chinese. Mr. Lo stood there, not moving or speaking.

One of the worst things about my job is talking to the families of victims—particularly right after a crime has been committed. But I sucked it up and walked over to them. I introduced myself and asked if we could go inside the restaurant and sit down. The female patrol officer helped guide Mrs. Lo into the restaurant, which, like most of its kind, was decorated in red and gold. Red for good luck, gold for strength and wealth. I tried to ignore the irony as we sat down at a booth.

"Restaurant close one o'clock," Mr. Lo said. "Susie, she leave right away, out back door. She live few blocks away, share apartment with cousin."

I wrote down the address and the cousin's name, Peter Hung. "Peter good boy," Mr. Lo said. "He go UH. Become engineer."

Susie wasn't dating anyone, not that Mrs. Lo knew of. "She play computer a lot," her father said. I made a note of that.

According to her parents, there had been no angry customers, no one who paid a little too much attention to Susie Lo. She was a good student, a talented artist, studying computer animation at Honolulu Arts College.

In response to an urgent text message from his uncle, Peter Hung showed up at the House of Lo just as the medical examiner's van carrying the body of his cousin pulled out of the parking lot. After a quick conversation with his aunt and uncle in Cantonese, of which I understood about half a dozen words, he turned to me.

He was a skinny, pimply kid, and reminded me a lot of what my friend Harry had looked like when we were in high school. He was wearing baggy pants that looked like pajama bottoms and a UH T-shirt. He didn't look sleepy; he'd probably been up late studying.

Mr. and Mrs. Lo wanted to close the restaurant, so Peter and I walked out to the parking lot and I leaned against my truck while we talked. "Your aunt and uncle told me Susie was a sweet girl," I said. "I don't mean any disrespect here, but I have to know anything I can about her in order to find out who killed her."

He shrugged. "There aren't any hidden secrets, detective. Susie was just who everybody thought—a sweet girl, a little nerdy, a good artist. She's had a couple of boyfriends but nothing serious. We never got threatening phone calls and she never told me she was frightened of anybody."

"How about when she found that body at Christmas?" I asked. "Did she get upset about that?"

"Sure. It freaked her out. But she didn't know the guy and she got over it."

I made arrangements to meet him the next day at the apartment they had shared, and he left. By then, the crime scene techs had gone over the parking lot and packed up and Jimmy Chang had left for another call. Susie's body had gone to the morgue, and her parents had shut the restaurant down. The parking lot was empty except for me and my truck, lonely and a little scary in the late night. I stayed there for a few minutes, trying to get a feel for Susie Lo and who might have killed her, but I didn't get anything.

The next afternoon I met Peter Hung at a small two–bedroom a few blocks off University, in a neighborhood of low–rise buildings, both residential and commercial, that catered to the UH student body. The campus itself was just down the hill. "How come you don't live in the dorm?" I asked Peter after he led me inside.

"My parents and Susie's parents all wanted us to live at home. The only way they agreed to let us out of the house was if we kept an eye on each other." He gave me a half grin. "Neither of us were troublemakers, but you know parents."

The art on the walls in Susie's room was disturbing—lots of dark swirls and evil creatures, but Peter assured me his cousin just liked the style. "She was sort of a Goth in high school, but she got over it."

He turned on her computer and showed me some of her school projects. In one Flash movie, a Chinese dragon hatched from an egg, grew to full size, and flew away. It was beautifully drawn and smoothly animated. "I've got to study, detective," Peter said. "I've got an exam tomorrow, and I'm going to have to spend a lot of time at my aunt and uncle's over the next few days."

He left me in Susie's room and I started clicking on stuff on her desktop. I opened a text file labeled "Chat," and started to read a transcript of a session between two people, one called Li–Chi and the other Ultimareus. At first it was a lot of the "Hey, how you doing," stuff, but quickly it got racy, describing sexual positions and adventures in graphic detail. Both Li–Chi and Ultimareus were male—which made me wonder how Susie had gotten hold of their chat transcript.

As I read I had to remind myself that I was investigating a murder, not surfing some gay chat room. When I finished, I asked Peter what he knew about it.

He glanced at the beginning of the file. "Li–Chi was the name Susie used when she was playing *The Last Emperor*."

"What's that?"

"An online role–playing game. It takes place around the turn of the century, when there were factions warring for control in China, and the last emperor was a little boy. You can be a warrior, or a courtesan, or pretty much anything you want."

"What was Susie?"

"I don't know. We didn't talk about the game much."

"Did she play a lot?"

"Every day. Don't get me wrong, she always did her homework first."

"I'm not going to tell on her," I said. "Can you get me into the game?"

"I think so." I moved over, and he clicked a few things. Susie had saved her password, and soon we were facing a picture of The Forbidden City on the screen. Peter was navigating us along a pathway when a text message box popped up.

"I'm sorry, I'm sorry, I'm so sorry!" the message read. It was from Ultimareus, the person Susie had been communicating with in the chat transcript. "I was so sure I hurt you and I've been feeling so bad."

"Is that the guy who killed her?" Peter asked.

I shrugged. "Don't know." I applied my fingers to the keyboard. "You should be," I typed. "You really hurt me."

We waited. The next message appeared a minute later. "I just expected you to be, you know, a guy," the message read. "You freaked me out."

"Can we find out any info on this character?" I asked Peter.

He right–clicked on the character's name, and a personality profile window popped up, with some basic information:

Character: Ultimareus

Occupation: Sword maker

There were a few other things specific to the game, and at the bottom was a place where you could put in anything you wanted. It read, "Honolulu GAM ISO same."

My dabbling online helped me interpret that—Ultimareus was a gay Asian male in search of someone like himself.

A new message popped up on screen. "Can we still be friends?"

"Maybe in the next life," I muttered. But I typed, "Have to work again tonight. Meet me same time same place."

The letter "K" appeared on the screen, followed by a system message that Ultimareus had signed off.

"Susie the only one who used this computer?" I asked.

"Mostly. Sometimes I did."

"You ever sign on to the game? Pretend to be Li–Chi?"

"Nope."

"Not even late at night? I know how it is, you know. You get so horny sometimes, and if you're not out of the closet, it's hard to meet somebody, and so you go on line…"

"I'm not gay," he interrupted me.

"You can be honest with me, Peter. I won't tell your family, and I'll do my best to keep it out of the police records on the case."

"Don't put yourself out, detective. Like I told you, I'm not gay. I may still be a virgin, and I may stay a virgin until my skin clears up and my wallet gets fat, but when I do have sex, it'll be with a girl."

"What about Susie? You think maybe she was gay?"

He shook his head. "I've seen her moon around over guys."

"So how'd she hook up with this Ultimareus guy? And why all this explicit messaging back and forth?"

Suddenly there was a light bulb going off over his head. "I remember this time—not in *The Last Emperor*, but in this other game she used to play. Her character was a girl there, some kind of martial arts warrior, and guys were always hitting on her. It freaked her out. She said when she started playing TLE that she was going to be a guy."

"Why a gay guy, though?"

"The gays have their own scene in these games," he said. "The straight guys never even talk to them, if they can help it. I mean, this guy, Ultimareus? He says he's a sword maker. As far as I know, that's a kind of a code, some gay thing, where the sword is like a dick. I don't know what it is. But if I were in the game and I needed to buy a sword, I'd look at the profile for every sword maker to make sure I wasn't sending the wrong message."

I took Susie's computer into evidence and brought it down to the station, where I left it sitting on my desk. We'd been seeing a lot of complaints lately, people pretending to be someone else on line, and the department had just sponsored a seminar a week before. Whereas in the past, we'd seen pedophiles pretending to be teenagers to get close to their prey, now we were also seeing kids as young as eight or nine creating online identities in their late teens. It reminded me of a cartoon I'd seen once, a dog sitting at a keyboard typing. The caption was, "On the Internet, nobody knows you're a dog."

I hadn't understood it at first, had to get someone to explain it. But as I started hanging out in gay chat rooms, I got it. You could be anyone you wanted to be online—add years or pounds or shave them off. Change your gender or your sexual orientation if you wanted to see what that was like. Even the most honest men I'd met online lied about something, whether it was penis size, employment, or HIV status. It was enough to make me want to turn the damn thing off and just head for a gay bar. At least there you had a visual to go with your gut reactions.

By then, it was Sunday evening, and I called Harry Ho and asked if he could meet me for dinner.

"Thought you were working the late shift," he said.

"I am. I need your help."

We settled for a sushi bar a few blocks away from the station. "I might need you to come in and look at this computer for me."

I was already sitting at a table looking over the menu when he came up. "You don't want to sit up by the chef?" he asked, nodding toward the bar, where a sushi chef was making custom creations for diners. That's usually where we sat in any sushi place, so we could make friends with the chef and make sure we got the best, freshest sushi.

"I need to talk to you about a case, remember?"

"Oh, yeah." He sat down. We ordered a selection of *maki–zushi*, rice and seaweed rolls, and *nigiri–zushi*, rice topped with slices of cooked or raw fish. After the waitress left he asked, "Your case?"

I told him briefly about Susie Lo. "House of Lo?" he asked. "Didn't we used to go there when we were in high school?"

"That was House of Ko. On the other side of the campus."

"Oh. Or should I say Ko."

"Ho ho. Or should I say ko ko." I leaned forward. "Seriously, Harry, you ever play any of those online games? Like *The Last Emperor*?"

He shrugged. "A couple of times. I get cranky if the graphics don't move smoothly, or the game play is dumb, and I give up."

I told him about how Susie Lo had pretended to be a gay man on TLE. "I'm not surprised," he said. "The kind of guys who play those games have no social skills and they hit on every girl. I can see why she'd pretend to be a guy."

"But why a gay guy?"

"Who knows? Maybe the last guy she dated treated her badly, and she didn't want anything to do with straight guys for a while."

I thought of Jimmy Chang and wondered if there was more to his story than he had told me. "How do I find out more about Ultimareus?"

"Not easy. I mean, give me a day or two, I can hack into their database, but you can't use anything I find to get a warrant on the guy, you know that. And these companies are really careful about giving out personal data. You'll have to get a warrant, and that could take a while."

"I made a date with him for later tonight."

He nearly dropped his California roll. "A date? As yourself?"

I shook my head. "As Susie. He doesn't know he killed her."

"What's your take on all this?"

"I don't know. I'm thinking maybe Ultimareus met Li–Chi on line, and they hit it off. They had at least one smoldering sex chat, and either he hacked the database, like you said, or he figured out where she worked from something she said. It was Saturday night, he was horny, and he decided to meet up with her."

"Thinking she was a gay man?"

"Either that, or maybe he figured her out and got mad."

After we finished eating, we went back to the station. It took him a couple of minutes to hook the computer up and connect it to the station network, but eventually I saw that Forbidden City screen and knew we were in.

While I rounded up backup for my appointment behind the House of Lo with Ultimareus, Harry printed out some archived chat sessions between Ultimareus and Li–Chi. Li–Chi was a gardener on the grounds of the Imperial Palace, which gave Susie the chance to watch what was going on. She went to some kind of virtual fair where the sword maker was showing off his wares, and he approached her—first to see if she wanted a sword.

Their conversations were far–ranging. He liked an artist called Geiger, and so did she. From the way Harry described Geiger's work, I recognized the posters I'd seen on Susie's walls. Soon, they were online chatting every day, sometimes for an hour or more at a time. Reading through the logs, I found small clues— she mentioned working at her family's restaurant once, then the restaurant's general location another time. Several times she complained about working Saturday nights, saying that by the time she got off work at one a.m., she was tired and her clothes smelled like soy sauce and ginger.

Ultimareus was much cagier. There was almost nothing personal about him—some generic messages about work sucking, and a few comments sympathizing with the restrictions Li–Chi's family placed on her.

Harry went home around eleven, and I headed up to Mānoa to stake out the parking lot behind the House of Lo. There were half a dozen cops in various places, from inside the restaurant to lurking in the shadows at the edge of the lot. Jimmy Chang was in a van on University, along with a detective from Vice, ready to monitor my conversation from a wireless mike.

I peeled off my aloha shirt and strapped my bulletproof vest on. With my shirt back on, my gun in its holster and a can of mace strapped to my belt, I was ready to meet Ultimareus.

The whole set up reminded me of a blind date. I had, on a couple of occasions, met guys I'd connected with online. I always started out being careful and cautious—I'd only meet someone in a public place, without any commitment, giving both of us the chance to walk away if we didn't click. But usually those "dates" ended up with me going back to his place, or him to mine, and all those safety features went out the window. I was no longer so quick to judge when a complainant or victim said, "But he seemed so nice and trustworthy."

I was thinking of that bad dating practice when one of those "dates" came walking through the parking lot of the House of Lo. I'd met Louie Nakayama online one night when I was horny—and we'd agreed to meet at a 24–hour Zippy's in Waikīkī.

From there it was a quick jump back to my apartment, where we had some bad sex. He had strong body odor, which I didn't notice until we were both laying, spent and naked, on my bed.

He wasn't a great conversationalist, and when he said he wanted to see me again, I waffled. I gave him my cell phone number—with one number changed. Pretty mean, I know, but I didn't know how else to get him out of my apartment.

"Kimo! Hey, man, I tried to get hold of you but I must have written your number down wrong," he said.

Shit. Here I was on a stakeout, and I had to figure out a way to get rid of Louie quickly before Ultimareus showed up.

He was even less attractive than I remembered him. He was heavy, and the tank top he wore showed off his flabby arms and highlighted the roundness of his belly. It was no surprise that he spent his time online trolling for anonymous sex. I didn't know a gay man who would have given him a second look.

"Hey, Louie, how's it going?"

He came right up to me and hugged me, then kissed me on the lips. He still smelled bad and I could imagine the guys in the van and in the shadows were either laughing their heads off at me or grossed out.

"What brings you out this late?" I asked. "Meet up with a hot date online?"

"Not really. I mean, yeah, I met somebody online, but not a hot date."

Okay, I guess I was slow on the uptake. Seeing Louie there in the parking lot, the first thing I thought of was our own embarrassing encounter. I didn't make the connection to Susie Lo until that moment.

"What do you mean?" I asked, trying to think. I'd never expected that Ultimareus and I would have any kind of history.

"I thought at first it was a guy. We were grooving, then I found out it was a chick. Really messed with my head, you know."

"Weird. What happened when you found out?"

"I went a little crazy. It was right here in this lot last night. I knew that Li–Chi worked at this restaurant, and I knew what time his shift ended. I was determined I was going to meet up with him, you dig? But then the only person who came out of the restaurant was this little Chinese chick. She must have seen my picture, man, because she knew just who I was. She came up to me and started talking, and I was like, get away from me, girl, I'm meeting a man. Then she said, 'Ultimareus, it's me. Li–Chi.' And I realized she was he. I mean, she was this person I was so into online."

"Must have made you upset."

He nodded. He leaned in close. "I wasn't even thinking. I just grabbed this concrete block and swung at her, and then I was so freaked out I ran away. But she was back online today, so I guess she's okay."

"Bad news for you, Louie," I said. "That wasn't her online today, and she's not okay. Not at all." I pulled the handcuffs off my belt and snapped one on each of Louie's wrists before he could react. I was reading him his rights when my backup emerged from their hiding places.

"Be easy if you could date all our suspects," Jimmy Chang said, coming up with a smile on his face.

"You want to talk stink, Jimmy?" I asked. "How about you dating Susie Lo, giving her such a bad experience she started to pretend she was a gay man online?"

That shut him up. Louie Nakayama blubbered all the way down to the station, even after I'd read him his rights, trying to explain how much Susie Lo had hurt his feelings by pretending to be something she wasn't. "It's bad enough the gay guys all dis me," he said, making me feel bad. "Now even the straight women don't want anything to do with me."

I walked Louie through processing, and I was back at my desk just as my shift was ending when Jimmy Chang showed up. "Yeah?" I asked him.

He looked like he was ready to cry. "You really think I hurt her feelings so bad she gave up on men? She was a sweet kid, but after two dates she was talking about me meeting her parents, maybe her cousin moving out so I could move in with her. I'm not ready for that stuff."

"I'm not one to judge." I told him how I'd given Louie a wrong number.

Usually I feel good when I lock up a bad guy—but sitting there with Jimmy, I felt lousy. It wasn't Jimmy's fault that Susie had lied about her identity on line, and my ditching Louie hadn't turned him into a killer. But neither Jimmy nor I had acted honorably, and the fact remained that a woman he'd dated was dead, and a guy I'd dated had killed her.

There was a sour feeling in my gut, and I reached into my drawer for a couple of antacids, though I knew they wouldn't do much good. Jimmy left and I closed out the file on Susie Lo, though I had a feeling I'd be thinking about her for a while to come.

Jason Tupua answered his door in a faded University of Hawai'i T–shirt that stretched tight across his chest, and a pair of gym shorts so skimpy they might have been worn by a go–go boy at a gay club. "My name's Kimo Kanapa'aka," I said, showing him my badge. "I'm a detective. You filed a missing persons report?"

"Come in, please," he said, stepping back. I followed him into the living room of a small apartment, dark but cozy, in a rundown three–story building just outside downtown Honolulu, in a residential neighborhood near the Pali Highway.

I sat in the living room, and as Tupua got me a glass of water, I looked around. The furniture was old but the wooden coffee table shone with polish, and the room was adorned with knickknacks and personal memorabilia, including a sawed–off shotgun mounted on one wall over a series of family photos. The dark brown walls were hung with vibrant, impressionistic paintings that looked like sugar cane, brown stalks topped with bright green foliage. In some paintings the stalks glistened in sun, in others they shimmered with raindrops. A couple looked like they'd been painted in a hurricane, the stalks bent over in the wind. In some you could see a horizon, while in others it seemed like the artist had been lying on the ground looking forward through acres of cane. Looking closely at one, I saw the name 'Tupua' scrawled in a corner.

The missing man was named Abram Kastner; in his call, Jason Tupua had indicated they had a personal, sexual relationship, and so the case had been routed to me.

"When was the last time you saw your boyfriend?" I asked, as Jason came back into the living room and I accepted the water. I wasn't really thirsty, but I wanted Jason to think of me as a guest, and often letting someone get you something gives them that feeling. In missing persons cases, it's important to establish a rapport with those who are left behind; it helps them feel someone who cares is on the case, and you may find out information they wouldn't feel comfortable revealing otherwise.

"We prefer the term life partner," Jason said, a slight frown crossing his face. He was in his late twenties, and I couldn't pin down his ethnic identity; he had a Polynesian last name, but light skin and straight brown hair. "The last time I saw Abe was Monday morning, when he left for work."

It was Wednesday morning by then; you can't file a missing persons report on an adult unless the person has been gone for at least forty–eight hours. Kids are different; you can call in a missing child immediately, and we issue what we call a Maile alert, after a little girl who was abducted from a party and killed in 1985. But for a thirty–eight–year–old man like Abram Kastner, we make you wait two days.

It's not a great rule; if there has been foul play, you've already missed the window during which most crimes get solved. But human beings are quirky and unpredictable, and the missing persons workload would double or triple if we had to investigate every guy who was late home from work or every woman who just needed a few hours to herself without anyone knowing.

"Do you know of anyone who saw Mr. Kastner after he left you Monday morning? Somebody at his office? A neighbor who might have seen him leave?"

Jason Tupua shook his head. "He didn't go to his office. His boss called here a little after ten, worried that Abe was sick. We talked, and we both assumed that he had a meeting somewhere that he hadn't told either of us about."

He rubbed his nose. I went to a seminar where we learned to interpret body language, so I knew that was a sign of rejection, doubt, or lying. My experience had shown me that these signs were valid, so either Jason Tupua wasn't telling the truth, or he couldn't believe that his partner of two years had disappeared on him.

"Mr. Kastner worked for the Department of Corrections?" I asked, going back to my notes.

"Indirectly. He worked on a project funded by the University of Hawai'i to help parolees adjust to the outside world."

Not a good sign. People who spend a lot of time with the criminal element put themselves at risk, no matter how careful they are. "Did he often go to meetings at other locations?"

"Not without telling someone. Most of the time, his clients came to his office, but occasionally he met with a parole officer or went to court." He picked up a picture from the coffee table—him and Abram Kastner at a party somewhere—and his hand shook. "I started to worry when he didn't call before I left for work, like he always does."

"He never called you at all?"

"No. And he didn't call his office, either, which isn't like him at all." He rubbed his nose again, then ran his hand over his forehead and into his hair. The worry seemed to be etching lines into his face.

"Any chance he could have just gotten disgusted with things, decided he needed a breather? People do that sometimes, you know."

"Not Abe." Tupua was firm about that. "Abe likes to take care of people. It's like his reason for being, you know? I mean, even if we were having problems, and I'm not going to lie to you, we did have problems now and then, and he went somewhere to cool down, he always went to work. Always. He felt he had a responsibility to those people. And Abe took his responsibilities very seriously."

"You say he used to go somewhere to cool down. You know where?"

"His ex–boyfriend's place." I raised my eyebrows at that, so Tupua went on. "It's not like you're thinking. They're just good friends. Abe didn't like confrontation. He said it was counterproductive. So when he got mad, instead of letting it out, he'd go over to Gus's place and stay there until he cooled down."

"You checked with Gus?"

"Gus hasn't heard from him either."

I collected the rest of the information I needed— address and phone numbers for Kastner's office, his friend Gus, and a few other friends in the islands and back on the mainland. "How about his car?" I asked. "You know the license number?"

"We share a car," Tupua said. "It's parked outside. But we both go to work on the bus."

"Any places Mr. Kastner liked to hang out—places I could check for him?"

Kastner, it turned out, was a homebody. After he and Jason Tupua moved in together they'd stopped going out. Nesting, Tupua called it. They didn't have a lot of money and they both worked long hours, so in their free time they just stayed home.

I put away my notepad and stood up. "I'll start making some phone calls," I said. "Please let me know if you hear anything—a neighbor who might have seen him waiting for the bus, a friend who might have spotted him somewhere. Did he have a cell phone?"

Tupua nodded, and gave me the number. "I've called it a dozen times but I never get an answer."

I asked if I could take a look around the apartment, and Tupua agreed. The place was tiny but clean, just the living room, galley kitchen, a bedroom with a queen–sized platform bed, and a pink and gray tiled bathroom with a leaky toilet. Most likely, I could eliminate a kidnapping for ransom from the possibilities.

Tupua followed me downstairs, where he walked me over to the car he and Kastner shared. As a formality, I had him open it up, including the trunk, though there was nothing there to see.

"You'll call me as soon as you find him, won't you?" he said, as I climbed into my truck.

"I'll be in touch as soon as I have anything to report." I gave him a little wave as I pulled away.

I headed back downtown, parking in the police garage and then walking the couple of blocks to Abram Kastner's office, in a nondescript office building just down Beretania Street. His boss, a short, plump woman named Mabel Tseng, showed the same kind of concern that I had found in Jason Tupua.

"Abe is the soul of reliability," she said. "He's never once been late to work or missed an appointment in four years."

"Tell me about his job." I sat down next to Mabel's desk and she started looking through Abe's case files. "Any clients threaten him lately?"

She shook her head. "Abe's a case worker with offenders on parole. He helps them find housing, find jobs, get reintegrated into the community. His clients like him because he genuinely cares about them. He has a real feel for the underdog."

Even so, she found a half dozen cases where Abe was either working with someone who had served time for a violent crime, or with a parolee with a history of mental instability. She gave me their names, phone numbers, and home and work addresses, and I started checking.

Louis Akana was a mildly retarded man the size of a small mountain. He was twenty–five and had recently finished a ten–year sentence for the killing of a neighbor girl, which his family had maintained all along was simply an accident, Louis unaware of his own strength. He was living with his mom again, working as a bag boy at the Safeway in Aiea. His time card showed he had clocked in at seven and clocked out at eleven for a fifteen–minute break. Assuming Jason Tupua had seen Abram Kastner leave for work around eight, Louis Akana was in the clear.

Frankie Chang and a couple of his friends had been growing dope in an isolated plot off the Likelike Highway. A couple of hikers stumbled on the plot, and Frankie's buddy shot them both dead. For helping to dispose of the bodies, Frankie served four years at the Oʻahu Community Correctional Facility in Kalihi. He had nothing but good things to say about Abram Kastner.

"He solid, brah," he told me, outside the warehouse facility in Salt Lake where he assembled circuit boards for a Japanese company. "He get me this gig, get me taking college courses.

Without him, my life be *pau*." An ex–con's life could easily be finished if he got on the wrong path, and I was glad Kastner had been able to help. Frankie's alibi checked out, too; he had taken an exam in his 8 a.m. algebra class at Honolulu Community College. His professor marked the time the student finished on each exam, and Frankie hadn't handed his in until the bell rang at 9:15. Though the college wasn't far from Kastner's apartment, there was no way Frankie could have made it in rush hour traffic.

By Wednesday evening I was beat, but I had an appointment to meet Gus Weir at his apartment, just a few blocks from where Abram Kastner and Jason Tupua lived. My shift had long since ended, but I got Lieutenant Sampson to authorize the overtime because I had a bad feeling. I was worried that some nutty parolee had Kastner tied up somewhere, torturing him. Too much time had passed already, and the uncertain vibe I'd gotten from Jason Tupua didn't make me feel any better.

Sometimes a case catches you, and you have trouble letting it go. I was single, and looking for a boyfriend, and what Abe and Jason had, from the outside, looked good to me. I had to find out what happened to keep that dream of my own a possibility. Either that or I felt Abe's *akua*, or spirit, pulling at me, demanding that I find out what happened to him.

Weir met me at the open door of his bungalow, light spilling out from behind him. He was a heavyset guy in his mid–forties, wearing sweats and a T–shirt that read "I don't know what your problem is, but I'll bet it's hard to pronounce."

"Abe was a caretaker," he said, once I was sitting in his living room, echoing what Jason Tupua had told me. "When we met, I was a drunk." He laughed. "Hell, I'm still a drunk, I just don't drink these days. Abe helped me get sober, and then…" He shrugged.

"But you were still friends?"

"Oh, sure. You couldn't help but be Abe's friend."

"How about Jason? He told me he used to fight with Abe sometimes, and Abe would come here."

"Abe refused to let himself get too angry. So rather than let loose on Jason, he'd walk out. He'd come to me because he knew I couldn't have anything in the house—no drugs, no liquor. Hell, I don't even smoke cigarettes."

"And you never…"

"What? Fucked each other?" He laughed. "Hell, look at me. You think I can compete with Jason? Abe didn't come here for sex. No, he had his hands full with Jason. In more ways than one."

"What do you mean by that?"

"Jason tell you about his past?"

I shook my head. "We didn't talk about him at all. He's the one who painted the paintings, right?"

"Yup. Every time I go over there he's done another one." He paused. "I don't know all the details, but I know his dad killed his mom, then committed suicide. You see that shotgun up on the wall?"

I remembered it. "Yeah, up above some family pictures."

"That's what his dad used. Jason's the one found the bodies, in his dad's van out in the cane fields. Some little piece of land his family owned. When his folks showed up missing, it was Jason who led the cops out there. Jason cleaned it all up, too. Sold the van, kept the gun."

"Kind of creepy. Is that the field he's always painting?"

Gus nodded. "Abe's a caretaker," he repeated. "Jason needs a lot of taking care of."

I thought about that on my way back to my apartment in Waikīkī. "Every pot has its lid," I remember my mother saying when I was a kid. Was that all relationships were, one person's neuroses complementing the other's? Abe Kastner was a caretaker, and Jason Tupua needed someone to take care of him. What did I need, I wondered, and what could I give to the man who needed me?

The next morning, as my shift was starting, I googled Jason Tupua, and then looked up the old case files. It was pretty much as Gus had described; Viti Tupua, who had emigrated from Samoa, had married Grace Edwards; they had one child, Jason. Twelve years before, when Jason was sixteen, Viti had taken Grace out to a piece of cane field her family had once farmed, which by then had been leased out to a large operation. Once there, he had shot her, and then himself.

The article I read speculated that Viti had been depressed and jealous. He was a possessive husband, always had to know where Grace was and when she'd be home. A sad kind of love for Jason to witness growing up.

Jason probably knew more about the case than he had ever said, either to a journalist or to the police. He came home from high school that day to find the house empty. When his parents didn't come back for dinner, he called the police, worried. An officer went out to the house, and Jason convinced him that he knew where his folks were.

The officer drove him out there, and the resulting story made the news for at least a week. I was in college in Santa Cruz then, so I had missed the fuss. I looked up the ownership of that land; it was still registered to Jason Tupua, and the deed showed there was a small building out there. Creepy, I thought, to hold on to the land for so long, and creepier still to keep painting it, over and over again.

Jason's paintings bothered me, and once I had wiped the most likely of Abe's clients off my list, I was left with his partner. I worried that perhaps Jason had Abe locked up out at the cane fields, trying to hold onto him in a way that he hadn't been able to hold onto his parents.

I had a little experience myself with obsessive love. When I first came out of the closet, I was so desperate to make all the trouble I'd gone to make sense that I grabbed onto the first guy who showed some interest in me. It was tough to let him go, when it became obvious that we both had to move on. I felt that kind of heart–rending angst that comes on you when you think no one will ever love you again.

From everything I'd heard, Jason was just as emotionally fragile. I needed to talk to him again, gay man to gay man, to see how obsessive his love for Abe Kastner was. Could it drive him to do something harmful?

There was no answer at the apartment, so I drove over there. The car he and Abe shared was gone from its parking space, and there was no response when I rang the bell. I looked in through the window and saw the shotgun was gone from its place on the wall. I got a sinking sensation in my stomach.

I took Kam Highway through town, heading toward the north shore and the piece of land Jason Tupua still owned. As I got closer, I noticed that there was no sugar cane. Anywhere. Coffee, papayas, and some tall stalks that looked like corn stretched out all around me. I branched off on a dirt road that headed up toward Wilson Ditch, and then I stopped short.

Jason and Abe's beat–up Toyota Celica was parked at the edge of the road. I used my cell phone to call the Wahiawā station for backup, then, my senses on alert, I drew my weapon and eased out of my truck. Using its body for cover, I moved alongside until I could see into the field. Jason Tupua sat next to a mound of earth, his shoulders slumped, his hands dangling. I wondered where the shotgun was.

I kept my gun in my hand. "Jason?"

He looked up at the sound of my voice. "Detective?"

I stepped slowly into his field of vision. "You knew where Abe was all along."

He looked up at me. "I know you won't believe me, but I didn't," he said. "I must have blocked it out. It wasn't until this morning that I remembered."

I wanted to believe him, but I didn't. "What made you remember?"

He held up his left hand. The palm was swathed in gauze. "I broke a glass in the sink and cut my hand picking it up. It was the blood." His gaze shifted toward the horizon. "This is where he did it, you know. My dad."

"Why do you think he did?" My senses were on super–alert, watching Jason for any indication that he had the shotgun handy and might use it.

"He loved my mom so much, but he never had a clue what she was all about," Jason said. "I used to wonder about that—was it that they came from different races, different backgrounds? Was it just that he was a man and she was a woman? But men and women have been marrying each other forever, and there's lots of mixed–race families that are just fine."

He looked down at the ground. "She was starting menopause, and she would get all weepy sometimes, and then angry for no reason. She bought all this sexy lingerie to wear for him, but he thought it meant she was having an affair."

"That's why he killed her? He suspected she was cheating?"

"That's what he said in the note. And that he couldn't live without her." He looked over at me, and his cheeks were glistening. "I thought that was so romantic, you know? I mean, how dumb is that? I wanted someone to love me that much."

"And Abe didn't?" I said gently.

"He did," Jason insisted. "I know he did. But he loved me for the wrong reasons. Because I was a project. Because he thought he could save me."

"Why don't you let me drive you back to town," I said, moving toward him.

"No!" he shouted, jumping up. "Stay away from me." That's when I saw the sawed–off shotgun behind him. He grabbed it with his right hand.

My adrenaline level soared. Where was my backup? I hoped I had given the dispatcher good enough directions.

"Come on, Jason," I said, as calmly as I could. "Put the gun down and let me help you. You need help. Abe saw that. He wanted you to get help."

"Abe couldn't help me."

He waved the shotgun at me and I pulled my gun up and pointed it at him. "You don't want to do that, Jason. Put the gun down."

"I figured something out, you know. My dad wasn't dumb. He was crazy, and so am I. Broken. Can't be fixed."

"Nobody is so broken that they can't be fixed. Put the shotgun down and we can talk some more."

He shook his head, clenching his eyes shut and grimacing. I thought about tackling him but I didn't want that shotgun to go off. "Abe tried, and he couldn't. Look at me—I did just what my dad did. I killed the one person who loved me."

"Why? Did you guys have a fight? Was he going to leave you?"

I remembered, with a sudden twist of my stomach, when that first boyfriend told me that he wasn't ready for the level of commitment I wanted, that he was breaking up with me. I struggled to put that memory aside and return to the moment, there in the cane field with Jason, mosquitoes buzzing around us.

"He told me I needed therapy. That I was more messed up than he could handle." In the sunlight streaming down on us, I saw tears staining his face. "I couldn't do it. I was afraid that if I talked to a shrink, I wouldn't be able to paint any more. Abe couldn't understand that, even though he knew me better than anyone. He could only see what therapy could bring, not what it could take away."

"You don't know that. I'll bet lots of people in therapy draw and paint and write stories and compose music." The shotgun dangled slackly from his hand, and I wondered if I could get close enough to him to kick it away.

"As therapy," he said. "Not as art. I couldn't take that chance." He wiped his nose on his left shirt sleeve. "Abe told me that if I wouldn't go to see a shrink, he'd leave me. That he couldn't stay with me if there wasn't a hope that I could get better." He looked up at me. "I was just another project to him. Like getting Gus to give up booze and weed. I thought he didn't love me at all."

I listened for sirens in the distance, but all I heard was the sound of a small animal moving around in the cane. "I'm sure that wasn't the case."

"I thought it was. Sunday morning, I told him that I wanted to come out here, to say goodbye to my parents one last time. That then I'd go for therapy. I'd do whatever he wanted, as long as he didn't leave me."

"It's going to be okay, Jason," I said, moving a little closer to him. "Why don't you come with me. We'll go down to my station, and you can tell me all about it. You can write it all down."

"I have to be with Abe. He was the only one who really loved me, and I killed him." He pulled the sawed–off shotgun up to his head, and before I could move, he pulled the trigger. His body toppled backward, falling over the open grave that contained Abe Kastner's body. If I could have, I would have left them both like that, together forever.

I ran into an old girlfriend the other day, one of the last women I dated before I finally acknowledged my desires and stepped out of the closet. Mindy Kerner was a secretary at a law office, and we met when her boss defended a guy I arrested for grand theft auto. I went to the office to give a deposition, and while I was there, Mindy asked me out.

She was that kind of take–charge girl, and we'd dated for a couple of months, until lack of interest on my part corresponded with her meeting someone new. I wasn't sorry we broke up, and I wasn't all that happy to see her again, either.

I dated – and slept with – a lot of women while I was trying to be straight. Seeing any of them again is awkward; I'm afraid one will accuse me of wasting her time, or worse. But Mindy came running up and gave me a big hug and a kiss.

"Kimo, I'm so glad to see you!" she said. "I read about you in the paper and I've been meaning to call, really." Since my coming–out made the news in Honolulu, I've gotten a mixed reception from friends and acquaintances. None as enthusiastic as Mindy, though.

"I want to hear about everything that's happened to you," she said. We were standing outside the Takashimaya store at the Ala Moana Center, and streams of Japanese tourists passed us as Mindy enthused about seeing me. I agreed to stop by her apartment that evening just to get her to shut up.

Don't get me wrong, I like Mindy. She has a good heart, even if her personality comes on strong. We had a lot of interests in common—we went roller blading together, to alternative music concerts and the zoo at Kapi'olani Park. I figured I'd spend an hour at her apartment, talking about our lives and our history, and then be on my way.

She still lived at the same address, a second–story walk up in the Salt Lake neighborhood, out by the Aloha Bowl stadium.

It was called a garden apartment complex, but the only gardens I ever saw were the potted plants on her neighbor's balcony. I pulled into a parking spot in front of her building just as night was falling, a few stars beginning to twinkle against the darkening sky.

We sat on the couch next to each other and we were soon chatting away like old friends—which I guess you could say we were. About a half hour passed, going over the things we'd done and the people we knew. It was all very innocuous.

Mindy still used the same perfume, Elizabeth Taylor's White Diamonds, which smelled like sandalwood. I'd always liked it, liked the way the fragrance clung to my body after we had sex. She wore a low-cut light-green blouse with cap sleeves, and a white leather miniskirt so short I could tell she wasn't wearing anything under it. I wondered if she'd dressed that way deliberately, trying to remind me of what I'd given up.

Her living room hadn't changed much since we dated. The same overstuffed couch in a floral print, framed posters of tropical flowers on the walls. It was a girly apartment, from the scented candles to the stained glass hibiscus hanging over one window.

My senses are always on alert, even when I'm off duty, so I heard the sound of someone setting a car alarm outside—a tiny whoop of a siren, then silence. It coincided with Mindy jumping me.

We were talking about a co-worker of hers I'd met, and suddenly she planted her lips on mine and swung over to straddle me, her leather miniskirt riding up to her waist. It took me by surprise; it had been a while since I'd had such intimate contact with a woman, and I was assaulted by sense memories, as well as the strangeness of it all. My dick didn't mind it, though; it popped up to attention. I remember marveling, in the middle of it all, at how confused I must be. Did I respond to any old stimulus? Was I really gay, if a woman's kiss and caress could turn me on? I always thought a bisexual was just somebody who couldn't make up his or her mind—was I one of them?

It only got stranger when I heard a key in the lock, and then the door swung open. A haole bodybuilder type stood there, framed in the light. He had a deep tan, and his dark hair was shaved down to a stubble. "Hi, honey!" Mindy said, looking up. "This is Kimo, my ex–boyfriend. Kimo, meet Bobby."

My dick was still standing at attention, though I hoped Bobby wouldn't notice. "Come on in, honey, close the door behind you," Mindy said.

"Hey," I said, trying to get Mindy off me, but she wasn't moving.

Bobby mumbled something, then stepped inside and closed the door behind him. "You remember, I told you about Kimo," Mindy said to him. "He's gay."

Bobby looked shell–shocked. What Mindy said next, though, shocked me, too. "Come on, honey, take your clothes off." She started unbuttoning my aloha shirt, running a lacquered fingernail down the center of my chest.

She was still straddling me on the couch, and she leaned over and began kissing the edge of my chin. The evening's surprises weren't over yet; to my astonishment Bobby began doing just as she said.

My eyes fastened on his body and wouldn't let go as he began to unwrap himself. First he pulled his T–shirt above his head, revealing washboard abs and biceps as thick as my leg. He kicked off his sandals, then unfastened his shorts and dropped them to the floor.

My body was going nuts, and I wasn't sure if it was the pressure of Mindy's ass on my stiff dick, her nibbling on my chin, or the show going on in front of me.

Bobby was wearing a pair of white Calvin Klein briefs, and his dick was already hard and pressing against them. Mindy began rocking her ass over my dick and I started to worry I was going to come in my pants. "Come on, honey, the shorts, too," Mindy said.

I was having trouble catching my breath, between seeing Bobby's body and the pressure of Mindy's body against me. The overhead light shone on Bobby like a spotlight as he peeled the white fabric down, shimmying the tight shorts over his well–muscled thighs and calves. He stepped out of them, and took a few steps closer to us on the couch. He was like some Greek sculpture come to life, the musculature so clearly defined. A spot of precum glistened at the head of his dick.

I wondered if this was the first time they'd played out this scenario. Was this why Mindy was so happy to see me at the Ala Moana Mall that afternoon?

"Bobby has a nice dick, doesn't he, Kimo?" Mindy said. "Do you want to suck it? I suck it sometimes, but I think Bobby really wants a guy to do it for him."

Maybe my jaw dropped open a little farther because of the weirdness of the scene, or maybe because I did want to suck on that fat, juicy dick, but Bobby came closer and somehow his dick found its way into my mouth. I grabbed his firm ass cheeks and began pumping his dick in and out.

Mindy must have sensed how close I was to shooting a load, because she slid off me and sat sideways on the sofa, watching me suck her boyfriend's dick. "I'll bet you want to kiss Bobby, don't you, Kimo?" she said. "With the taste of his cock in your mouth. Bobby likes that."

Who was I to argue? I stood up, letting Bobby's fat dick bounce around in the air for a bit, and we locked lips. He kissed with a bit too much tongue for me—but then, I remembered Mindy had kissed that way, too.

When I looked over at Mindy, I noticed she had opened her blouse and her tits were hanging free. She was peeling off the miniskirt, and I decided I didn't want to be the only one left clothed, so I stripped, too. Mindy stood up next to Bobby, wrapping one leg around him like a flamingo, and they began making out.

Once I was naked, I asked Mindy, "You got a condom around here? I want to fuck your boyfriend's ass."

"He'll like that," Mindy said, backing off Bobby's mouth. She reached over for her purse.

"How about you, Bobby?" I asked, reaching over to pinch his left tit. "You ever speak for yourself, or you let Mindy do all the talking? You want me to fuck your ass?"

He panted as I flicked my index finger over the other tit. It was hot in the apartment, and he'd started to sweat. "Yes, sir," he said. "Please, fuck my ass with your big cop dick."

If I hadn't been so horny I would have burst out laughing. The dialogue sounded like it had come from some cheap porno flick—but then, wasn't that what we were acting out, there in Mindy's second–floor living room?

She unwrapped the condom, squirted some lube on my dick, and slipped the sheath on me as Bobby and I kissed again. "Bobby's going to need some loosening up," I said. "I'll bet he'd like your tongue to do that for him."

She got right to work, kneeling on the floor behind Bobby and sucking and tonguing his ass noisily. Bobby's dick and mine were dueling as we pressed our bodies together. He was very hairy, and I loved the feeling of that hair sliding against my skin. All the Asian in me has made me pretty smooth, though I've got a nice patch of pubic hair, and hairy guys really turned me on. He was such a hot guy, a little on the short side, but those muscles more than made up for it. And he was enthusiastic, even if he didn't say much.

"He's ready for you," Mindy said, backing away. I turned Bobby around and bent him over the back of the sofa. With my right hand, I guided my condom–coated dick up to his ass.

"Just relax, Bobby," I said. "This is going to hurt for a while, but then it's going to feel really good."

I felt him suck in a deep breath as I plunged my dick into his ass, sliding past the sphincter and up into his chute. He was whimpering and panting, but I went slow, and kissed his neck as

I did, and soon he was relaxed enough to start enjoying himself. I was just starting a rhythm when I felt Mindy's mouth at my own ass, starting to lick and suck.

I'd been part of a threesome once, in college, but then the girl had been the center of our attention, and the other guy and I had barely touched each other, scrambling around trying to position ourselves around her mouth, vagina and ass. This time, I was in the middle, and I wasn't minding it at all.

I was getting into fucking Bobby, so much that I hardly noticed when Mindy stopped her attentions to my ass. I noticed quickly, though, when I felt something hard poking at me back there. Looking over my shoulder I saw Mindy had strapped on a dildo and was preparing to fuck me as I fucked her boyfriend.

There's a kind of delirium that comes over you when you're in the middle of a good fuck. Things you'd ordinarily never do seem perfectly acceptable. So I didn't mind when Mindy's painted fingernails wrapped around my hips, and she slid that dildo— fortunately a skinny model—up my ass. I wondered how many times she had fucked Bobby before stumbling on me at the Ala Moana Mall.

I reached around in front of me and grabbed hold of Bobby's dick. It was leaking precum, so it was easy to get it lubed up, and I started pulling on it as I pumped his ass. It didn't take long before I started shooting, and that triggered him to come as well.

I pulled out of him, and Mindy backed off me, and the three of us collapsed in a heap on the floor. Bobby's dick was limp until Mindy leaned down and started sucking on it. Then she backed off, and leaned back with her legs open. As I watched, Bobby slipped another condom onto his dick and then plunged into Mindy.

I was feeling a little left out until Bobby said, "Feed me your dick, man," motioning me to come around to where he could suck me. I stood over Mindy's head, my balls hanging low, and Bobby swallowed my dick. Mindy reached up to stroke my balls, and it wasn't long before we all came again—this time the three of us in quick succession.

They invited me to stick around for pizza and beer afterward, but I'd had enough strange sensations for one evening. It was one thing to fuck your ex–girlfriend's boyfriend, then have him suck your dick while he was fucking her. I decided it would be just too weird to stick around for casual conversation.

So I begged off, and ducked into Mindy's bathroom for a quick cleanup. When I came out, my overworked dick stuffed into my pants, buttoning my shirt, I found them on the sofa deep throating each other while they waited for the pizza to arrive.

"Great to see you again, Mindy," I said. "Nice to meet you, Bobby." I gave them a little wave as I let myself out the door—polite to my hosts as ever.

On the way home, I thought about what had happened, about the confusing feelings and emotions that had taken over me. And I wondered about Mindy—did she have a taste for soon–to–be–gay boyfriends? Had this whole interlude been her way of pushing Bobby out of the closet? But then I turned the radio on, letting Israel Kamakawiwoʻole's sweet tenor wash over the car. Some mysteries, I decided, didn't need to be investigated.

The Sun God and the Boy He Loved

It was late afternoon, nearly the end of my shift, when I got a call on a questionable death at Queen's Medical Center. I found the patrol officer, a middle–aged Chinese guy named Frank Sit, whom I had worked with before, out in the corridor, and he gave me the rundown. "Victim's name is Hy Nguyen, ethnic Vietnamese. Twenty–six years old, HIV positive, in the middle of an attack of something called *pneumocystis carinii*. His lover found him dead in his bed here at the hospital."

"You think it's a homicide?"

He nodded. "For now. The lover is the suspect, Caucasian male named Paul Ford, forty–two. Ford spent a lot of time at the boy's bedside. Nurses verify he was very devoted. After the doctor was in this morning, Ford got pretty upset. Nurse says she saw him leave the room, crying. About a half hour later, he returned to the room, and called for help. The boy was dead, and Ford told the nurse several times, and I quote, 'I killed him. It's all my fault.' The nurse called 911 and I reported."

"Any indication of foul play?"

"I just secured the room with the body, called you and called the ME's office —I leave the investigating up to you guys. You want to take a look?"

Sit led me down the hall to a single room overlooking the highway, and pulled the sheet down off the body in the bed. The deceased was a willowy young Vietnamese man. The ravages of the virus had accentuated his slimness, and given his skin a pale, almost translucent quality.

Together, we examined the body carefully, looking for any sign of trauma. The boy's eyes were closed, and I took a Q–tip from the bedside and used it to slide open one eyelid. Leaning close, I saw what I was looking for—tiny red veins in the eye, the sign of a petechial hemorrhage. I pointed it out to Frank. "You think the lover suffocated him?" he asked.

"Somebody did. And unless this guy prefers otherwise, let's call him the partner, Frank." I threw the Q–tip in the trash. "Let's talk to him."

I hate being some kind of language police, but it's part of the sensitivity training sessions I help facilitate for the force every few months. We say "sexual orientation," not "sexual preference." We say "partner," or, if more appropriate, "boyfriend," rather than "lover."

Two months before, I had started dating Mike Riccardi, a fire inspector I'd met on a case, and I was just getting accustomed to calling him my boyfriend. I hoped that some day we would move on to partner.

Paul Ford was sitting at a wooden table, a chunky guy with sandy blonde hair thinning at the top. He looked like he'd been through hell. His hair was rumpled and his eyes were red and teary, and it looked like he'd slept in his clothes the night before, probably at Hy Nguyen's bedside.

I introduced myself and sat down across from him. "I know you," he said. "You're the gay cop, aren't you?"

"That's what they call me these days. I want to tell you how sorry I am for your loss. You must be going through a lot of pain."

"He was such a beautiful boy," Ford said. "Have you seen him?" I nodded. "He hasn't been the same for a while. I have a picture in my wallet, the way he used to look. Here, let me show you." He pulled a photo out, worn thin and slightly frayed at the edges. Ford sat on a beach somewhere, shirtless, in a pair of orange print swim trunks. His arms were around a dark–haired Vietnamese boy whose face glowed. Nguyen was thin but he had a strong chest and features that anyone would have called handsome.

"He was," I said. "Beautiful."

"And I killed him," Ford said. "I was pretty wild before I met him. When I was in San Francisco, I almost lived at the baths. I sucked and fucked more guys than work in this whole building.

Who ever heard of a virus then? You couldn't get another guy pregnant, and they could clear up VD with a shot of penicillin. Then I came to Hawai'i and I met Hy, and I stopped all that. It was just him, just him and me."

His eyes filled with tears and he pulled a rumpled tissue from his shirt pocket. "A year ago we both got tested. Both of us were positive. He hadn't been around much before he met me, so we knew he got it from me."

"And that's why you said you killed him?"

"Well, I did, didn't I?"

"Did you try to ease his suffering? He must have been in a lot of pain."

"I did whatever I could. Then this last episode. I couldn't keep him at home. I had to bring him in here."

"Did you suffocate him? To put him out of his misery."

He stared at me as if I'd announced I was a police detective from Mars. "I didn't suffocate him."

"But you said you killed him."

"I gave him that goddamned virus. I infected him."

"The disease got loose in his body and started running wild with his cells. But that's not what killed him. I can't say until the medical examiner performs the autopsy, but it looks like what killed your partner was suffocation."

I went back to Hy Nguyen's room and took photos of the crime scene. Then one of the assistant medical examiners arrived and transferred the body to a gurney for transport. Paul Ford saw the toe tag on the body, sticking out from under the cover of the sheet, and broke into sobs. I put my arm around his shoulders and led him out to the parking lot. I told him not to leave town, that I would be in touch with him after I did some investigating. By the time we reached his car, he had stopped crying and told me he was okay to drive home.

"Be careful," I said, closing the driver's door for him and watching him leave the parking lot. Then I went back upstairs to talk to the nurse on duty, a petite Vietnamese woman named Khanh Le.

She verified the account she had given to Frank Sit. I asked if anyone else had gone into Nguyen's room while Ford was away. She shrugged. "There are four of us on this floor, and twenty–four patients. Nobody monitors who comes and goes."

I had a feeling she wasn't telling the whole truth, but I figured it was because she had slipped away from her post and didn't want to get caught. There was nothing I could do to challenge her.

The crime scene techs took all the linens into evidence, as well as dusting the room for prints. While they were working, I went around to each nurse, and as many patients and visitors I could talk to, asking about anyone going in or out of Hy Nguyen's room. I got nothing.

There was nothing else I could do without evidence, so I tabled the case until I got the medical examiner's report, which came in the next afternoon. In addition to the petechial hemorrhaging, cotton fibers had been found in Hy Nguyen's airway.

I drove out to Paul Ford's house, where I found him agitated, pacing around the living room of the bungalow he had shared with Hy Nguyen. I expected Ford to have rested, but he still looked like a wreck.

"Do you know a good lawyer?" he asked me, as I walked in. "This shouldn't be happening. Hy left a letter, goddamn it. One of those durable powers of attorney. He wanted me to plan the funeral. He didn't want that asshole family of his around."

He looked at me. "That's supposed to be the law, isn't it? His goddamn family can't just march in and take over."

I felt like I'd been flipping channels and landed on some program right in the middle, not a clue what was going on. But when a suspect wants to talk, you let him. "Tell me what's going on," I said.

"Hy didn't even want them coming to visit him, not while he was in the hospital. His mother, she's a real bitch. He said it made him too weak to have to deal with her when he was already sick."

"Let's start from the beginning," I said gently. "Come on, sit down, try and relax. Tell me how you met Hy."

"It was a lecture at UH. About four years ago. Hy had just graduated from UCLA and moved to Honolulu. We both loved Greek mythology, and there was a lecture up there about finding the gay characters behind the myths. You know the story of Apollo and Hyacinthus?"

I shook my head. "I'm not really up on my Greek mythology. Apollo, he's the god of the sun, isn't he?"

Paul Ford nodded. "He drives the chariot of the sun across the sky every day. In this myth, Apollo loved a boy named Hyacinthus. There were only about a dozen guys there, and afterward Hy said something about the coincidence of his name—you know, Hy and Hyacinthus." He paused. "I've got a book around here somewhere—I could lend it to you."

"That's okay. So you and Hy started talking?"

"Yeah. We really hit it off. One thing led to another, and after we'd been dating for a few months I lost my lease, and he invited me to move in here."

"This was his house?"

That set him off again, and he was up, pacing and gesturing. "His goddamn family. They're trying to evict me," he said. "The house is in his name, but I'm supposed to get it in the will. He told me that. He wanted me to have it." He looked up at me. "I've never had much money, see. I drive a courtesy van for Sun Tours, taking people back and forth from the airport and so on. I took some time off to take care of Hy this last time. Hy paid for most everything we did anyway."

"Let's get back to yesterday," I said. "Did you spend the night in Hy's room?"

"Yeah. I mean, the nurses there are great, don't get me wrong, but they're overworked. I slept in the chair by his bed in case he needed anything."

"You said that you left for a while?"

He sat back down on the sofa. "I got upset when the doctor was there—the infection just wasn't healing. So I went down to the cafeteria to get some coffee. When I got back to the room, I figured he was asleep, but I walked over to him, just to check. He wasn't breathing, so I quick buzzed for the nurse. She couldn't get a pulse out of him. It was so sudden, so unexpected. I lost it for a while. That's when I started saying it was all my fault."

"The medical examiner's report says he was smothered with a pillow."

He was flabbergasted. "Who would do that? He was the sweetest guy in the world. There wasn't a person on earth who could say a bad word about him."

"You said you get the house in his will. Anybody else stand to inherit?"

He laughed. "Inherit what? Hy had some money— he bought this house, at twenty–two, and he had a passion for nice clothes. Everything European, beautifully made. He mentioned a couple of times that his grandfather had been a rich man in Vietnam, that he'd gotten a lot of money out when the family moved to Switzerland. But we never talked about bankbooks or anything like that, if that's what you're asking. I can't imagine there's that much left. He hasn't worked for a year, and he's paid all his own hospital bills."

"Tell me about his parents."

"His mother's name is Vo Giap, and his father's name is Nguyen Le Duc. Mrs. Vo, she's definitely a bitch. She didn't approve of me and she didn't like that Hy was gay. The father and the sister, they basically just do whatever Mrs. Vo says."

I took some more notes, and he told me the attorney who'd written Hy's will was Sandra Guarino, a friend of mine. Sandra worked in a high–rise office building in downtown Honolulu, a few blocks from my office, and when I called I found she was in a meeting, but her secretary said she could squeeze me in if

I could get there in half an hour. I said I could, and I was there about twenty minutes later.

The receptionist directed me down a long corridor paneled in mahogany with small offices opening off each side. Sandra was almost at the end, in an office lined with law books on mahogany shelves.

"Hi, Kimo," she said, standing up to kiss my cheek. She was a stocky woman in a gray business suit with a white blouse. Her hair was a non–descript shade of brown, and she wore it tucked behind her ears in a way that made her look younger than I knew she was. "To what do I owe the pleasure?"

"Business call, I'm afraid, not pleasure. You have a client named Hy Nguyen?"

"More properly Nguyen Hy," she said, sitting in a plush leather chair behind her desk. Next to her, a narrow floor–to–ceiling window looked out over the Ko'olau Mountains. I sat in a mahogany visitor's chair. "Vietnamese last names go first."

"You know he died yesterday?"

"No, no one notified me. I'll have to call Paul."

"Well, that's why I'm here."

I explained Paul's situation briefly, and she said, "I might as well tell you up front that Hy had a lot of money. About $5 million, as a matter of fact, and he left almost all of it to Paul."

"Paul says he has no idea about the money. He thinks Hy spent whatever he had on his medical care."

"Not likely. He hasn't been sick that long. You know anything about his background?"

I shook my head. "Fill me in."

"His grandfather was some big mogul in South Vietnam. In the late sixties, he saw the writing on the wall and moved the family to Switzerland. Hy was born there and sometime during his childhood, I'm not sure when, the family moved to California. He went to UCLA and moved here after graduation."

She paused. "I understand that relations were strained between the grandfather and his daughter, that's Hy's mother, Mrs. Vo. The grandfather cut Mrs. Vo out of most of the money, leaving it directly to Hy. That's been a bone of contention between Hy and his mother."

She motioned to the cappuccino maker and small refrigerator in the corner of her office. "You want anything?"

"You got a bottle of water in there?" She nodded, and I got the water while she continued to talk. "I met Hy at an AIDS fund–raiser about six months ago, and he came in shortly thereafter for some estate planning advice. He wanted to make sure his family didn't cut Paul out of his care decisions if he became ill."

"Does his family live in Hawai'i now? Sounds like they're on Paul Ford's case."

"Yeah, Hy bought them a restaurant in Iwilei after he got his inheritance," she said. "It really upset him that they didn't approve of him being gay, that they hated Paul, but he was still a good Vietnamese son, taking care of his parents."

I explained that Hy's parents were now trying to evict Paul from the home he believed he was to inherit, and Sandra's anger flared. "They can't do that. Hy's will is very specific about the house, as well as the rest of his estate."

"The parents get nothing under the will?"

"There are a few separate bequests, mostly charities. There's a clause mentioning the parents, that Hy took care of them during his lifetime. That's to keep them from challenging the will, saying he just forgot to mention them. His sister gets a big chunk, but almost $4 million goes to Paul."

"Do you think Paul knew how much money was involved?"

Sandra shook her head. "I swore not to tell him. Hy was afraid it might change things between them."

"I'll say. But if he didn't know, then the money isn't a motive for murder."

"I'm not sure Hy's family knew about this will," Sandra said. "He would never tell me how honest he was with them."

"So maybe Mrs. Vo thought she was going to get the money? She's certainly acting like she's the heir."

"I can see I've got my work cut out for me. Anything else I can tell you?"

I shook my head. "I'll call you if I think of anything."

We both stood up, and kissed goodbye. "Let's have dinner sometime, you, me Cathy and Mike. I want to get to know him better."

"Sure. I'll call you."

By then, my shift was over, and I headed for home. I pulled my clothes off and dropped them in a pile, and put on a pair of board shorts. I took my surfboard down the street to Kuhio Beach Park and managed to catch a few quick waves before night fell.

I met Mike for dinner at our favorite Italian restaurant on Kuhio Avenue in Waikīkī, and over the antipasto, I told him about the case. "That's tough," he said.

Mike's mother is Korean, and she'd had some trouble about his being gay at first, so I knew he could relate to Hy Nguyen's problems. Fortunately, Mike's mother had come around. I had not met his parents yet; Mike was closeted, and he was uncomfortable with anybody, family or coworkers, knowing about his private life.

That was tough for me. Since I got dragged out of the closet, I've tried to be as open as possible, and I'm often recognized, the way Paul Ford had known that I was the gay cop. Mike didn't like that.

He spent the night at my apartment, and after we'd made love I lay there in the moonlight watching him sleep. What would happen if he got sick? Would his parents try to shut me out? I doubted they knew he was dating anyone. I snuggled close to him, and he shifted his body to accommodate me. I fell asleep like that, wondering how long I would be able to hold him.

In the morning, as I drove to work, I thought about the case. Somebody had killed Hy Nguyen, and I didn't believe it was Paul Ford; he didn't ring my bullshit detector when we talked. That left me looking for other suspects, and the prime ones seemed to be his family, who thought they were inheriting.

I drove out the Nimitz Highway toward Hilo Hattie's aloha shirt factory, and found Saigon House in a seedy neighborhood of warehouses, a homeless shelter and the cream stucco mass of the medical examiner's building with its extra powerful fans and refrigeration units. The restaurant occupied a nondescript storefront, with a faded menu taped to the inside of the window. I peered through the dusty glass and saw someone in the back, so I knocked on the door.

An ancient woman, hunched almost completely in half, shuffled forward and said, through the closed door, "Closed now. Open eleven."

Before she could turn to go I held my badge up to the door. "Police," I said. "I'm looking for Vo Giap and Nguyen Le Duc."

She looked up at me with cloudy eyes, then shrugged and turned back into the restaurant. She called something in Vietnamese and unbolted the door, then shuffled down the linoleum corridor.

A tall woman with sharp features and raven hair pulled into a bun came through the beaded curtain at the back of the restaurant and walked toward me. "I'm Vo Giap," she said. "Who are you?"

It was hard to connect this homely woman as the mother of that beautiful young boy. Her face looked frozen in a perpetual sneer, and she wore an apron over a white cotton blouse and a pair of light blue polyester pants.

I introduced myself and extended my condolences. I said that I was investigating the murder of her son, and she said, "Ridiculous. My son was not murdered. He chose that lifestyle. If anything his death was a suicide."

"He didn't hold a pillow down over his own face until he stopped breathing," I said, and I noticed a faint tremor in her right hand when I said it.

"You mean it wasn't that...that disease?"

I shook my head. "The doctor was expecting him to recover. And you know, with the new drugs they have now, the protease inhibitors, he might have had years ahead of him."

"It must have been him," she said. "That freeloader. That bum who lived with him. He got tired of Hy and killed him."

"He is a suspect. I just want to tie up some loose ends. You know, before they close the cell doors on him. When was the last time you saw your son?"

"Months ago. I didn't approve of his lifestyle and I refused to tolerate it."

"Even though he bought you and your husband this restaurant?"

She glared at me. "My foolish father chose to leave his money to Hy instead of to me, as was proper. So Hy felt obliged to take care of us." She waved her arm around at the small, dingy restaurant. "Though he could have done better."

I didn't say anything. "You know, the hospital did not even call me to say he died. My daughter Angelique had to call them to find out. We had a big fight to get him to a proper funeral home."

"I understood your son left instructions about his care, and his funeral," I said, trying to keep my voice as neutral as possible.

"My son is dead. I don't care what he wanted any more."

"Are you familiar with the terms of your son's will?"

Now she looked surprised. "Will? My son had no will."

"He did. According to his attorney, the bulk of his estate passes to Mr. Ford."

Her surprise turned into alarm. "That's impossible. We are his parents!"

"I'm afraid the law is the law. In the meantime, I suggest you stop trying to evict Mr. Ford from the home that now belongs to him."

"This is all the fault of my foolish old father. He had no business leaving that money to Hy. It should have come to my husband and me. That money belongs to me, detective." She stood up. "I get what I deserve."

"I hope you do." I got up and walked out.

I knew then that Mrs. Vo had gone into her son's room and, just as she had given him life twenty–six years before, she had taken that life away. I knew it as certainly as I knew that Paul Ford was innocent. But how could I prove it? The evidence lab had told me that there were no fingerprints on the pillowcase, and no witnesses could place Mrs. Vo in her son's room.

On my way back to headquarters, I thought about the sister, Angelique, who had called the hospital about Hy. That meant she must have cared about him, to defy her parents. What could she tell me about her brother?

She was a student at UH, so I called a friend over there and asked him to check her schedule. She had classes in the morning, and worked evenings in the English department. I went back to the office and spent the rest of the afternoon on paperwork, including reading a copy of Hy Nguyen's will that Sandra Guarino faxed over to me. He had left $250,000 to Angelique, ownership of the restaurant to his parents, and the bulk of his estate in a trust for Paul Ford. Upon Ford's death, any of the principal that remained went to Angelique. I wondered if she knew about the will.

At five o'clock I took off for Mānoa. I had a slice of pizza at an outdoor cafe on campus, and watched the passing crowd. There were quite a few Vietnamese students, always walking with other Vietnamese. It reminded me of the cliquishness I had experienced in college myself, at UC Santa Cruz, where all the Hawaiian students hung out together, helped each other study, shared papers. A bell was ringing in my head, and it took me a while to answer it. But once I did, I knew who had killed Hy Nguyen. I just had to hope that I could get the proof I needed.

A few minutes before six I was lingering in the hallway in front of the English department as a pretty, young Vietnamese woman came toward me. I could see her brother's face in hers, though she didn't have the same luminous beauty he had. I felt sorry for her in that instant, knowing her grandfather had favored her brother and wondering if that was the story of her life.

"Excuse me, are you Angelique Nguyen?"

She stopped and looked at me. I held out my badge and introduced myself. "I'd like to ask you a few questions about your brother."

"Of course," she said. "Let me just check in here."

She walked in the door of the English department, leaving it open behind her. She spoke briefly to one of the secretaries, and left her black leather knapsack behind the secretary's desk. Then she came back out to the hallway, pulling the door shut behind her. "There's a little conference room down this hall. Nobody uses it after hours."

She wore her long black hair in a ponytail, and I could see she had her brother's taste for fine clothes. I didn't know much about women's clothing, but I could tell when something was expensive, and her black leather mini–skirt and pink sweater said money to me. I wondered why she had a part–time job if she could afford fancy clothes.

"Tell me about Hy," I asked, when we were sitting at a big round table in the conference room. She was about ninety degrees away from me.

"My brother and I were very close. We talked almost every day." She motioned to her sweater. "He bought me clothes all the time. He loved to come up here to the campus and hang out." She smiled. "We used to rate the boys together. Of course, he loved Paul, and I know Paul was dedicated to him."

She paused, but I didn't say anything. "My mother didn't approve of Hy, so I didn't tell her how much I saw him and spoke to him. When I heard he was in the hospital, I wanted to visit him, but she wouldn't let me go. She was afraid I was going to catch AIDS just by walking through the halls."

She got up and walked to the whiteboard on the wall behind me. Someone had been writing lecture notes on it, in red and blue magic marker, and she picked up an eraser and started to clean the writing. "Did you ever have to make a decision between people you loved?" she asked. "Like the movie *Sophie's Choice*, when Sophie had to choose which child she loved best?"

"It's always hard to have to do that."

"My mother didn't have to make that kind of choice," she said. "She and my father left Vietnam before either of us was born. If Hy had been born there, I think she might have left him behind." She turned to me. "Surprised, Detective? Everyone else loved Hy. He was a beautiful baby, a beautiful little boy, even a beautiful man. Have you seen his picture?"

I nodded.

"Even my mother loved him, in her fashion. But she was also jealous of him. He was my grandfather's only male heir, you see, and that made him special. She felt that took something away from her." She put the eraser down, but remained standing. "I had it easier than Hy; I was just another responsibility, another mouth to feed and another body to clothe. My grandfather was rich, but he kept us all on a tight leash. My mother isn't the type to accept a gift graciously. She resented everything."

"Some people find it very hard to be happy."

"My brother made me happy. I'm not sure if I can be happy again."

Her face crumpled then, and she began to cry. I sat her down at the table and found her a paper towel to dry her tears. "I'm sorry," she said, when she had stopped crying. "This is very hard to do."

"It's always hard when someone dies. Especially someone so close to you."

She nodded. "I loved him a lot."

"Did you see him the day he died?"

"I did. I have never challenged my mother, not on anything important. Minor adolescent rebellions, nothing more. But I wasn't going to let my brother lie there in the hospital without knowing that I loved him. I told her I was going to go, and she insisted she had to come with me."

She blew her nose and dried her eyes. "My mother wouldn't even consider talking to Paul, but she knew the nurse, a woman who comes to the restaurant sometime. We waited in the car until the nurse called and told us Paul had left. When we got to the room, my mother told me she wanted to speak to Hy alone, first, and I let her, but I stayed out in the hallway."

She took a long time to continue. "I didn't hear anything so I pushed the door open a crack. I saw my mother standing over my brother's bed, holding his pillow in her hands. It was so frightening that I couldn't move, couldn't even speak. I tried, and only a little croak came out. I watched his body shake and quiver under the pillow. He reached his hands up toward her but he was just too weak. Then he didn't move any more."

I reached over and held her hand. "I watched my mother lift his head up and slide the pillow underneath. If you had just looked in you might think it was a loving gesture. I let the door close and walked down the hall. She was just a few steps behind me but I don't think she knows I saw."

Her eyes brimmed with tears again. "I lost my brother, and now I've lost my mother, haven't I?"

"I think she was lost a long time ago," I said gently.

I drove Angelique Nguyen down to police headquarters where she could give a formal statement, and sent a pair of uniforms out to Saigon House to pick up Vo Giap. I drove over to the hospital myself and picked up the nurse, Khanh Le, and she confessed that Mrs. Vo had paid her to call when Hy was alone in his room.

After my shift was over, after both Vo Giap and Khanh Le had been put into the system, I drove over to Paul Ford's to let him know in person what had happened. He was a lot calmer by then. "Hy didn't want a funeral," he said. "He saw how his parents got all bent out of shape over the whole ancestor worship thing. Especially since he knew he wasn't going to have children, he didn't want to be stuck in the ground where his mother could come and complain about him."

"So what are you doing?"

"As soon as they release the body, he's going to be cremated. And then I'm going to sprinkle his ashes in the ocean." He smiled. "He always liked dolphins. He used to have these dreams about leaving Vietnam—even though he was born in Switzerland. And there were always dolphins in the dream, guiding him."

I told him about the arrests.

"I'm glad you caught them. Both Mrs. Vo and that nurse. I always got a bad feeling from her." He reached behind him and pulled a book out. "I've been reading the myth again," he said. "The story of Apollo and Hyacinthus."

"The sun god and the boy he loved?"

He nodded. "You know, in the story, Apollo killed Hyacinthus. He was throwing a discus or something and it hit Hyacinthus, and killed him."

"Those old stories, they're tough."

"The new ones, too," he said.

By the time Ray Donne became my partner, I'd gotten accustomed to working on my own. I paired up for the occasional case with different detectives as one or another was out on vacation or sick leave, but there was never anybody available to partner with me on a permanent basis. Being the only openly gay homicide detective on the force didn't help; nobody was scrambling to be my best friend, either.

Ray didn't have a choice. Newly hired, he took what was offered to him—and that was a spot in the Criminal Investigation Division, at police headquarters on South Beretania Street in downtown Honolulu. Lieutenant Sampson partnered him with me because I was the only detective working solo.

Sampson called me in to his office, where he introduced me to Ray, then dispatched us to interview Doc Takayama at the morgue about the suspicious death of an elderly man. I drove, Ray in the passenger seat, staring out the window like a tourist, marveling at the palm trees.

The medical examiner's office is on Iwilei Road, just off Nimitz, in a two-story concrete building with a slight roof overhang. The paint on the exterior is peeling and the landscaping is overgrown— after all, the dead don't vote. Alice Kanamura, the laughing receptionist, buzzed us through to Doc's office, where his diplomas from UH and its medical school shared space with gruesome photos of dismembered corpses Doc had managed to identify.

After I introduced Ray, we all sat and Doc ran the case for us. "Caucasian male, aged 82, discovered by his daughter bleeding from his mouth, rectum and ears, and rushed to The Queen's Medical Center, where he was diagnosed with an intracranial hemorrhage. He died within twenty-four hours. My autopsy revealed a high level of warfarin, a blood thinner, in his body."

I asked Doc to spell the medication. "Brand name is Coumadin," Doc said, and he spelled that, too.

"He have a prescription for it?" Ray asked.

Doc nodded. "He had a heart valve replacement a couple of years ago. Coumadin thins the blood, allows it to flow more freely. Downside is, patient bleeds more easily, so the Coumadin level has to be monitored carefully."

"Any chance this was accidental?" I asked.

Doc shrugged. "Old folks sometimes mix up their medications. And there have been cases where the pharmacy provided a higher strength than was called for. You'll have to check with the physician."

"Why call us?" I asked.

"Something smells fishy. Maybe I'm wrong, maybe it was just an innocent screwup. But I thought somebody ought to check it out."

We took down all the information Doc could give us, including the name and phone number of the daughter who'd found him. On the way out of the office, I called her and arranged to meet her at her father's home later that afternoon.

"ME's kind of young, isn't he?" Ray asked, as we were getting into my truck. "Looks like he barely graduated high school."

"That's why he became the medical examiner," I said. "Doesn't have to worry about instilling trust in his patients."

Ray nodded. I called the cardiologist's office and the receptionist said she could squeeze us in between patients, so we headed over to his office, at the Queen's Outpatient Center. The waiting room was filled with elderly men and women—and in some cases their aides—and a sign next to the receptionist's window indicated that patients who were rude or abusive to the staff would be removed from the premises by the Honolulu Police Department and their records deleted from the doctor's system. "Tough crowd," Ray said, noting the sign.

"You'd be surprised," I said. We waited in the lobby for about fifteen minutes before a nurse showed us to the doctor's office. He came in a minute later, apologizing for the delay.

Dr. McDonough was a red–headed haole in his mid–thirties, wearing wire–rimmed glasses. His name was embroidered on the pocket of his lab coat, followed by a whole alphabet of initials that meant nothing to me, but seemed impressive. "You're here about Milton Bishop?" he asked.

I nodded. Bishop was an honored name in Hawai'i, indicating at least collateral descent from one of the islands' oldest families, with connections to Hawaiian royalty.

"Damn shame," Dr. McDonough said. "He had a mitral valve replacement two years ago and he'd been doing very well." He opened up the chart he'd brought in with him. "He was here two months ago, and we checked his Coumadin level at that time. Everything was fine."

I looked at my notes. "Doc Takayama found a Coumadin level of 18.5 in Mr. Bishop's blood. Is that high?"

"Astronomical," McDonough said. "Therapeutic level is anywhere from 1–2. Levels of 4–6 can be reduced through medication; anything over that requires immediate hospitalization, and injections of potassium, along with careful monitoring."

"How does a level get that high?" Ray asked.

"I see patients with elevated levels all the time. Patient mistakes one pill for another—takes a second Coumadin instead of something else, like a heart pill or a diabetes pill. Patient forgets he took his pills and takes another set. Never this high, though. A level like this requires prolonged exposure to higher doses."

"Could this be criminal?" I asked.

"I suppose," McDonough said. "You need to get hold of the pills first, and make sure they were dispensed correctly—that the pharmacy gave him the right strength." He looked at the chart. "Mr. Bishop was to take three milligrams once a day. Those pills are tan. It's possible that the pharmacy mixed something up and gave him the highest dosage, ten—which are white. Or that he mixed up his instructions and started taking his threes twice a day."

"How long would it take to build up to the level he demonstrated?" Ray asked.

"Probably no more than a couple of weeks."

I looked at Ray. Neither of us had any more questions, so we said goodbye to the doctor and went back to my truck. It was almost one o'clock by then; the daughter, Melanie Bishop, taught English part–time at the UH campus in Mānoa, so she wasn't free to meet us at her father's condo until three. "You want to get some lunch?" I asked. "I'll introduce you to Zippy's."

"No chance they sell Philadelphia–style hoagies, is there?" he asked. "I've been Jonesing for one since we landed in Honolulu."

"Probably come close. Zippy's has the kind of menu, you make it what you want."

We got our sandwiches and sat down. "So how'd you wind up in Honolulu?" I asked.

"I grew up in Philly, and always wanted to be a cop. My dad, two of my uncles and three of my cousins are on the job." He took a bite of his sandwich. "Not as good as a hoagie, but it'll do."

He took a swig of his lemonade. "I met my wife when I was a patrolman and she was in college. We got married when I got my shield and she got her degree in East Asian Studies." He laughed. "And before you ask, she's as white as I am. She just got hooked on this Asian stuff."

"UH is a good school. That why you ended up out here?"

"Yeah. She spent a couple of years working at jobs that had nothing to do with her degree. And all the time, she was champing at the bit to go back to school. She got in to this program for her master's in Pacific Island Studies, so I started applying for jobs. Lieutenant Sampson liked my background."

I nodded. "He's a good guy."

"So I hear you're gay," Ray said. "How's that working out, in the department?"

I shrugged. "Some guys are okay with it, some not." I looked at him. "How about you?"

"I worked with gay guys in Philly," he said. "It's all right by me."

I waited for a punch line, something like, "As long as you don't make a pass at me," but none was forthcoming. All right, I thought. I could deal with Ray Donne.

We talked about his wife, about how they had to share a car for now, how they were struggling to find an apartment they could afford. "How about you?" Ray asked. "You seeing anybody?"

"I am. But he's pretty closeted, so I don't like to talk about him."

"Wow. That must be tough. On him, and on you."

"It is sometimes." I crumpled up my wrappers and napkins. I'd met the guy all of about four hours before; I wasn't quite ready to share my secrets with him. At least give me a couple of days.

We drove over to the condo, in a tall, 1960s building near the 'Ilikai Hotel. Bishop's apartment was on the twentieth floor. "Man, must have a hell of a view," Ray said, as we pulled up outside the building.

"And a hell of a price tag. You're looking at a couple million, even in this market."

Melanie Bishop met us at the apartment's front door. She was a solid-looking woman in her mid-forties, short blonde hair, wearing slacks and a tailored jacket. She ushered us into a living room with an expansive view of the ocean and downtown Honolulu.

As we sat on a U-shaped couch covered in faded gold velvet, I said, "I'm very sorry for your loss."

"Thank you. It was a shock finding him like that, and then to lose him so quickly afterward."

"You found him," I said. "Did you come here to your father's home often?"

"Once a week," she said. "Every Thursday afternoon. I went through the mail, paid his bills, and put his pills out for him in plastic containers. That's why I don't understand how he could have overdosed—I'm always very careful."

"Is it possible you could have made a mistake?" Ray asked. "I know my dad takes a ton of pills, and it's easy to get them confused."

"I could have," Melanie said. "Once. Not week after week."

"We'd like to perform a search," I said, trying to be gentle. "And take in all his pill bottles for examination."

"You think I killed him?"

"I don't think anything yet, Ms. Bishop," I said. "We can get a warrant, if necessary, but since you're here, you could just give us the authority."

"Should I talk to a lawyer?"

"That's up to you, ma'am," Ray said. "But the lawyer's going to tell you that you have to honor a warrant, and that if you have nothing to hide, your best course is to cooperate fully with us."

"Everyone has something to hide, detective," Melanie said.

"Let's get the rest of our questions out of the way," I said. "Then you can decide about the search." She nodded. "Now, who else had access to this property?"

"He had a maid come in once a week." She motioned around the room. "As you can see, she didn't do much, but it was another person to check on him. I have a brother, but I don't know that he's been to see Dad for years." She gave us her brother's name, address and phone number. "I haven't spoken to him in eight years. I assume he hasn't moved."

"Any particular reason why you and your brother are estranged?" Ray asked.

She looked at him, and she looked at me, and I could see she was calculating how much to tell us. One of those secrets she alluded to earlier, I figured.

"I'm a lesbian, detective. My brother doesn't approve. And I think he's an alcoholic, a loser and a leech."

"How about your father? How did he feel about your brother?"

She shrugged. "My father thought both of his children were disappointments, but he still split his estate between us. And I know you'll find out sooner or later, so I might as well tell you, it's a substantial one. Not just this condo, but acres on the North Shore, stocks and bonds. Based on the last time I checked my brother and I will split about ten million dollars."

Ray whistled softly. "We'll need a copy of the will," I said.

Melanie picked up a pad and pen from the coffee table and made a note. "I'll have our attorney send one to you."

We went through a few more details, and finally Melanie said, "If you come with me, I'll show you where he kept his pills."

"I'm glad you decided to cooperate," Ray said. "We'll try and make this simple."

"I just don't have it in me to fight," she said, standing. "I'm going into the hospital myself in a couple of days. I need to get all this wrapped up."

"I hope it's nothing serious," Ray said, walking next to her as we headed toward the kitchen.

"Breast cancer. I need a mastectomy, and then chemotherapy. Unfortunately I haven't been going to the doctor as often as I should have, so the lump is larger than I would like. That's the downside of not having insurance."

"You don't get insurance through the university?" I asked.

"Not as an adjunct." She paused, weighing how much to include. "My partner's company doesn't offer domestic partner benefits either. But at least they let her cover our daughter."

"I have a friend who had a lumpectomy last year," I said. "She and her partner went through it all. I'd be happy to give you her number, if you'd like to talk to someone."

"That's very kind, detective," Melanie said. "But unfortunately, I know all too many lesbians who've had breast cancer. It's the AIDS of our community."

We came to the kitchen, and Melanie pointed to a couple of zip–lock bags crammed with pill bottles. "My father's collection," she said. "I filled those big pill cases every week for him."

Ray brought out a couple of evidence bags, slipped on a rubber glove, and started collecting. "No one else helped him with his pills?"

"Not that I know of."

We took the bottles and cases, and said goodbye to Melanie Bishop. Ray looked at his watch as we got back in my truck. It was nearly four. "How long you think it'll take us to get back downtown?" he asked.

"You got a hot date?"

"My wife found an apartment that we just might be able to afford. She's got an appointment to see it at 4:30. It's near something called Kamehameha Community Park. We're sharing a car, so I've got to get a bus out there."

"Not the best neighborhood, but it's okay. If you get Julie to drop you off on her way to UH, you can hop right on the H1 at Kalihi Street and be at work pretty quickly. She'll keep going to the University Avenue exit." I looked at my watch. "Tell you what. I'll run you out there, then I'll drop the evidence off at the station. We'll meet up tomorrow morning and go over what they find."

"You're the man, Kimo." He waited a beat. "So, what's it look like to you? She did it?"

I shrugged.

He started ticking things off on his fingers. "She had the means—the pills. The opportunity—every Thursday. Motive—five million bucks."

"Let's just see how the evidence stacks up," I said. "You never know who else's prints we'll find on those bottles."

I dropped him off at the apartment building, and as soon as he was out of the truck I stuck the Bluetooth on my ear and called Mike on my cell phone. "Hey, it's me."

"Hey, me. How'd your day go?"

"Got a new partner. Finally."

"Really? I want to hear all about him."

"Over dinner?"

"Can't. Command performance at my folks. How about tomorrow?"

"Sure." We chatted some more and I hung up, wondering if I would ever get to meet his parents. He had met mine, and both my brothers and their families. Everybody liked him—but what was not to like? He was a sweetheart. A couple of inches taller than me, handsome, with black hair and piercing blue eyes. Kids and dogs gravitated toward him; guys were impressed that he was a firefighter, and women swarmed him, even those, like my sisters–in–law, who knew he was gay.

I dropped the plastic bags off at the Scientific Investigation Section, the only full–service forensic laboratory in Hawai'i. We'd also taken Melanie Bishop's fingerprints for comparison, and she'd called the maid and asked her to come by the SIS office at headquarters to supply her prints as well.

I went home and grilled myself a burger on my little hibachi. The next morning I was at my desk at eight, reviewing a copy of Milton Bishop's Last Will and Testament. Ray came in a few minutes later and I started passing him pages.

"So, what did you think?" I asked when he finished.

"Seems pretty straightforward to me. Just like she said. Split down the middle with her brother."

"What about if the brother dies first?"

"His share goes to his kids."

I leaned back in my chair. "And if Melanie dies first?"

Ray paged through the will to proper section, then whistled. "If she dies first, the entire estate goes to the brother."

"Cutting out her partner and her daughter."

Ray nodded. "So?"

"So she told us she's got breast cancer."

"And she's got no health insurance and big medical bills coming up."

"Gives her a good motive." I hated the idea even as I said it. I liked Melanie Bishop, and I didn't see her deliberately overdosing her father so she could inherit. Unfortunately, I did see her doing it to safeguard her inheritance for her partner and her daughter.

"We still have to talk to the brother," I said. "Let's see if we can get hold of him."

"And the maid," Ray said.

We left messages at Henry Bishop's home and office. The maid, a tiny dark-haired Filipina named Encarnacion Rodriguez, came up to our office on the second floor after leaving her prints with SIS on the B1 level. She had worked for the Bishops for many years, since before Melanie's mother had died. "You ever have reason to touch Mr. Bishop's medication?" I asked.

She shook her head. "Not even to dust?"

"He leave his pills on the table, on top of whole pile of newspapers. Mostly I mop the floor, I clean the bathroom and the kitchen counters. The table, I don't even touch."

"Okay. Anybody else come by?"

"Miss Melanie, she come every week. Sometimes I see her, sometimes not. Mr. Milton, he leave a big pile of mail on the coffee table for her, he just drop the bills there for her to pay. I always know when Miss Melanie just been there."

"How about her brother?"

Encarnacion frowned. "Mr. Henry not nice man. Always lotta yelling when he come by."

"He come over a lot?"

She shrugged. "Not like Miss Melanie. And I tell you something, when he there, I stay in bedroom 'til he gone."

"You see him at the condo in the last couple of weeks?"

Encarnacion thought. "I see him once, maybe two, three weeks ago. But I think maybe he there more, I just don't see him."

"You remember when you saw him?" Ray asked. "What day it was?"

"Had to be Friday. I always go Friday." She slapped herself on the mouth. "But wait, last two weeks, I had doctor appointments for my son, Fridays. My son, he have cerebral palsy. Got to take him to doctor all the time. So last two weeks I go on Saturday instead."

Ray was taking notes. "So you think you saw Mr. Henry Bishop at his father's house three weeks ago, on a Friday."

Encarnacion nodded. "And then you think maybe he was there once or twice more in the last two weeks, but not on the Saturdays when you were there."

"That right."

"How did Miss Bishop get along with her father?"

"Mr. Milton was not nice guy, not after his wife die. He get old, you know, cranky and sick. But Miss Melanie, she always put up with him. Sometimes he yell at her, call her names, but she just keep taking care of him."

Ray thanked her and walked her out to the elevator. By then the fingerprint results were back; the only prints on the bottles matched Melanie and Milton Bishop. Lieutenant Sampson came by as Ray came back. Sampson wore his signature look—a polo shirt and chinos. This one was hunter green, with some kind of embroidered crest that I didn't recognize. Once you get past the polo player and the little alligator, I'm pretty clueless about labels.

We laid the case out for him. "You going to pick up the daughter?" he asked.

"I still want to talk to the brother," I said. "She's got a job at UH and she stands to inherit $5 million if she sticks around. I don't think she's going anywhere."

"I'll hold you to that," Sampson said dryly.

Ray and I decided to stake out Henry Bishop's apartment on the edge of Chinatown. "Not exactly what I'd expect of a guy who's about to come into five million," Ray said, surveying the run–down building, the lone scraggly palm tree, the crumbled newspaper blowing along the gutter.

"Expectations don't pay the rent." I was just settling back into my seat when I saw a guy I knew. "Stay here," I told Ray. "I'll be right back."

My father's lifelong best friend was a career criminal I called Uncle Chin, who had died a few months before. One of his friends was Hang Sung, a weaselly Chinese bookie in his late fifties. Hang worked out of a lei stand on Hotel Street, taking bets on everything that gave odds—including things like would Prince Charles ever accede to the throne of England, and how long Britney Spears' latest marriage would last.

He tried to get away when he saw me, but I said, "Hold up, Hang. You know I can outrun you, so why make me break a sweat?"

"What you want, detective?" He was wearing a white brocaded shirt with yellowing stains under the armpits, and a little porkpie hat that should have seen the dumpster years ago.

"I'm looking for a guy lives around here. Henry Bishop. You know him?"

Hang's nose twitched and I could see him trying to formulate a deal. "How much is he into you for?" I asked.

"Into me? What you mean, into me?"

"You know what I mean, Hang. I couldn't care less what you do over on Hotel Street. But I'm looking for this guy, and I think you know him."

"I do you a favor, you do me a favor, detective?"

I put my hand on his shoulder in a friendly way. "Hang, Hang. You were a friend of my beloved Uncle Chin. You need a favor, you come to me."

Hang didn't believe me, and he was right not to. But he said, "Henley Bishop owe me 100 large."

"One hundred thousand dollars?" I asked. "Hang, how do you let somebody get so far down?"

"He long time client. Always get money from his father before. This time, father no give him money. I tell him, Henley, everybody got to pay. Even poor son of rich father." He looked down the street. "Here he come now. You pick him up, you ask him when he going pay me. Save me the trouble."

A tall, skinny haole was coming toward us. When he saw Hang, he turned and started to hurry away. "Mr. Bishop," I called, starting after him. "Police. I need to talk to you."

Bishop ran and I gave chase. Behind me, I heard Ray start up my truck, and moments later he zoomed past me, executing a turn that blocked Henry's path. Ray jumped out of the driver's seat when I was half a block away, pointing his gun and shouting, "Freeze, motherfucker!"

Henry Bishop froze.

"That the way you do it in Philadelphia?" I asked, coming up to them.

"Nah, I just always wanted to say that."

"Why'd you run, Henry?" I asked. "We just wanted to talk to you about your dad. Give you our condolences."

"Yeah, right," Henry said.

"But now, your running, that seems suspicious to me. I think that calls for a little chat down at headquarters. What do you think, detective?"

"I agree, detective." Ray patted Henry down for weapons, and finding none, bundled him into the tiny back seat of my truck, really more of a cargo compartment. Since he wasn't a suspect, just a guy we wanted to talk to, we didn't bother to cuff him. My previous partner had a Ford Taurus with a full back seat, easy for one of us to ride in the back with anyone we were taking in. I had to hope Ray got his car situation worked out, or I'd be giving up my truck very soon.

At headquarters, Henry Bishop asked for his attorney before we could ask him anything. That made me suspicious, so I read him his Miranda rights, just in case he said anything while we were waiting. I got him a cup of coffee, and he said, "So, you talk to my dyke sister yet?"

I nodded toward Ray, letting him take the lead. "Yeah, looks like an open and shut case against her," he said. "That's why I don't understand why you were running."

"Not from you guys; from that bookie I saw your partner talking to."

"In a little over your head?" Ray asked.

"You could say that. Bastard was trying to squeeze me."

"You dad wouldn't bail you out this time?" I asked.

He shot me a look. "Hang told you that?"

I nodded.

"It wasn't that big a deal. I told him my dad was old and sick, he just had to wait a little while. Hell, charge me the vig, I don't care. I knew I was going to inherit a bundle."

"Even more if your sister died first."

He laughed, a sharp almost barking sound. "That carpet—muncher? She'll live to be a hundred."

"Not with breast cancer, she won't," I said.

Henry's head swiveled toward me. "You didn't know? She's going in for surgery next week. Apparently the tumor's big, and it's spread."

"Good for her." Then a light bulb went off. "Jesus, you mean if I'd waited a few more weeks I could have had it all?"

His mouth dropped open as he realized what he'd said. "Waited for what, Henry?" I asked. "Waited to switch your dad's pills around?"

"I want to talk to my lawyer."

"Not much your lawyer can do at this point," I said. "We already read you your rights. The thing is, though, if you explain to us what happened, maybe we can put something together for the DA that swings in your favor."

"You in pretty deep to the bookie?" Ray asked. "I know what that's like. My cousin back in Philly got into trouble like that. And the asshole bookie, he wouldn't cut my cousin any slack at all."

"Sounds like Hang Sung," Henry grumbled. "Kept upping the interest on me. Every other day it was 'ask your father.' Asshole didn't know what kind of jerk my father was."

He sighed. "My father didn't know what he was taking," Henry said. "I just went in and added a couple of Coumadin to his morning pills and his night pills. I figured nobody'd ever investigate, and if they did, they'd put the blame on Mel."

"What did you do about fingerprints?"

"Rubber gloves. I'm not stupid, you know."

"No, Henry, you're not. You know, you might as well write it all up now, put in about how the bookie was squeezing you. Might get you some juice with the judge." I pushed a pad and pen over to him.

"You think?"

"You never know." By the time his attorney arrived, Henry had already written up his statement and been taken down for processing.

"Say, you get that apartment?" I asked Ray, as we were filling out the paperwork.

"Nah, she found a sublet for us in Waikīkī instead. Some professor from UH who's going to the mainland to pick up a grant. She thinks the guy might not come back at all, which means we could just take over the lease."

"Whereabouts in Waikīkī?"

"A couple of blocks from Kuhio Beach Park," he said. "You know, I heard they surf out there. I was thinking I might get myself a board, and learn."

"Ray," I said, "this might be the beginning of a beautiful partnership."

"Fancy neighborhood," Ray said, as I drove us up into Black Point to respond to a homicide call.

"All lava underneath here," I said. "Hence the name. They say when King Kamehameha arrived from the big island, his war canoes stretched all the way from here to Hawai'i Kai."

"The homicide department doesn't work out for you, you could always get a gig as a tour guide."

"You like this neighborhood? Cause I'm happy to let you out."

"No, no, continue the tour," he said, holding up his hand.

It was a gray, rainy day, another in a long line that had besieged Honolulu. We're accustomed to blue skies and the occasional quick, tropical shower; this prolonged spell of bad weather had everyone on edge, the crime rate spiraling. Husbands and wives were battling, kids who had been cooped up indoors for too long were sneaking out to cause mischief, roads were flooding and roofs were leaking.

Both of us were short–tempered after the non–stop deluges, and cranky about working on a Sunday. The fact that I'd broken up with Mike Riccardi a month before didn't help my mood, either. "Neighborhood first developed in the 1930s," I said, trying for a lighter tone. "Some of the most expensive houses on the island. We're talking ten to fifteen million bucks."

"I guess a lot of cops don't live over here." The sublet Ray and his wife had in Waikīkī was running out, and they were house–hunting again. Even though they'd sold a home in Philadelphia before they moved, their budget was still too thin to get them much in Honolulu.

This was the third murder we'd responded to in a residential neighborhood in the last two weeks. The first two had been clear cases of domestic violence, passed into the system quickly. As we drove up and parked in front of a sprawling ranch, I hoped the third time would play out the same way.

The house looked like no one had mowed the lawn for weeks, but then, lawns all over Honolulu were growing fast due to the constant rain, and our legions of yard workers couldn't cut them in downpours. But there was more to the distressed look of the house than just an overgrown yard. No one had trimmed the hibiscus, which were running rampant with plate–sized red blossoms, or picked up the dead leaves under the kiawe tree in the center of the yard.

The house needed a paint job, and there was a broken shutter hanging loosely next to a front window. I stopped my truck behind the black–and–white parked in the driveway, and the medical examiner's van, which had come up behind us, parked on the street. A couple of neighbors were standing in their driveways, under umbrellas, watching what was going on.

Ray and I hurried into the house, getting soaked on the way; we were both too macho, or too stupid, to carry umbrellas. Inside, we met the two cops from the 780 who'd responded to the initial call, a haole named Cooke, and a Japanese named Okada. "What've we got?" I asked Cooke.

"Caucasian male, forty–eight years of age, named Michael Paterson. Significant blunt trauma to the head. Lots of blood."

"Who made the call?" Ray asked.

"Visitor. Jane Shiner. Friend of the deceased, worried that he hadn't shown up for a lunch. Drove over to check on him, found the front door open, and walked in. She's in the kitchen."

"Paterson live alone?" I asked.

Cooke shook his head, then appeared to change his mind. "Well, not exactly. Mrs. Shiner said he lived here with a boyfriend, partner, whatever you want to call it. But the partner was cheating on him, living in Waikīkī."

I looked at Ray. "Body first?"

He shrugged. "Sounds good to me."

Michael Paterson had been in bed, most likely asleep, when somebody had beaten him over the head with a hefty stone statue of a male nude. There was blood everywhere—on the bed, the floor, the walls, even the ceiling. Bloody footprints tracked to a pair of open French doors, where the shoes themselves stood. Beyond the doors I could see an equally overgrown back yard and a lap pool littered with fallen leaves.

The crime scene unit stepped into the room and began gathering evidence, taking photographs, collecting samples and so on. "Pretty brutal attack," I said, as we stood to the side taking notes. "Crime of passion?"

"Wonder where the boyfriend, or ex–boyfriend, is," Ray said. "This one may work out as easily as the last two."

"We can only hope," I said. "At least this one's indoors." The call that had come in just before, which another team of detectives had caught, had involved the body of a homeless man found in Kapiʻolani Park. Those detectives were going to be very wet by the time they got back to headquarters.

I called over to the evidence tech, who was gingerly handling the sculpture of the male nude. "Any prints?"

He shook his head. "My guess is gloves."

The other tech was on the floor examining the footprints. "And don't get your hopes up on these," he said. "There's a bit of a slide on each footprint. Looks like someone with smaller feet stepped into big shoes to get through the blood."

"Any other good news?" Ray asked.

"Give us some time," the first tech said.

"Come on, let's go talk to the friend," I said. We walked out to the kitchen where we found a heavy–set middle–aged haole woman sitting at the kitchen table with Lidia Portuondo, a beat cop I knew from my days in Waikīkī. Lidia was trying to get the woman to drink some tea.

Lidia stood up, organizing two chairs across from Mrs. Shiner for us, and then stepped to the doorway. We introduced ourselves and sat down. "Can you tell us what happened this morning?" I asked.

"Mike was supposed to meet me for lunch, at eleven–thirty. When he didn't show up, I called the house, and his cell phone, and neither answered. I got worried, so I drove over here."

She began crying, and Lidia handed her a tissue. After a minute or so, Mrs. Shiner said, "How could he do this? Be so brutal."

I said, "When you say, 'he,' you mean…"

"Grant. His life partner. Grant Buckley. I know he's an awful shit, but I never imagined he'd be capable of something like this."

"What makes you think Mr. Buckley did this?" I asked.

"Who else would? Mike was a sweet man. Never said a hurtful word about anyone. He taught special needs children at the Kamalei School." She started crying again. "Those poor children. How devastated they'll be."

"What can you tell us about the relationship between Mr. Paterson and Mr. Buckley?" Ray asked.

Jane Shiner dried her eyes. She looked like she had regained her purpose in life. "My husband Wolf owns Island Appliances," she said. "Grant was Wolf's chief financial officer until recently."

Wolfgang Shiner was a prominent businessman, owner of a chain of stores throughout the islands. When I was a kid, my family bought hedge clippers, TVs, blenders, and every other kind of electrical appliance from Island. I remembered walking the aisles of the Island store on Fort Street in downtown Honolulu, before it became a pedestrian mall, picking out a portable tape player with headphones for my tenth birthday.

My father's construction business regularly bought washing machines, refrigerators and the like from Island. As the digital wave hit Honolulu, Island boomed, becoming the go–to place for printers, MP3 players and game systems, with a flourishing wholesale business as well.

"Wolf and I used to socialize with Grant and Mike all the time," Jane Shiner continued. "That's how Mike and I became such good friends."

"Used to?" Ray asked.

"Until Grant met Wili," she said. "One L, two I's. A Filipino boy half Grant's age." She shuddered. "He abandoned poor Mike. He set Wili up in an apartment in Waikīkī and spent most of his time there." Her mouth set in a frown that looked like it was a permanent feature on her face. "His work suffered. Eventually Wolf thought it best to replace him."

"Let me guess," Ray said. "Grant didn't take kindly to that."

"He was very angry. With Mike and with me." Her eyes widened. "Oh, my. What if I'd come in while it was…happening. I might have been killed."

Ray and I both took a lot of notes. "Why wasn't Mike Paterson sleeping in the master bedroom?" I asked.

"Grant snored. Mike couldn't sleep and Grant wouldn't do anything about it. So Mike moved into the guest room a few years ago." She must have sensed my disbelief, because she said, "Even happy couples sometimes sleep apart," she said. "My husband and I have separate bedrooms for the same reason."

She didn't know Wili's last name, but she was sure that the apartment was listed in Grant Buckley's name. She didn't know much else. "We'll need to speak with your husband as well," I said.

"He's very busy."

"I'm sure he is, ma'am," I said. "But I know how many contracts Island Appliances has with the City and County of Honolulu, so I'm sure he'll be quite willing to help out the police with our inquiries."

Jane frowned again, but gave us Wolf's office phone number and said, "His secretary's name is Lois Roeper. Talk to her tomorrow morning and she'll set something up for you." She stood up to go, but hesitated. "Mike didn't have much family," she said. "I'd like to take care of the arrangements for him."

I gave her the medical examiner's phone number. "They'll let you know when they release the body," I said. She took the card, put it in her Coach bag, and left.

By then the crime scene guys were finished, and we watched the medical examiner's team pack up Michael Paterson's body for transport to the morgue. Before they left, I asked the assistant ME if she had a time of death for us.

"Six to twelve hours ago," she said. "Doc may be able to narrow that down after the autopsy, though."

That gave us a window between midnight and six a.m. I thanked her, and as they were leaving I called Harry Ho and asked him to check the property appraiser's database for me and find any property registered to Grant Buckley. I could have done it myself, back at the station, but I didn't want to wait, and there wasn't anyone there who could do the search for me as fast as Harry could.

He was back on the phone a minute later with the address in Black Point and another, on Ala Wai Boulevard. "Just down the street from me," he said. "It's a condo called Diamond View."

"Thanks, brah."

I was about to hang up when he said, "Hey, you and Mike want to meet Arleen and me for dinner this weekend?"

I hadn't told Harry—or anyone else—about my breakup with Mike, or the reasons behind it. I just said I'd get back to him and flipped the phone closed.

Ray looked over at the address I'd written down. "I know that street," he said, as we walked back to the truck. The rain had let up, but gray clouds still loomed overhead. "It's not bad, but it's a few steps down from this place."

I knew the street, and the building—not just from living on Waikīkī myself, but from having patrolled its streets when I was in uniform. "Maybe Grant Buckley's finances were getting stretched, especially without a job."

"You think he had an insurance policy on his partner?"

I shrugged. "If I were Paterson, I'd have one on Buckley, knowing I couldn't afford to stay in that house on a teacher's salary. So I'd guess Buckley had one on Paterson."

We went back up the driveway and into the house, looking for insurance information. Michael Paterson had been found in the house's second bedroom, but there were no papers there or in the master suite, which had an unlived–in feel, so we headed directly for the third bedroom, which had been fitted out as an office.

Ray found the policies in a file cabinet drawer. "Bingo. Million–dollar policies on each other."

"So that would help Buckley's financial situation. Plus, with Paterson out of the way, he and his new boyfriend could move back up here."

It only took us a few minutes to drive from Black Point into Waikīkī. We hoped the weekend, and the bad weather, would mean that Buckley, or his boyfriend, would be at home. We left my truck in the Diamond View driveway and badged the doorman, who buzzed us through without calling upstairs.

Wili's apartment was on the third floor and faced *makai*, toward the ocean, rather than *mauka*, over the canal and toward the hills. Since there were four blocks and a dozen buildings between Diamond View and the ocean, it was the less valuable side.

I knocked on the door and said, "Police. We're looking for Grant Buckley."

The door opened a moment later and a tall, hefty haole in a long–sleeved Ralph Lauren dress shirt over shorts said, "I'm Grant Buckley."

He had dirty blonde hair, fair skin, and a spider web of red veins on his nose. I introduced myself and Ray and asked if we could come in.

"What's this about?" Behind him I saw a slim Filipino in his late twenties whom I assumed was Wili.

"Michael Paterson," I said.

Buckley shook his head. "Jesus. What's that drama queen up to now?" He stepped back and motioned us in. "You'd better come inside."

He introduced us to Wili, who perched on the arm of the overstuffed armchair where Buckley sat. Ray and I took seats on the white leather sofa across from them.

The apartment was low–budget, with cheap carpeting, used furniture, and only a couple of posters of the Philippines tacked up on the walls. A little love nest.

"What can you tell us about your relationship with Michael Paterson?" I asked.

"I thought he was the love of my life. For fifteen years."

"Until you met Wili," Ray said.

Buckley shook his head. "Mike moved out of the master bedroom nearly two years ago," he said. "We hadn't had sex for, jeez, two or three years before that. We were more like brothers than lovers. A year ago I gave up, told Mike it was over and I was going to start dating again. I met Wili and he reminded me what it was like to be in love. I moved out of the house and down here about six months ago."

"How would you characterize your relationship in the last few months?" I asked. "Since you met Wili and moved in here."

He frowned. "Not good. That house, that's where I grew up. My parents' house, which I bought from them. Mike makes pennies teaching retarded kids. He never paid a dime in rent, never bought a piece of furniture or paid for a vacation. He bought groceries sometimes, and he'd take me to dinner for my birthday." He paused to catch his breath.

"I wanted him to move out. It wasn't fair that he was living in the house and I was paying all the bills. But he refused. I even offered to sign this place over to him, as a gift."

"He was very selfish," Wili said. "And stupid. He got Grant fired."

"How did he do that?" Ray asked, innocently.

"Mike and I used to socialize a lot with my boss and his wife, Jane the bitch. Since they're both big drama queens, Mike and Jane hit it off. When I moved out, Mike got his revenge by getting Jane to have me fired."

"It's not that you were doing a crappy job because you were obsessed with your new boyfriend?" Ray asked.

Grant Buckley looked shrewdly at Ray. "You've been talking to Jane, haven't you?" he asked. "What's this all about, anyway?"

"Jane Shiner discovered Michael Paterson's body earlier today," I said. "He'd been beaten to death in his bedroom."

Grant Buckley's mouth dropped open, and Wili took his hand. "My God," he said. "Poor Mike. Who could do such a thing?"

"Jane Shiner suggested you," I said. "And you did have a million–dollar life insurance policy on Mr. Paterson. Killing him would get him out of your house, and give you a financial windfall that might help you out of your current difficulties."

Buckley looked angry. "That bitch," he spat. "She didn't tell you I have a new job, did she? That I'm making more than her cheapskate husband ever paid me? Did she tell you that I've started legal proceedings to remove Mike from the house? No, of course she didn't."

I looked at Ray, and he stood. "Wili, can I talk to you in the kitchen, please?"

Wili looked at Buckley, who nodded and said, "Go on."

When they'd left, I asked, "Where were you last night?"

"I get it. You want to see if Wili's story and mine stack up. That's fine. We've got nothing to hide. We were at the Rod and Reel Club last night for the drag show. Hefty gal in blue spangles lip–synched to Donna Summer's "MacArthur Park" and then danced with the crowd. We stayed 'til about midnight and then walked back here. The bartender, Fred, will remember us. I'm a good tipper."

We talked for a few more minutes, and he gave me the name of the woman at his new job who could verify his employment status and his salary. He also passed on the address of the Kamalei School and the name of the principal. "He wasn't a bad guy, you know," Buckley said. "We loved each other for a long time, but then we just fell out of love, and it wasn't fair to either of us to stick around when things weren't working out."

Ray and Wili returned from the kitchen, and after giving Grant Buckley my card and asking him to call if he thought of anything else, we left. "What was Wili's alibi?" I asked Ray, when we were in the elevator.

He told me the same story that Buckley had, though his description of the drag queen was more flowery. "Still doesn't mean they didn't do it," Ray said.

"True. You notice Wili's feet and his upper arms?"

"Not particularly," Ray said dryly. "Don't tell me you're falling for him, too."

"Nope. But he has small feet—which would slide if he stepped into a pair of Paterson's shoes. And he works out, too; he has the upper body strength to pick up that statue and slam it into Paterson's head."

"My bad," Ray said.

There wasn't much else we could do on a Sunday. Buckley's new employer was closed, as was the Kamalei School. Fred the bartender didn't come on duty at the Rod and Reel until eleven, and we wouldn't get the autopsy results, with a narrower window of time of death, until Monday or Tuesday. It was nearly the end of our shift, so I dropped Ray at his apartment and then drove the few blocks to mine.

It began raining again. I couldn't surf, or run, or ride my bike, or do any of the other outdoor activities that relieve the stress of investigating homicides, without risking getting sick, so I curled up in bed with a gay mystery by Anthony Bidulka, a Canadian whose work I liked, made some dinner, then dozed a bit, until it was after eleven and I knew Fred would be behind the bar at the Rod and Reel Club.

The rain had stopped, but the night was still cloudy. I dressed a little better than I would for an ordinary witness—tight white pants that hugged my ass, and a short–sleeved black shirt that was nearly see–through. Black belt, black shoes, and a black choker of neoprene rubber around my neck.

The Rod and Reel was packed, an island's worth of gay men breaking out of rain–driven isolation. I could hear the back beat a block away, and when I got to the club it was an oasis of light and color in a drab, gray world. When Fred brought me my first Longboard Lager, I told him I needed to talk to him when he got a break. It was nearly an hour later, though, and I was deep in conversation with a muscle–bound hottie, when Fred tapped me on the shoulder.

The sacrifices I make for my job. I told the hottie I'd see him later and walked out to Kuhio Avenue with Fred, where he lit up a cigarette and I asked him about Grant Buckley and his boyfriend Wili.

"Last night?" he asked. "Yeah, they were here. Helen Wheels was doing her Donna Summer routine. She doesn't stop munching crack seed, she's going to be doing a Mama Cass impression soon."

Being an island boy myself, I knew that he was talking about preserved fruits like rock salt plum and honey mango, rather than non–prescription drugs. "You notice what time they left?"

He frowned, a sure sign there was thinking going on inside his pretty head. Blond, with a sexy physique always displayed in wife–beaters and shorts, Fred was a flirt and a slut, which resulted in great tips and a to–die–for sex life, but he wasn't the sharpest toothpick in the box. "Around midnight," he said finally. "I remember asking if they weren't going to stick around for Helen's second show, and Grant said something about a cake that he had left out in the rain."

How could you sit through a Donna Summer act and not listen to the words, I wondered, but that was Fred. Too busy pouring drinks and criticizing the size of Helen's ass to pay attention to what she was singing.

I expected him to ask why I needed to know, but instead he said, "I get off tonight at two. You still gonna be around?"

I shrugged. "Depends on whether I get lucky," I said.

"You might get lucky at two."

In the pool of light from a street lamp above us I saw a sly grin on Fred's face. Why hadn't he and I ever gotten together? Oh, no brain. Right. "Maybe I will," I said. I put my arm around his shoulders and he leaned in for a kiss. His mouth tasted like rum and tobacco.

"Consider that a down payment," he said. Then he crushed his cigarette out and went back inside.

I stood there for a moment. I'd established the truth in Grant Buckley's story. I could go home. But who was I kidding? I went back into the bar. If the hottie wasn't still there, I always had Fred to fall back on.

It had started to rain again by the time I got home, sometime after four in the morning, and I fell into a deep, dreamless sleep, recovering from the night's exertions. The next morning I called my father and asked him about Island Appliances, curious about Wolfgang Shiner. My father made a noise—the one I'd heard so often as a kid and a teenager, the one that expressed disapproval. In my mind's eye, I could see his face, handsome still in his sixties, a mix of features inherited from his Hawaiian father and his haole mother. When he wasn't happy with me or one of my brothers, his lips flattened and his eyebrows raised.

"Late deliveries twice this month," he said. Though he'd been slowing down, he still ran the construction business that had supported three sons, put food on the table and paid private school and college tuition. "Other contractors too. We think money problems."

Were those problems related to Grant Buckley's departure? Had he been fired, as Jane Shiner had said, because of fiscal improprieties? Or, as Grant suggested, had his firing been because of his problems with Mike Paterson?

Ray and his wife were still sharing a car, so I picked him up and drove us to the Kamalei School, a private school for special needs kids on the outskirts of Aiea. I was expecting to see a bunch of happy little Downs syndrome kids, maybe a couple in wheelchairs or on crutches.

I was wrong. When we sat down in her office, Sylvia Chu, the school's principal, said, "We pick up kids who fall through the cracks. They've been kicked out of their original schools, and many of them are in foster care or live in group homes. Some have graduated from high school but their families have nothing to offer them during the day."

"What's the age range?" Ray asked.

"Fourteen to twenty–one," Sylvia said. "Many are profoundly disturbed or have low intellect. Mike Paterson was one of our saints."

"Did you know Grant Buckley?" I asked.

She nodded. "Of course. Not only was he Mike's partner, he's one of our biggest donors." She leaned across the desk. "Normally I wouldn't betray a personal confidence, but I think in this case Mike would forgive me. He and Grant had grown apart, and when Mike told me that he had moved into the second bedroom at the house, I was sure that Grant's support would stop. But he's made the same generous donation every year."

"Another saint," Ray said dryly.

"Any students who have a history of violence?" I asked.

"Of course. But we're very careful about our faculty privacy. We'd never give out a teacher's home address or phone number, and frankly, our students don't have the mental capacity to find that kind of information on their own."

"What if someone found the information for them?" Ray asked.

Sylvia Chu was a smart lady, and she saw where Ray was going. "You think Grant Buckley hired one of our students to kill Mike?"

"We have to look at every possibility," I said.

Something sad settled in Sylvia's face. "It's a terrible world. We shelter these kids for a few years, and sometimes all we do is put off the inevitable. There are a half–dozen boys who have the strength to do what you suggest and who could be influenced by someone with money and authority. If you give me your fax number I'll have my secretary put together a list."

"I hope we're wrong," I said, as I gave her the card.

"Right or wrong, Mike's still dead," she said.

Before we left the Kamalei school, I called the headquarters of Island Appliances and spoke to Lois Roeper, Wolfgang Shiner's secretary. She told me that Shiner could see us for a few minutes at ten.

"We have a lot of possibilities," Ray said, as I drove us toward a Starbucks on the way to Shiner's office. "Too many."

He began ticking them off on his fingers. "Grant and Wili leave the club on Waikīkī on Friday night and drive to the house in Black Point. They wait until Paterson's asleep and then Wili goes into the house, grabs the statue, and brains Paterson. He steps into Paterson's shoes to get to the French doors, and then slips around to the front where Buckley picks him up."

"Buckley doesn't even have to be involved," I said. "Suppose Wili sneaks out after Buckley's asleep. He's been to the house, he could take Buckley's key."

"That's possibility number two," Ray said. "Number three is that Buckley knows some of the kids Paterson works with. Sylvia Chu said he used to go over to the school all the time, before he and Paterson split up. He could have dropped Wili at the condo and gone off by himself—or the two of them could have worked together. Pick up the kid at home, drive him out to Black Point. Give him step by step instructions."

"True."

"You think we have to eliminate Buckley as the killer?" Ray asked. "Because of the shoes?"

"I think so. Buckley's feet were pretty big."

"You know what they say about foot size," Ray said, leaning back in his seat and pointedly propping his size twelves against the dashboard.

"You mean the one about the inverse relationship with IQ?"

"Hmph." Ray put his feet back on the floor as we pulled up at the coffee shop, and while he ordered the coffee, in lieu of paying me for gas, I used my new Blackberry to check for email and phone messages. Doc Takayama had emailed his results; blunt trauma to the head had caused Paterson's death, and the closest fix he could get on time of death was between three and four a.m.

I told Ray when he came back with the coffee. "Nothing we didn't already know," he said. "Buckley and Wili are still each other's alibi."

We went back and forth over the details of the case, but nothing new occurred to either of us. At a quarter to ten, we pulled into the parking lot at Island Appliance's headquarters, a massive one-story box just off the Pali Highway. It looked new, and one side of the building was dedicated to loading bays. There was only one truck in a bay, though.

We walked inside and were directed down a hallway to a lavish executive suite—thick carpets, koa wood furniture, sepia prints of old Hawai'i on the walls.

"I'm just sick about what happened to Mike," Lois Roeper told us. She was a trim blonde in her early sixties with a Bluetooth headset nestled in her bouffant hairdo.

"You knew him?" Ray asked.

"Of course. Grant used to bring him to all the office functions, and he and Mrs. Shiner were such good friends, too."

She pressed a button on her headset and spoke to Shiner, and then a moment later a door to an inner office opened and the man himself was there to lead us inside. He was smaller than I'd expected, a trim 5'8 or so, and carried himself with a military bearing. "What can I do for you, gentlemen?" he asked, pointing us to chairs and sitting behind a massive mahogany desk.

The room was as lavish as the rest of the executive suite, with framed photos of Shiner and various dignitaries, a state of the art computer, and carpet so thick you could lose a small dog in it. "We wanted to understand the terms of Grant Buckley's separation from Island Appliances," I said.

"We came to a parting of the ways." Shiner crossed his arms over his chest.

"Could you be more specific?" Ray asked. "Was it related to his personal life?"

"That was certainly a big part of it. We're a family here at Island Appliances. And both Grant and Mike were a part of that family. I had no problem with Grant's sexual preference, but I believe in fidelity. A man who cheats on a partner is just as likely to cheat on a boss."

"Were you aware that he and Paterson were living apart before Buckley met his new boyfriend?" I asked.

"As far as I knew they were both still in the house in Black Point."

I nodded. "But in separate bedrooms."

"I didn't like to pry," Shiner said. "And Jane—my wife—had some definite ideas, and I guess I listened to her."

He looked sad. I figured we'd gotten what we needed, and Ray and I stood up. "Thanks for your time, sir," I said. We all shook hands, and then Ray and I drove back to headquarters in a pouring rain. By the time we arrived, the fax from Sylvia Chu was waiting for us.

We had just finished going through the list, one by one, without coming up with a single solid subject, when my cell phone rang. I saw the call was from my father. "Hey, dad. Howzit?"

"You asked about Island Appliances," he said. "So I made some calls this morning. Everyone I called said there were problems."

"Really? What kind of problems?"

"Sounds like money. Shiner built a big building, but sales have been dropping. Now I hear he's slow to pay suppliers, so shipments to little guys like me and my friends run late."

"Any idea when these problems started?" I asked, looking around for my notes. I saw that Buckley had been fired four months before.

"Maybe three, four months," my father said.

I thanked him for the info, then hung up and explained it to Ray. We both thought about it for a while. "Suppose Shiner regrets firing Buckley now," I said. "Buckley was his CFO, ran all the money side of things. Now the money's a problem. And he blames Paterson."

"He should blame his wife," Ray said.

"But he can't kill his wife. But Paterson—he could get away with that. You saw all those photos on his walls—he's got a pretty high opinion of himself."

"So you think he killed Paterson? How would that solve any of his problems?"

"With Paterson out of the way, his wife wouldn't object if he tried to get Buckley back. Maybe he sees Buckley as the way out of his financial troubles."

Ray looked skeptical, but he said, "I looked at his shoes. Small feet. And even with a suit on, he looked like he was strong enough to beat somebody up."

The Shiners lived in a gated development in Hawai'i Kai. The kind of place that keeps records of who goes in and out, even down to the use of gate clickers. After jumping through a few hoops with the security company, I got a manager to fax us the log, which showed that someone using the Shiners' clicker had left around two and returned around four.

"And didn't Jane Shiner tell us she and Wolfie slept in separate bedrooms?" I asked, paging back through my notes. "So she can't alibi him."

"Could Jane be the killer?" Ray asked. "She's a hefty gal. She could swing that statue. And her feet are undoubtedly smaller than Paterson's."

"But she doesn't have a motive," I said. "She was Paterson's friend."

"Well, there's that."

"So let's say Shiner did it," I said. "How can we catch him?" I remembered the crime scene, and how much blood had been spattered there. "Luminol," I said, citing the chemical that can pick up traces of blood. "We check Shiner's car."

"How are we going to get a warrant?" Ray asked.

I shrugged. "Have to think about that one." While we were thinking I called over to a friend at Motor Vehicles to ask what kind of car Wolfgang Shiner drove.

My friend left me on hold for a while. "Sorry it took so long," she said, when she came back. "Seems Mr. Shiner just traded his car in, and we got a VIP request to expedite a change in the records."

She gave me the new information. "Hold on. When did he swap the cars?"

"First thing this morning."

"Who's got the old one?"

"Palm Mercedes," she said. She gave me the VIN number and I called the dealership. They still had the car, hadn't even had a chance to get it detailed. "Hold off on that, will you?" I asked.

The abrupt trade of the car was suspicious enough to get us a warrant, and Ray and I were slogging through another downpour to Palm Mercedes at the end of our shift that Monday with an order to have the vehicle towed to the police impound lot. By the end of the next day we had the Luminol results and a match to Mike Patterson's blood type. We got a warrant for Shiner's arrest first thing Wednesday, and picked him up at his office. Lois Roeper looked personally offended as we marched Wolf out.

"We won't be on her Christmas list this year," Ray whispered to me.

Wolf Shiner never admitted a thing, and all he'd give us in the interrogation was his name and his attorney's phone number. But I was sure the evidence we'd found was damning.

Jane Shiner showed up to bail her husband out that afternoon and on her way she stopped by the detective bureau. Ray and I were working on paperwork, waiting for another call to come in, and it was pouring again. "Are you sure it was Wolf?" she said, standing in front of my desk. "And not Grant?"

"Was your husband with you between two and four on Saturday morning?" I asked in return.

She shook her head.

"There's your answer, then."

"Mike was a sweet man. He didn't deserve what Grant put him through."

"Then he certainly didn't deserve to die," I said. "If you hadn't pressured your husband to fire Buckley, Island might not have gotten into financial trouble. Buckley would have eventually gotten Paterson out of the house in Black Point, legally, and Paterson would still be alive."

"You don't know that," Jane Shiner said defiantly.

"I know that," I said. "The other thing I know is that if I could lock you up as an accessory I would, but sometimes the judicial code doesn't let us do what's right, only what's legal."

Jane Shiner stalked away. "Little harsh on her, weren't you?" Ray asked.

"It's the rain," I said. "Makes everybody grouchy."

THE SECOND DETECTIVE

Honolulu District 6 Patrol Officer Lidia Portuondo was beginning her fourth straight day of 12–hour patrols when she found the naked man behind the new sports bar on Kuhio Avenue. It was just before seven a.m. on an early November day, and I was walking out the door of my apartment on Waikīkī, on my way to work, when she called my cell phone. "I think you'll want to catch this case, Kimo," she said. "Naked male, bleeding from the rectum, confused and non–responsive."

"But is he cute?"

She gave me the address and hung up. She had patrolled Waikīkī early in her career, and then after some problems been transferred out to Pearl City, a much less desirable beat. She had worked hard to get back to Waikīkī, and I appreciated her initiative in calling me directly.

It looked like it was going to be another tourist office day— temperatures in the 70s, sunshine and offshore winds. I'd already been out on the surf for an hour just at daybreak, so I was in a much better mood than Lidia, who normally worked three twelve–hour shifts in a row, then had four days off. Once every three weeks, though, HPD throws a fourth shift into the mix, to average out to a 40–hour week. When I was a patrolman, I hated that fourth shift—all the crazy stuff usually happened during it.

I called Ray, and we met a few minutes later at the sports bar, Da Kine. We rounded the corner to find Lidia squatting on the ground in a narrow alley, talking to a beefy blonde haole in his early twenties who was, as she had said, completely naked. "Sir, I think you need to go to the hospital," she said. "An ambulance will be here any minute. Can you tell me your name?"

The guy just stared at her in a daze. Lidia stood up and came over to me. She's just thirty, three years younger than I am, and getting ready to take her sergeant's exam. She's a tough, no–nonsense cop, sturdy but not stocky, with her long dark hair pulled up into a neat bun on the back of her head.

"This is the third guy I've found like this," she said to us. "Always on Tuesdays, and always behind this bar."

"How do you remember that well?" Ray asked.

"It's always been just after a Monday night football game," she said. "The first case, the guy told me his friends got him drunk and stole his clothes. The second guy had no clue what happened to him. I didn't see a pattern until this guy."

"Why'd you call me?" I asked.

"The bleeding. I thought it might be a sexual assault."

"Sounds like a good call." I went over to the guy. "I'm Detective Kanapa'aka," I said. "But you can call me Kimo. Can you tell me how you got here?"

The guy just stared at me. He didn't seem to realize he was naked, lying in an alley that commercial trucks used to service the bars and stores along Kuhio Avenue. The ambulance pulled up then, and as the EMTs were coaxing the guy up and into the back, Lidia said, "Does this look like roofies to you?"

Ray and I both nodded. The scientific name for the drug is Rohypnol, but its street name is roofies. We see it sometimes up at the university, where a guy slips a pill into a girl's drink, gets her tranked up, and then takes her back to his room and rapes her. That's why they call it the date rape drug. It's tasteless and colorless, and dissolves easily in alcohol. I hadn't seen a male victim before, but I knew that roofies had been found in gay bars on the mainland.

Before we followed the ambulance over to The Queen's Medical Center, I asked Lidia to track down the reports on the two previous cases, to ensure that she was remembering the facts correctly. Da Kine wasn't a gay bar; it was a sports bar. I couldn't see a gay man going in there, chatting up some cute football fan, then drugging and raping him in the back alley.

We stopped at police headquarters and checked in, then drove over to the hospital. The doctor on the case was a Japanese woman named Lois Fujimoto, who often dealt with sexual assault victims. "I took blood and urine samples, and I'm going to test for FNP metabolites," she said. I knew that meant the presence of Flunitrazepam, the chemical behind Rohypnol. "Evidence of sedation is clear from his unresponsive state."

"You think this was a sexual assault?" I asked. "Lidia noticed he was bleeding from the rectum."

"It's not hemorrhoids," she said dryly. "He has a small anal fissure—that's a tear in the lining of the anus. A fingernail could have done it, or someone inserting a penis into the rectum roughly or without proper lubrication."

"Presence of semen?" Ray asked.

She shook her head. "No. But we found a couple of pubic hairs that are not consistent with the victim's own hair."

"Is it your medical opinion that he was the victim of a sexual assault?" I asked.

She pushed a lock of black hair out of her eyes. She looked like she'd been on duty all night. "Based on my examination, I'd say he was in no condition to provide informed consent to anal penetration, and that some sort of penetration did occur. That means sexual assault to me."

"Me, too," I said. "Thanks, Lois. Can we talk to him now?"

"He's recovering. But go easy on him; I don't think he understands what happened yet."

I pushed the door open, Ray behind me, and found the guy sitting up in bed, dressed in a hospital gown and looking agitated. "I have to call my wife!" he said.

"It's okay," I said. "I'll get you a phone in a minute." I introduced us and asked his name.

He looked confused. "Okay. How about your phone number. Do you know that?"

I could see the agitation mounting. "Take it easy. It looks like somebody slipped something in your drink last night that might be affecting your memory. But it'll come back to you soon, I promise."

"But my wife. She'll be worried about me."

We worked on that for a while. He did remember he was married, though he couldn't remember his wife's name or his phone number. "You live here in Honolulu?" Ray asked.

"Honolulu?"

"Guess that means you're not a local," Ray said. "I know what that's like."

I called Lidia and had her check every hotel within a few blocks of Da Kine to see if any guest had been reported missing. "I'm thinking newlywed," I said to her. "If that's true, his wife is probably going crazy."

Ray and I sat with the guy for about an hour, trying to keep him calm while at the same time coaxing details from him. Then Lidia called to say she had his wife and they were on their way.

"Is your wife's name Regina?" I asked, after I hung up.

Relief seemed to wash over him. "Yes, Gina," he said. "Yes! My wife! Gina!"

"And your name?"

"Bob." The name seemed to startle him. "I wanted to watch the game."

It took another hour, and the visit from his wife, before a few details came back to him. After an early bird dinner at a Chinese restaurant, Gina had returned to their room and Bob had stopped off at Da Kine, where they were showing a football game on a big-screen TV. When he didn't come back to the room, Gina figured he'd found some guys to get drunk with and she had gone to sleep angry.

She had woken up alone and been immediately concerned. "Bob likes to drink," she said to us, as we stood in the hallway outside his room. "I was hoping he'd grow out of it once we got married."

They were both twenty–three, graduates of the University of Nebraska, in Honolulu on their honeymoon. Bob was a manager for a fast–food chain, and Gina was a social worker. They had arrived on Saturday and were staying 'til the following Saturday.

I didn't tell Gina about the possible sexual assault. I figured it would only agitate both of them. "Has Bob ever ended up without his clothes at the end of a night of drinking?" I asked.

She blushed. "Once. When we were sophomores. He was rushing a fraternity, and they got a bunch of the guys drunk, made them strip, and then dropped them off a few miles from campus. But nothing like this."

I got her to go back to their room and call the credit card companies. Bob was still a little disoriented, and he agreed to stay at the hospital until Lois Fujimoto said he could go. Ray and I went back to the station and looked over the records Lidia had pulled on the other two victims. In both cases, they had been taken to Queen's, but treated only for the aftereffects of intoxication. No one had done a rape kit on either man.

Ray and I went back to Queen's at noon, just as Bob Wolsey was being discharged. His clothes hadn't turned up anywhere around the bar, so Lidia had run Gina back to the hotel to pick up something for him to wear.

I gave him my card and asked him to call me if he remembered anything further. I also took a couple of digital pictures of him to show around the bar.

Da Kine's manager was an island guy named Louis Pito. It was impossible to tell what race he was, though there was clearly a mixture in there. He recognized Bob's picture and said he'd been drinking alone, then joined a group at the bar as the game progressed. Louis didn't remember any guy in particular paying much attention to Bob.

"Did you see him leave?"

Louis shrugged. "We get pretty busy during a game. It went on at six-thirty and was over by nine, but we stayed open until two."

"Was Bob still around then?"

"Nope. The last hour, we only had half a dozen guys in the house, and he wasn't one of them." He told us that he parked in the alley behind the club; Bob wasn't lying naked on the ground when he closed up at three.

Back at headquarters, Ray and I tracked down the two previous victims. The first was a tourist from California, and I reached him at work. His name was Ed Newton, and he'd been in Honolulu alone. "I just got divorced," he said. "I figured the cure for my broken heart was a pretty little Hawaiian girl. The only ones I ended up meeting were nurses, though."

"Do you remember anything about that night?"

"Just that I had a massive hangover the next day. I remember drinking, and then I woke up in the hospital."

"Do you know how long you were out?"

"Most of the next day." I looked at the file, and saw he was five–eight and weighed a hundred ninety pounds. When I asked he told me that he was blond, and agreed that somebody might say he was beefy. "Though I'd prefer muscular."

"Do you remember who you were drinking with?"

"Just a bunch of guys at the bar."

No one had used his credit cards, though he'd lost about a hundred dollars and had trouble boarding his flight home without his driver's license. "Do you remember experiencing any rectal discomfort?"

He laughed. "The beer went down my throat, not up my ass, Detective."

I thanked him. The second victim was a student at UH, and his roommate said he'd be back after his last afternoon class, so Ray and I drove up to Mānoa. Chris O'Connor looked like he'd come from the same gene pool as Bob Wolsey, and probably Ed Newton as well. He was twenty–one, blond and buffed. He wrestled and played flag football; he'd gone down to Da Kine two weeks before with a couple of buddies to watch the game.

"But they both had exams the next day, and they cut out early," he said. "I hung around to watch the rest of the game."

"You remember anything about who you were drinking with?"

He shook his head. "It's a blur." He assumed that his buddies had come back and been messing with him. "I wouldn't have even reported it if I'd woken up before that lady cop found me. She made me go over to Queen's and get checked out."

"They do any tests on you?"

He shook his head. "Just figured I was a drunk who got rolled." He hadn't carried any credit cards with him to the bar, and had only lost a few dollars, his student ID, and his room key. "Had to call my roommate to bring some clothes to the hospital for me. That was embarrassing."

We were about to leave, but before I did I had to ask him the rectal discomfort question. That's when he looked closely at me, and something clicked. "You're the gay cop, aren't you?"

"I am."

"I'm not gay, dude. This was not some gay crime."

"I didn't say it was, Chris. I just asked if you…"

He interrupted. "Yeah, I know what you asked. And the answer's no. Now I've got some studying to do."

"So, does the whole island know about you?" Ray asked, as we walked back to my truck.

"Pretty much. But it's usually gay people who bring it up."

"So what do you think? The guy's really gay?"

"I think he remembers being assaulted, but he's not going to talk about it."

Lidia Portuondo joined Ray and me to bring the case to Lieutenant Sampson the next morning. He's older and heavier than the victims, but given the right conditions thirty years ago I could see he might have had the right look. I knew he'd pitched for a minor league team on the mainland before busting his knee and coming to the islands to recover.

Sampson's polo shirt that day was a glossy dark green, the color of banana leaves. After the three of us laid the case out for him, he asked, "What do you want to do?"

"Set up a sting. We know where the guy finds his victims, and we know what they look like."

"He does this every Monday night?"

"At least three of the last five Mondays," Lidia said. "The other Mondays, I was off duty. I asked around and no one else on the beat saw anything similar. But the vic could have woken up and left before anybody found him."

Sampson nodded. "Tough for a big blond guy to walk around Waikīkī naked after dawn, though." He considered. "All right, see if you can find a cop who looks like our victims and get a sting set up for next Monday night. Get me the paperwork and I'll sign off on it. And follow up with the honeymooner, see if he remembers anything more."

"Now where are we going to get a big, blond haole?" I asked, as we walked back to the detective section. "Ray, you feel like a dye job?"

"He's not big enough," Lidia said. Ray frowned at her, and Lidia covered. "Sorry, but you just don't fit the profile. There's a guy I worked with in Pearl City, though. A rookie." Back at my desk, we got hold of a picture of the guy, whose name was Billy Stephan, and I agreed he looked right. I called his sergeant, talked it over with him, and got Stephan assigned to me on Monday. "Hope he likes football," I said to Lidia, when I hung up.

"I think he's what you're looking for," she said.

Then Ray was shifted to a task force at the airport for a while, and I got called out to a homicide, and I didn't think about our potential rapist until Billy Stephan showed up, in uniform, at my desk at noon on Monday. After the introductions, I laid the case out for him. "So you just want me to hang out at this bar and watch a football game?" he asked.

"Pretty much."

"But you don't expect me to let this guy stick his dick up my ass, do you?"

"No more than a female cop in a prostitution sting does," I said.

"Because I'm not gay, you know."

I was losing my patience. "Billy, I don't care if you like to fuck goats in your spare time. I need you to go to this bar, order yourself a beer, and watch a football game. I'm going to be watching you, watching out for you. I'll make sure nobody gets in your pants."

Billy didn't look like he trusted me. "But what if somebody recognizes you?"

"So? Cops watch football games in their off time."

"But people know you're a fa—I mean, gay."

I really hate being some kind of ambassador from the world of gay to the world of straight, and I was tempted to give Billy a smart–ass response, but I held back. "First of all, lots of gay men like sports. Some of them watch football because they like the game, and some watch because they like to see well–built guys in tight pants falling all over each other." That was not the answer Billy wanted. "And yes, lots of people in Waikīkī know I'm the gay cop. But most people either don't know or don't care. So I'm pretty sure I can blend in at Da Kine. But if I get made, and I have to leave, then you leave, too, and we try again next week, okay?"

He agreed. I sent him home to change out of his uniform. "I don't have to like, wear anything goofy, do I?" he asked.

"How old are you, Billy?"

"Twenty–three."

"And how long ago did you graduate from the academy?"

"Nine months ago. I just finished my fourteen weeks on foot patrol in Chinatown last month."

"I'm going to cut you some slack, even though you're starting to get on my nerves. I want you to dress like a twenty–three–year–old guy who wants to go to a sports bar and watch a football game. You think you can manage that?"

Billy looked like a puppy who had been scolded for peeing in the corner. He nodded his head. "Good. The game starts at six-thirty. I suggest you get there around six. How many beers can you drink before you start to get wasted?"

"I can usually manage a six–pack."

I was tempted to say something about the beginning of a beer belly under his uniform shirt, but I was trying to be nice. "Then don't drink more than four. I want this guy to see you drinking and think he can take advantage of you."

At the end of my shift, I headed home, where I changed into an aloha shirt and jeans, topped with a UH ball cap. By the time Billy Stephan arrived, I was already in place at Da Kine, sitting in a back corner with my friend Akoni, who had been my partner when we were both working out of the substation on Waikīkī. He had transferred to a special task force shortly after I left, and the short–lived department plan to base detectives there had fallen apart.

With Ray on the task force for the foreseeable future, Akoni was just the guy I wanted as my backup. Plus, he liked football and was delighted to get overtime for hanging out at a sports bar watching a game on the big–screen TV.

Billy started walking toward us, and for a minute I thought he was going to blow his cover and come over to join us, but halfway across the floor he remembered what he was there for and headed to the bar, where he ordered a beer.

Akoni and I enjoyed ourselves, hanging out and talking about old times, while keeping an eye on Billy and anyone who talked to him. The bar got crowded, and eventually Akoni and I had to split up, taking opposite sides of the room to keep Billy under surveillance. There wasn't anyone else in the bar who matched the description of the victims, so Billy was the only game in town. But nothing unusual happened, and after the game was over the bar emptied out. Billy was left alone at the bar, nursing his last beer.

I sent Akoni over to tell him to call it quits, and met up with both of them down the block from Da Kine, free of anyone who might have been watching. "I did just what you said, detective," Billy said. He didn't seem drunk at all.

"We'll try again next week. We don't know this guy's pattern all that well. He might only go out every other week, or every third week."

During the next week, people kept on committing crimes with the same depressing regularity, and with Ray on the airport task force I was up to my ass in alligators. I confess I'd forgotten all about Billy Stephan and the rapist until the following Monday afternoon, when I found Billy waiting patiently outside my office after I returned from a visit to the medical examiner's office. He was already dressed for action, in an oversized 49ers T–shirt, board shorts and flip–flops.

"Shit," I said. "It's Monday, isn't it?"

He just nodded. "Well, you might as well hang out here for a while. I've got some paperwork to do before I can get out of here."

"Can I help?"

I'm never one to pass up an offer like that. I set Billy to sorting a series of auto theft incident reports by location and type of vehicle for a case I was investigating, and sat down to read the autopsy report I'd brought back with me from the medical examiner's office.

"Was that guy who was with you last week at the bar gay, too?" Billy asked, after a few minutes.

"Not according to his wife," I said. "That reminds me." I called Akoni, and found that he had a stakeout of his own that evening. I made a few more calls, and couldn't round up another cop to go with me. Ray was on a stakeout himself and couldn't bail out of it. "Looks like we might have to cancel," I said to Billy. "Try again next week."

"You don't need backup," he said. "I can watch out for myself."

"I don't know, Billy. You're still just a rookie."

"What if some other guy gets raped because we're not there?"

He had me there. "All right. But you're gonna have to be extra careful."

We worked for a little while longer. "Do you play sports?" he asked me.

"I surf, I run, I roller blade. I played football in high school, but only because I could run."

"But most gay guys aren't into sports, are they?"

I was starting to regret ever pulling Billy Stephan into this investigation. "I can't speak for most gay guys."

"Did you always know you were gay?"

I put the autopsy report down, because I wasn't getting much chance to read it. "Come on, Billy, let's hit the road. I've got to swing by my apartment and get changed. You might as well ride along with me." I looked at him. "Unless you're worried I might try something."

He turned red. "I'm sorry. I just don't know any gay guys."

"You do. You just don't know they're gay."

We took my truck back to Waikīkī. I thought I could make better time—and reduce the time I spent with Billy Stephan— by swinging over to Ala Moana Boulevard, which moves more quickly than taking South Beretania through downtown—but got stuck as the traffic cops cleared an accident in front of Ala Moana Beach Park, where Gilligan left on his three–hour tour, and where unsuspecting tourists are likely to get mugged after dark.

I was drumming my fingers against the steering wheel when Billy said, "You never answered my question."

It took me a minute to rerun the last hour across my brain. "Oh, yeah. Did I always know I was gay." I looked over to him. "You really want to talk about this stuff?"

"Not if you don't want to."

I shrugged. "It's an old story to me. I first started thinking something was strange when I was in junior high. I didn't get excited about girls the way other guys said they did. But I got a hard–on sometimes in gym class, or seeing a guy jogging in just a pair of shorts." I looked over at Billy out of the corner of my eye. He was hanging on every word.

I remembered what Lidia Portuondo had said. "I think he's what you're looking for." At the time I'd thought she meant just that he was blond and beefy. Now I was wondering if there was something else. "I slept with a lot of girls, mostly because I didn't know any better," I continued. "I mean, there were signals, I just wasn't paying attention. I'd see a porn magazine, but I only wanted to look at the guys, not the girls. I fooled around a couple of times with guys, but I was too caught up in my own head to see what I was doing."

Billy made a sort of strangled noise in his throat and I thought, oh, shit. He was gay, damn it, and trying to figure out how to come out. I knew I'd have to move very carefully—to let him know that I was there for advice, but not for sex; to be a friend, not a lover.

It would have helped if I had a boyfriend or a partner I could drop into the conversation, but I still wasn't comfortable discussing Mike and why we broke up.

Billy was sexy, in a straight–guy frat–boy way, but he was ten years younger than I was, and I was his supervisor, on this case. There was no way I was getting in his pants—or letting him into mine.

Traffic finally started to move again. Billy didn't say anything more, and I took my time figuring out what I wanted to say.

"Listen, Billy. I don't know what's going through your head right now, but I think I've got a damn good idea. I just want you to know you can feel free to ask me about anything, and whatever you say stays between us. All right?"

"All right."

He was quiet for a minute, and then he cleared his throat. I was expecting another general question, something about gay identity or meeting other guys, but he asked, "Have you ever had another guy fuck you?"

I lost my concentration for a minute and nearly banged into a tourist in a rented convertible who'd slowed down to gawk at *wāhine* in bikinis along the side of the road. I slammed on my brakes, and Billy said, "I'm sorry. Was that too personal?"

"It is pretty personal. But I told you that you could ask anything. If you're the guy who does the fucking, or you're the one who gets the blow job, you're the top. If you're the one who opens up his ass or his mouth, you're the bottom. I've done my share of both."

Billy didn't say anything, so I took a deep breath and continued. "To me, it's not about being the man or the woman, if that's what you were going to ask next. You get together with somebody you like, and you start exploring. What gives you pleasure, what gives the other guy pleasure. I'm not going to lie to you—getting fucked up the ass hurts sometimes. But it can also feel really good."

Billy was still in silent mode. I could tell by the tension in his shoulders that this was a tough conversation for him. It was just about to get tougher. "Have you ever fooled around with another guy?"

"I'm not gay."

"Gay is a label, Billy. It's not an answer to the question."

We traveled half a dozen blocks down Kuhio Avenue before he said, "In college, I got drunk once with a buddy. We had these two girls with us, but they bailed. We ended up back in his room, drunk and horny."

"Did you like it?"

I looked over at him, and I was afraid he was going to cry. In a very small voice for such a big guy, he said, "Yes."

"So, what? Did it make you feel guilty? Did you want to do it again?" I half turned to him. "Not with me, Billy. There's no way anything sexual is happening between you and me, no matter how drunk anybody gets. This is safe territory. You can say anything you want without any fear, any judgment."

"Yes," he said, defiantly. "Yes, it made me feel guilty. And yes, I want to do it again."

"Good. I'm glad it made you feel guilty, and I'm glad you want to do it again."

He looked confused. "You thought you did something bad, and you felt guilty about it. That makes you a good person. Because you care about what you do. You have to recognize, though, that what you did wasn't bad. There's nothing wrong with two consenting adults having sex—no matter who they are or what they do to each other. I mean, within reason, of course."

I pulled up in front of my apartment. "I've got to go upstairs and get changed. You can come up if you want, or you can wait down here."

"I think I'll wait down here, if you don't mind," he said. "It's not that I don't trust you—"

"You've got a lot to think about. I'll be down in ten minutes."

I gave him fifteen. The first time I came out to somebody, my heart was beating faster than the pace car at the Indy 500, my palms were clammy and my mouth was dry. It took a long time before I could out myself comfortably.

When I came back downstairs, Billy was all business. "We should have some kind of signal," he said. "If I figure out who the guy is."

"Don't worry about signals. I'll be watching you. I'll know."

We walked over to the bar together. A block beforehand, I hung back, to let him get to Da Kine first and establish himself. A few minutes later, I entered, to find him already at the bar with his first beer in hand. I ordered one for myself, and retreated back to the same corner where I'd sat with Akoni.

Because I was paying attention, I noticed the dark–haired haole positioning himself near Billy. The way he offered Billy a dish of peanuts, engaged him in conversation about the game. It wasn't anything I could put my finger on, but it seemed predatory.

Billy was also drinking more than he should have. I counted three beers in quick succession, and remembered four was his limit. But the stress of coming out was weighing on him, and alcohol was a convenient way of forgetting. The dark–haired guy wasn't helping the situation, encouraging Billy to down the rest of his beer and order another.

The 49ers had just scored a touchdown, and Billy turned away from his glass for a minute to cheer with the rest of the bar. In a quick, fluid movement, one I registered more intuitively than actually followed, the dark–haired guy dumped something into Billy's beer.

I couldn't be certain, though. Maybe it was just my imagination. I could have jumped up, flashed a badge, and taken the guy in. But what if I was wrong? I'd been nursing one beer all evening, but I knew even one beer could impair judgment. I decided to watch the guy some more.

I didn't have long to wait. Billy lifted his glass to his mouth, then put it down. He seemed to wobble on his bar stool, and the dark–haired guy took his arm and said something. Billy laughed. The guy said something else, and then stood up. He helped Billy off his stool as the rest of the bar was engrossed in the game.

They headed toward the men's room, which was down a hallway that also led to the kitchen—and a back door, I remembered. I jumped up and crossed the bar. But the 49ers had recovered a fumble and everyone in the bar was on his feet, cheering. I struggled through the crowd, excusing myself, but one guy still took offense and wanted to get belligerent.

I pulled my badge out of my board shorts and flashed it. "HPD," I said. "Get out of the way."

He backed off. I rounded the corner to the hallway just as I saw the back door swing closed. "Shit!" I took off at a run, bursting through the door. I was responsible for Billy; I didn't want him to get hurt. And I knew that if the rapist did anything to him, it would slow his coming out process by years, or decades.

The guy was helping Billy into a black SUV as I came out the door. "Hold it right there," I said, holding out my badge. "HPD."

The guy held up his hands. "Hey, what's up? My buddy here just had a little too much to drink. I'm taking him home."

"Yeah, taking me home to fuck me, strip me and dump me," Billy said, coming out of his stupor, and flipping the guy against the side of the SUV. "Spread 'em, asshole."

He pulled a pair of handcuffs from his pocket and had the guy cuffed before I could react from my surprise. "I thought you were drunk," I said.

"So did he," Billy said. "So what's up, dude? You're a good—looking guy. You go over to the Rod and Reel Club or some other gay bar, you could get a guy to spread his cheeks for you. Why'd you have to dope up some poor straight guy's drink?"

"You fags," the guy said, nearly spitting.

"That's Officer Fag to you," Billy said.

"And Detective Fag," I added.

I opened up my cell phone and called for a black and white to take the guy in for booking. He had a bunch of roofies in his pocket, and Billy's glass, the one he hadn't touched after he noticed the guy slip the powder in, tested positive as well. Billy went out to see Chris O'Connor at UH and helped him remember what had happened between the time he left Da Kine and the time he showed up naked in the alley the next morning. The details were still fuzzy, but he was able to pick our suspect, Jerry Lopez, out of a lineup, and provide a deposition.

Ray came back from his special duty assignment about a week after we pulled Lopez in, and I debated how much of the story to tell him. I had promised Billy I'd keep his secret, so I shouldn't have said anything at all to Ray. He'd only been my partner for three months, but I was starting to trust him, and I knew how corrosive keeping secrets can be, so I told him everything.

"Lidia knew," Ray said. "What do you call that, gaydar?"

I nodded. I told him that Lidia was the first cop other than my partner I'd told my own secret to, and how she'd told her boyfriend at the time, another cop, and then how my secret had spread throughout the ranks. "I guess she's learned to be a little more discreet."

"You think she's – you know, a lesbian?"

I shook my head. "After Alvy, she hooked up with another guy."

Jerry Lopez cut a deal with the prosecutor a couple of weeks later, agreeing to a few months at the Hālawa Correctional Facility and a course of therapy. I didn't see Billy Stephan again until he stopped by my desk after seeing the human resources department about some paperwork.

"How's it going?" I asked, sticking out my hand. I didn't think Billy was ready for a hug, at least not in the middle of the Alapa'i Headquarters.

He shook my hand, and gave me a sly smile. "You remember Chris? O'Connor?"

I looked at him. "You and…"

"Uh–huh. Neither of us really knew what the hell we were doing at the start, but we've been practicing a lot."

I laughed. "Well, you know what they say."

We talked for a bit, and then he said, "Is it true you took the sergeant's exam right after you were eligible, and passed the first time?"

Three years was the minimum an officer with a college degree had to spend on patrol before taking the exam, but a lot of guys waited longer. And a lot never took the exam at all, content to stay on patrol. In our force, detective is an assignment, not a rank, so passing the sergeant's exam was a prerequisite.

"Yeah. I was lucky; they needed detectives just after I passed my exam."

"I'm gonna need your help to study," he said. "I pretty much suck at tests, but I've decided I want to be a detective."

"You want to be the second openly gay detective on the Honolulu force?"

He shrugged. "Maybe. If that's the way it plays out." He surprised me by leaning against me and hugging me. "Thanks," he said. "For everything."

I hugged him back. "You got it, brah."

I overheard the tall, lanky man in his early sixties asking the receptionist for me by name and stood up to greet him. He looked familiar, but I couldn't quite place him. "Ted Kiely," he said, reaching out to shake my hand. "I teach up at Honolulu Arts College."

"I remember." He wore a battered–looking plaid long–sleeved shirt, ancient khakis, and flip–flop sandals. His graying blond hair was a little unkempt. He reminded me of English professors I'd had in college.

I led him over to my desk, and called Ray over. We all sat down and I asked, "What can I do for you?"

"I got this email." He handed me a printout.

The message was just a paragraph long, from someone named Linda Moldovan. "Dear Ted," it read. "I am sorry; but I will not be able to teach English at HAC this winter. I am with my family back in New York and I will not be able to get back. I been thinking about this for a long time. I wish I could of set down with you before I left: unfortunately the time just ran out."

I handed the paper to Ray after I finished reading. "This person is an English professor?" I asked Kiely.

"Exactly!" he said. "I called 911 to report her missing, and they put me through to a Detective Chu, who treated me like I was crazy, but I remembered your telling me that you were an English major in college, and I dug around until I found your card and drove down here. I knew you would understand."

Unfortunately, I didn't understand at all. "Why don't we step back a bit. Who's Linda Moldovan?"

"Lovely woman. Has a master's degree in British Literature. Did her thesis on Mrs. Oliphant, I believe."

I just looked at him.

"Oh, yes. She's been teaching for us at HAC for the last year or so, as an adjunct. We might have a full–time position in the fall, and she'd be top of the list. So it's unusual for her to just disappear without notice."

"She did send you the email," Ray said.

"But that's just the point, you see. She didn't write it." He pulled the paper back toward him, and motioned at it with a long index finger. "It's riddled with grammatical errors—something Detective Kanapa'aka saw immediately. Linda would never have written such a terrible email."

"People get rushed," I said. "They make typos."

"My dear boy, these are not mere typos. Look here—misuse of the semi–colon. No English professor would make a mistake like that. And then here—'I been thinking.' How could she leave out the past participle? And type 'could of' instead of 'could have?'"

"And she used set instead of sat, and misused the colon in the last line," I said.

He smiled. "I knew you would understand."

I noticed he had a computer bag with him. "Is the original message on your laptop?"

He nodded.

"Can you show us?"

"Certainly."

While he opened the computer and turned it on, Ray asked, "Have you heard anything more from her beyond this letter?"

Kiely shook his head. "I even went to her address, an apartment in Mililani. The landlord said she and her son had just up and left one day."

"Did he see them leave?"

Kiely shook his head as he turned the computer around to face me. "There was a note slipped under his door telling him to keep the security deposit. I don't think he trusted me so he wouldn't show me the note."

I saw the message in his inbox and clicked to open it, then viewed the message header. Ray got up and looked over my shoulder. Most of the stuff was gibberish, but I could see that the message had been sent through ihawaii.net, an ISP with headquarters in Honolulu. I pointed it out to him. "It doesn't look like the person sending it was in New York."

"And Linda came to us from California," Kiely said. "She never mentioned family in New York at all."

I turned the computer back to him. "Tell us more about Linda Moldovan. What makes you suspect something might have happened to her—beyond the bad grammar in this message, and her leaving her apartment."

"She never told me the details, but I got the impression something had happened to her on the mainland. She had been married, you see, and had an adopted son, and both of them had used her ex–husband's name, until they moved to Honolulu and she had both their names changed back to her maiden name."

"This thing that happened…"

"I think it had to do with a place she worked." He sighed. "Teaching writing at a prison. Just one of those terrible jobs you have to take, you know, when you're an adjunct. I gathered she had a problem with one of the prisoners."

Kiely didn't know where on the mainland she had worked, and didn't know the last name she had used there. He did give us a copy of the letter she had sent him when she applied for the job as an adjunct professor of English at HAC, and copies of the recommendation letters she had submitted as well.

Both letters referred to her as Linda Moldovan, the maiden name Kiely said she had returned to when she moved to Honolulu. And one of them had come from Norman Haider, the chairman of the English department at UC Santa Cruz, my alma mater. I'd taken a course with him once, a long time before, on popular fiction, and I remembered it because I'd loved the chance to read a mystery, a western, even a romance—the kind of books I'd have read even without a syllabus.

"What do you think?" Ray asked, after Kiely left.

"I don't know. But he spoke to Ralph Chu first; let's see what he thought." I hoped that Ralph had changed his mind and started looking for her, so I could safely push Kiely's concerns out of my mind.

He was out on a call, but I reached him on the radio. "The lady left a letter for her employer and for her landlord. Without any evidence of foul play, there's nothing we can do."

I looked at Ray after I switched the radio off. "Well, there's something I can do," I said, dialing the English department at UC Santa Cruz.

I asked for Dr. Haider, telling the receptionist that I was a detective with the Honolulu police. A moment later he was on the line, and I reintroduced myself, asking permission to put him on the speaker phone, so my partner could listen to our conversation. "I'm sure you've got so many students passing through you won't remember me, but I took your popular fiction course a few years ago. I really enjoyed it."

"I don't get many students with the Hawaiian *okina* in the middle of their names," he said. "I can't say I remember your writing, but I remember your name."

I switched gears, and explained that I was following up on Linda Moldovan's disappearance. He sounded confused for a minute and then said, "Oh, you mean Linda Rieger."

I asked him to spell it.

"Now I remember," he said. "She asked for a reference in her maiden name."

"Can you tell me why?"

There was silence on his end for a moment. Finally he said, "I think she was being stalked."

I looked at Ray, who had raised an eyebrow. "One of her students?" he asked.

"Being an adjunct's a tough life," Haider said. "The pay is terrible, and you need to teach six or eight courses each term just to make a living. You scramble for whatever work you can find, and most colleges and universities won't hire you for more than three or four courses a semester because otherwise the government will consider you full–time."

Ray and I both waited. Like me, he understood the need sometimes to just shut up and let people talk.

"Linda taught at a couple of colleges in the area, and she also worked at a prison somewhere, teaching writing to inmates who were getting ready for return to the world."

"So it wasn't a former student stalking her, but an ex–con?" Ray asked. I could see he was taking his own notes.

"So she led me to understand. She didn't share any of the details with me. I guess it was too personal, or she was embarrassed, or frightened. I do know she kept a file of evidence, in case she ever had to go to the authorities."

"But to your knowledge she hadn't done so?" I asked.

"Not as far as I know. I think she thought by leaving California and changing her name she could make the problem go away."

"I'm starting to think that didn't happen," I said.

He gave me a few more details, and I thanked him for his help. "Do you still read?" he asked, just before we hung up.

"You bet. Mysteries, mostly. I can't read police procedurals because most of them get too many details wrong, but I read almost any other kind."

"Excellent! It's my own informal survey. I ask every former student I run across."

"And how are your results running?"

"Encouraging. We must be doing something right."

I thanked him, and hung up. "You want to talk to Sampson?" Ray asked.

I stared at my notes for a minute, thinking, and then nodded.

Lieutenant Sampson's polo shirt that day was emerald green, over dark slacks. I was probably the only guy in the building who'd call that a jewel tone. But I refrained from saying it out loud.

Ray and I sat across from him and explained the evidence we had so far. "Anybody file a missing persons report?" he asked.

I shook my head and explained why.

"But you're interested?"

"Just a bad feeling so far," I said. "Of course it's possible she and her son took off on their own, fast, and they're safe and secure someplace else. But…"

"You write well," Sampson said. "Would you make any of these mistakes?" He pointed down at the email printout.

"I doubt it. Maybe one of them, if I was in a rush."

"She depended on Kiely to see something was wrong," Sampson said. He thought for a minute. "Let's try not to let her down. See what you can find out."

"Start with the landlord?" Ray asked as we left Sampson's office.

"Sounds good to me." Julie and Ray were still sharing a car, and so I drove us up the H2 toward Mililani and the address on Linda Moldovan's letter of application to HAC. The Waipi'o Valley Apartments were a small complex on the north side of town, close to Wheeler Air Force Base and Schofield Barracks, and I guessed a lot of military families lived there. If I were worried about a stalker, it was a good choice.

The superintendent, a haole in his early sixties, with the close–cropped hair and military bearing of a former soldier, lived in a ground–floor unit near the street. He stood in the doorway propping himself on a single crutch, the right leg of his faded khaki pants pinned up below the knee. We showed him our badges and he invited us inside.

He told us his name was George Cunningham. "Having a problem with my prosthetic," he said, half hopping toward the kitchen table. "Hell to get an appointment at Tripler these days, so many boys coming back from Iraq with problems."

"Tripler's an Army Medical Center," I said to Ray. "My partner's new to the islands," I explained to Cunningham.

"Welcome to paradise," he said. "Stopped here on my way back from Vietnam and never left."

Ray and I sat across from him at the table, and I explained we were looking for Linda Moldovan.

"That English teacher send you over here? I told him, she left me a note."

"I understand," I said. "May I see it?"

He shrugged. "No skin off my back." He reached over to a file cabinet next to the table, opened a drawer and pulled out a folder.

Ray and I looked it over together. This letter was written perfectly—not an error I could find. As Ted Kiely had been told, it said that Linda was moving on and the complex could keep her security deposit.

I handed the letter back to him. "Did you see her move out?"

"She didn't. Move out, I mean. Left all her crap in the apartment, for me to get rid of." He motioned down to his missing leg. "Haven't been able to do it yet. Probably have to hire somebody if I don't get my appointment by next week."

"Can we see the place?"

"You got a warrant?"

"We don't have a crime," I said. "So no judge is going to give us a warrant. All I've got is a bad feeling, a missing single mom and a kid who might be in trouble."

He sighed. "I liked the boy. Good kid, needs a man in his life, though." He hoisted himself up, hopped over to a key case on the wall, and pulled a key off. "Bring it back, hear? Otherwise I've got to call a locksmith, and that's out of my pocket."

"I'll return it," I said. "Thanks."

"You see the boy, you tell him I've still got a few stories left to tell."

"I'm sure you do, sir."

The apartment was on the third floor, at the corner. No elevator; I could see why Cunningham hadn't gotten up there yet.

"Smart woman," Ray said, waving out at the view from the top of the staircase. "Good visibility of the parking lot. No elevator to get stuck in. Peephole in the door, so you can see who's there. If you're worried about a stalker, you could find worse places."

"And I'll bet a lot of her neighbors are military." I told Ray about the two installations in the neighborhood. Then we both pulled on gloves before I opened the door. If there was evidence there we didn't want to disturb it.

We stood in the doorway before walking inside. A large living room, with a galley kitchen to one side, a table and two chairs. A sofa, a TV, and a couple of cheap bookcases. It looked like Linda Moldovan and her son had cleared out in a hurry. There were dirty dishes in the sink, clothes strewn on the sofa, books tumbled out of a bookcase on the side wall.

"I'll start out here," Ray said. "You want to try the bedrooms?"

"Sounds good to me." I began with the bathroom, figuring to get it out of the way quickly. I moved slowly around the room in a clockwise manner, taking notes as I went. Time ticked by as I learned more about Linda and her son, whose name, Ray discovered, was Brian. I finished with the bathroom and moved into Brian's room.

He was a collector. There was a box of trading cards for a game called *Magic: The Gathering* on the top shelf of his closet, and stacks of books on the floor, leaving almost no room for shoes. He had half a dozen glass bowls filled with seashells on his dresser. I was surprised that he'd left all his collections behind.

There was nothing else to find in Brian's room, so I moved into Linda's bedroom. If she was keeping information on her stalker, it was probably in there.

An hour or more later, I had nothing. Some clothes were clearly missing, but others had been left behind. The same with toiletries, books, and personal belongings. A hurried exit—but no indication that the departure had been involuntary.

Ray hadn't found anything in the living room, and he came into Linda's bedroom to join me. While he lounged in the doorway, I sat down on the edge of her bed to think about keeping secrets. When I was a teenager, I'd owned a single pornographic magazine, one I'd shoplifted from a used bookstore on the Fort Street Mall in downtown Honolulu because I'd been too embarrassed to buy it.

There was a nearly naked man on the front cover, the shot cropped just below the waist so that only a hint of pubic hair showed. I hadn't known at the time that I was gay, but that cover photo had struck a bell inside me, and it was still reverberating sixteen or seventeen years later.

I'd hidden that magazine between my mattress and box spring. Far inside, at what I figured was the geographic center of the bed. I hoped my mother would never stumble on it, and as far as I knew she never had.

Had Linda Moldovan used the same hiding place? It was worth a try. "Give me a hand here," I said, standing up. The two of us tipped the mattress on its side, revealing the box spring beneath. Nothing.

I was ready to give up when I noticed a faded white folder that had been taped to the underside of the mattress. Bingo. Thank you, Linda. And thank God I was the kind of teenager who had secrets to hide—but then what kid didn't?

Ray and I took the folder into the living room and sat at the Formica–topped table to read through it. It was a series of letters from an inmate named Pat Brown, all addressed to Linda Rieger. The theme was the same in each letter. Pat thought he and Linda had a spiritual connection, and that they were meant to be together. Creepy.

Linda had been meticulous in keeping each letter and its envelope, and I noticed that she had moved three times in the space of two years—and that each time, Pat Brown had been able to track her.

"So," Ray said, when we'd both read all the letters. "Last letter was dated what, six months ago?"

I nodded. "That's the one that says he's getting ready to be released."

"Parole officer?"

"Have to wait til Monday," I said, looking at my watch. It was early Friday afternoon. "Already after hours in California. If we knew who we were calling, we might be able to reach him, but we'll have to go through channels."

"And Pat's probably in Hawai'i now, anyway, so doubtful he gave a forwarding address."

We were just about to leave the apartment when I noticed an odd shell, in a corner just inside the door. It was about the size of my index finger up to the first joint, striated in shades of red, white, blue, brown and black. I don't pretend to be a biologist, but it looked like a snail shell to me. I picked it up and showed it to Ray. The snail inside had long since died and fallen away, and there was a musty odor emanating from it.

"Think it's one of the kid's?" Ray asked. "He dropped it on the way out?"

"I don't know. It looks like this is a land snail, and the rest of the shells in his collection come from a beach, most likely one in California. Land snails aren't that common on O'ahu any more. Maybe he picked it up outside his school or in the parking lot—but maybe not."

On a whim more than anything else, I dropped it into an evidence bag and took it with me.

We stopped off at a Zippy's and picked up bowls of chili, which we took back to headquarters. As we ate, Ray and I started typing up our notes and filling out forms. "We really have nothing," he said. "Suspicions, but no leads."

I stared at the file in front of me. Idly, I began flipping through the letters and emails that Pat Brown had sent Linda Moldovan, hoping that there would be a clue in there somewhere.

My eyes weren't really transmitting what I read to my brain until the word "shells" jumped out at me. "I know a place to take your son," Pat had written. "There are lots of cool shells there. He will really like them."

"Look at this," I said, and Ray came over to my desk to see what I was pointing at. "Pat knew about Brian's shell collection. Maybe that shell I found is a clue after all."

Ray and I went downstairs to the Scientific Investigation Section. As we were walking in, I ran into Olive Kapai, one of the techs I'd worked with in the past. "You know anything about snails?" I asked her, showing her the shell.

"Maggots and blowflies, yes, snails, no." But she looked at the shell anyway. "Where'd you find it?"

I gave her a brief rundown on the Linda Moldovan story. She turned the shell around in her hand, peering at it from all angles. "Looks like a tree snail to me, too, but you need an expert to tell you more. There's a guy at the Bishop Museum who might be able to help you."

It was already near the end of our shift, and Friday afternoon's a bad time to reach people, but Dr. Anthony Li was available to see us if we could get right over to the museum. He was a Chinese guy around my age, in a blue chambray short–sleeved shirt and a pair of khakis. His round, wire–rimmed glasses made him look smart, and I hoped he was.

"Definitely a tree snail," he said, looking at the shell. "There used to be seventy–two different varieties of these on O'ahu, but we're down to seven or eight now, and all of them are endangered."

He turned to his computer and started punching in keys. After a few minutes, he turned the monitor toward us. "The snails live on the mountain ridges, and over time different groups evolved into different subspecies. The one you've found looks like *Achatinella byronii*, which was last seen in 1975."

"You know where?" Ray asked.

Li nodded. "A ridge just south of Honouliuli Forest Preserve. Just north of Makakilo."

"Leeward coast," I said to Ray. "Out beyond Ewa."

"I'll take your word for it," he said.

"Where'd you get this?" Li asked.

"An apartment in Mililani. Any chance there's a colony of these over there?"

He shook his head. "Like I said, there's so many different variations. Highly unlikely that a second colony could be found so far away from the main one."

"Can you pinpoint the location any more closely?"

In response, Li moved to a filing cabinet with a series of flat, shallow drawers and after a couple of false starts pulled out a topographical map. "Best I can suggest is to head up Makakilo Drive. There's a turn for a road called 'Umena, which runs into Pālehua Road, which leads up to a military reservation and an Army observatory. There's a gate there. I suggest you park near the gate and then head into the hills, along the Palikea Ridge."

"Anyone live up there?" Ray asked.

Li shrugged. "There's always folks off the grid in these back hills and gulches. If you're looking for someone up there, he probably doesn't want to be found."

There were still a couple of hours of light left, so after getting Sampson to okay the overtime, Ray and I left the Bishop Museum, taking the H1 out toward Kapolei. We drove through Makakilo, finding the road and gate Li had mentioned. Before we parked, though, I wanted to explore the area. We drove around a few twisting streets, hugging the side of the hills, and then Ray spotted a dirt road that veered off up into higher elevations.

We parked and got out. It hadn't rained in a while, and the road was dusty and nearly overgrown with low–lying vegetation. But we could see faint tracks of a four–wheeled vehicle.

We looked up the hillside where the track led. There was enough low–lying underbrush to give us some cover if we wanted to climb it. "Think we need to call for backup?" Ray asked.

"Let's do some recon first. There may be nothing up there."

"And we'd look like a pair of idiots."

"Exactly." I opened the glove compartment, pulled out my digital camera, and dropped it in my pocket.

We started to climb, staying low and trying to follow the trail. Though it was early evening, there was still a lot of light in the sky, with little cloud cover, so we had great visibility. In some places the tracks were clearer than others. Somebody had driven up there within the last week or so. Therefore, there had to be something up there.

"Could just be an old campsite," I said. "This ridge is high enough, probably get a nice view down to the ocean."

"Military installations all around, too," Ray said. "Could be soldiers on an exercise. Hell, maybe even terrorists."

"There's no military training up here," I said. "At least not now." The trail twisted and turned, following the natural curve of the hillside, so we could never see more than a few feet ahead of us. The higher we climbed, the slower we moved, careful to disturb as little as possible and to keep our steps silent.

Then I stopped. There on the tree branch ahead of me was a land snail, identical to the shell I'd found. I pointed it out to Ray, and he nodded.

We'd just begun to climb again when Ray and I both heard the noise as the same time—a slap, followed by a tuneless whistle. There were more noises, a squishy sound, followed by another slap. Was Pat Brown hitting Linda Moldovan? Or Brian?

We stopped in our tracks and listened. When the sounds continued unabated, we moved forward again, finally coming around the last curve. From the shelter of thick underbrush, we looked ahead.

A woman was washing a very old Jeep, more rust than chrome. The canvas flaps were long since gone, but she was swabbing the windshield, and then the hood, with loving care. I looked at Ray, and he raised his eyebrows back at me. I pulled the camera out of my pocket and snapped a couple of pictures of the woman.

She was in her mid–forties, old enough to be Linda Moldovan. She had broad shoulders encased in an old T–shirt, and stocky legs in khaki shorts, with flip–flops on her feet. Her hair was a faded brown, cut close to her head.

If it was Linda, she didn't look like she was being held captive. Unless someone was watching her from the cabin to see that she didn't run away—or unless someone was holding her son inside.

The building behind her was a one–room cabin built of old pieces of wood and sheets of tarpaper. It looked like it had been abandoned for decades. Its one advantage seemed to be its location next to a small pond, probably fed by rainwater, which trickled down the hillside as a stream. I saw a gas–powered generator next to the cabin, turned off.

Another woman appeared in the doorway of the cabin, and said something to the one washing the car. We couldn't hear the words, but I kept snapping pictures. The woman washing the car stopped and followed the other inside.

Ray and I turned around and climbed back down the slope, following the rutted track. "Dead end," Ray said.

"Looks like it." We got back to my truck just as dusk was beginning to fall. "You want to give it another try tomorrow?" Though it was a Saturday, we were both scheduled for duty.

"Sure. I'll bet there's a lot of those old trails we haven't even seen yet."

I dropped him at his apartment and drove home. There was something I wasn't seeing, and I didn't know what it was. It nagged at me.

I realized we didn't know what Linda Moldovan looked like, and decided we'd have to call Ted Kiely the next morning and get a description before we set out. Then I gave up and went to the Rod and Reel Club.

I stepped up to the bar and ordered a Longboard Lager. Fred, the usual bartender, had switched shifts with a slim-hipped lesbian with a pierced tongue and a shock of auburn hair running through what was otherwise black and close-cropped. Her name was Lisa, and she'd only been working there a couple of weeks, but she already knew who I was. But so did most of the gay population of Oʻahu.

"Howzit, Kimo," she said, sliding the beer in front of me, no glass.

"It's Friday."

"And that's not a good thing?"

"Not if I have to work tomorrow."

"Bummer. My girlfriend's a nurse at The Queen's. She has to work every other weekend." She nodded, then went off to serve another customer.

Lisa had a girlfriend, I thought. That was nice. Maybe at some point I'd have a boyfriend again.

I sipped my beer, and talked to a couple of guys, and my eyes kept going back to Lisa. There was something about her nagging at me. So I watched her move smoothly behind the bar, blending cocktails, uncapping beers, pouring wine, flirting with the male and female customers alike. I wondered if her girlfriend minded.

And suddenly the light bulb went off. Like a straight cop, I'd made an assumption about Pat Brown. Dumb. Back at home I did a quick Google search, verifying my idea about the prison where Linda Moldovan had taught.

The next morning, I carried my short board out to Kuhio Beach Park at first light. It's a tourist beach, but it's the closest break to my apartment, and if you get out there early enough you aren't competing with the clueless grommets. I caught a couple of good waves while I waited for the day to begin for the rest of the world.

I picked Ray up at seven-thirty, and a half hour later we were on our way to Kiely's house in Mānoa. "Have you found her?" Kiely asked, when he opened the door of his ranch–style house.

"Maybe."

I showed him the pictures I'd taken up on the ridge outside Makakilo. "That's not Linda," he said, when he saw the one of the woman washing the car.

"I didn't think so." I flipped forward, to the shot I'd caught of the woman in the doorway.

"Yes! That's Linda. Thank God."

I turned the camera off. "Thanks. That's what I needed to know."

"Is she all right?"

"I don't know," I said, as we headed back to my truck. "But I will soon."

I called Lieutenant Sampson and told him what we had discovered. He mobilized the SWAT team, and by the time Ray and I made it out to Makakilo, Sampson was parked at the foot of the dirt trail talking on the radio. Today's polo shirt was navy blue, over khaki shorts and deck shoes.

A short time later, the SWAT team was there. We climbed the dirt trail, and they fanned out around us on all sides. "It's your op," the team leader said, handing the electric megaphone to me.

From the shelter of the underbrush, I said, "Pat Brown. Honolulu PD has you surrounded. Release your hostages and step out of the cabin."

We waited. I assumed Linda Moldovan was inside with Pat; I had no idea where Brian was. After a few tense minutes had passed, I was about to speak again when the door opened.

A teenaged boy stumbled out, the door flapping open behind him.

"Brian," I said, and he looked around, trying to identify the source of the sound. "Keep walking slowly forward, down the track. Someone will meet you."

He was wearing a T–shirt, nylon running shorts, and flip–flops, and he looked scared as hell, but he kept moving. One of the SWAT guys grabbed him as soon as he reached cover.

"That's a good start, Pat," I said into the megaphone. "Now send Linda out."

"She doesn't want to leave," a voice called from the cabin.

"Let her step outside and tell me herself." There was no answer. "Come on, Pat. If she wants to stay with you, she can go right back inside."

I looked over at Ray. He shrugged. Then the door opened again, and the woman Ted Kiely had identified as Linda Moldovan stepped out. "Come down the hill, Linda," I said. "We just want to talk to you. If you want to go back up to the cabin after we're done talking, you can."

Linda Moldovan didn't answer. Instead, she took off down the hill at a run, reaching the underbrush in less than a minute. I hurried over to her. "Does she have any weapons in the house?" I asked.

"A handgun," she said. "I don't know what kind."

The SWAT chief motioned back toward the cabin. I picked up the megaphone again. "Okay, Pat, we need you to throw your gun out the door, and then step outside. Nobody's going to hurt you. We're going to make this all go away."

There was no response from the cabin. We waited, sweating in the hot sun. Linda Moldovan insisted on staying with us, her arm around Brian. After about ten minutes, a gun came flying out the door, landing at the edge of the clearing. One of the SWAT guys ran out and scooped it up, then hurried back to cover. Only when he was back in place did Pat Brown walk out the door, her hands up above her head.

When she was clear of the house, a pair of the SWAT guys moved in on her, getting her in cuffs. Ray joined them and read Pat her rights as they walked down the mountain.

I turned my attention back to Linda and Brian, who were hugging each other. "You guys okay?"

Linda was shivering, and Brian was squeezing her around the waist. "I was so scared," she said. "How did you find us?"

"The note you left for Ted Kiely. He was sure you were sending him some kind of coded message. And I guess you were."

"I didn't know what else to do. Pat had a gun, and she made me write the notes to Ted and the super. She even read them to make sure I wasn't pulling any tricks." She shrugged. "Good thing she didn't pay much attention to the grammar lessons I taught back at the prison."

"I love you, Linda," Pat called out, as she was being led down the hillside. "I'll always love you."

"Words I always wanted to hear," Linda said sadly. "Too bad they didn't come from the right person."

"Yeah," I said. "Too bad." I remembered the last time I'd heard those words myself, and when Mike had said them to me. I swallowed hard, feeling that old pain once more. Then I turned and guided Linda and Brian down the mountain.

Baseball fever gripped Oʻahu in February. Jeffrey Kitamura, a big real estate developer, was in negotiation with Major League Baseball to bring an expansion team to Honolulu. In an effort to demonstrate a market for baseball in the islands, he announced the Las Vegas Kings, a new expansion team, would be playing an exhibition series with the Indianapolis Racers, another expansion team.

Hawaiʻi Winter Baseball, a four–team league and the only one to feature international players, was already a feature at UH's Les Murakami Stadium, home to the Waikīkī Beach Boys and the Honolulu Sharks, and at Hans L'Orange Field, where the West Oʻahu Cane Fires and the North Shore Honu played.

My dad played second–string baseball for a few years at UH, and he'd raised my brothers and me with baseball fever. He told us stories of the first baseball game ever in Hawaiʻi, played July 4, 1866, where the "natives" beat the "haoles", 2–1. The great Babe Ruth had come to Honolulu in 1933, and in the 1940s, when my dad was a kid, he used to watch Major League All–Star games in the old wooden Honolulu Stadium, affectionately called "The Termite Palace."

Randy Johnson was the Kings' star pitcher, and his $12 million, three–year deal with the team was part of the publicity surrounding the exhibition series. His handsome face, bulked–up arms and slim waist adorned billboards everywhere in Honolulu.

The buzz accelerated when Johnson came out of the closet a few days before the series was to start. I heard two guys on the radio debating the issue as I drove to work. One felt Johnson was debasing a great American game, while the other guy said, "I don't care what he does off the field as long as he keeps pitching like he does."

I parked in the garage and was on my way up to my desk when the chief's secretary called my cell and summoned me to his office, pronto.

My heart started racing as I ticked off my most recent cases. What could Ray or I have done to attract the chief's attention? I called Ray and asked, "What do you think is up?"

"What do you mean?" Ray sounded like he was eating, probably a malasada, a kind of Portuguese donut that he'd fallen in love with.

"The chief's office. I'm on my way there now. Aren't you?"

"Nope. I'm just going through paperwork, waiting for you to saunter in." He took another bite and chewed noisily, then said, "Looks like this one's all on you, partner."

"I'll call you." I hung up, then took the elevator to the chief's office. Though I'd shaken his hand on a couple of occasions, he'd never said more than "Good work, detective," to me.

When I approached his secretary, she said, "Go right in, detective. They're expecting you."

I opened the door tentatively and stepped inside a plush carpeted, wood-paneled office that could have served any corporate mogul. The walls were lined with photos of the chief with the mayor, the governor, and various dignitaries, as well as him presenting checks to the many charitable organizations that the force supports with the proceeds of drug forfeitures.

"Good morning, detective," the chief said. He was sitting on the edge of his desk, and he stood and shook my hand. "Jeffrey Kitamura, Detective Kimo Kanapa'aka."

Kitamura looked like his news pictures—a handsome Japanese-American man in his mid-forties in an expensive suit, a few worry lines creasing his well-tanned face. "Randy Johnson's been getting death threats," he said brusquely. "I can't let anything screw up these exhibition games—they mean too much to me, and to the people of Honolulu."

"You want me to investigate?" I asked.

Kitamura shook his head. "I want you to keep an eye on him while he's here."

I looked questioningly at the chief. "Bodyguard? Aren't there private firms that could handle this better than I could?"

"Randy's something of a loose cannon at the moment," Kitamura said. "Drinking, hitting the clubs. He's going through a tough time. I know what happened when you came out of the closet and I think you can do a better job of helping him than anybody I could hire."

I knew first–hand the hell the media could mire you in— though Randy Johnson's situation was much larger than mine. For one thing, nobody was paying me $4 million a year. "I'll do whatever I can."

"His plane lands at Honolulu International in two hours," Kitamura said. "I want you there."

The chief assured me that he'd already cleared my temporary reassignment with Lieutenant Sampson, so I was free to head directly to the airport to meet Randy's plane.

On the way I called Ray. He was a baseball fan, too, and wasn't happy to have been cut out of the duty. "See if you can wangle me some good seats." The tickets had sold out fast, though my father's connections had come through for him, my brothers and me.

"You can probably have mine. I doubt I'll be able to enjoy the game."

"Dude, you're the bomb."

"Dude, get a life," I said, and hung up.

The media had gotten hold of Randy's flight, and there were news cameras waiting in the arrivals area. Fortunately all the enhanced security after 9/11 prevented them from mobbing him at the gate. I badged my way in and introduced myself to the gate agent. Randy was among the first off the plane.

There weren't many guys in baseball as handsome as he was. Close–cropped blond hair, a face that resembled Brad Pitt's, chest and biceps bursting out of a royal blue polo shirt that matched his eyes. Narrow waist, slim hips, thighs and calves honed by running bases.

I stepped up and introduced myself. Up close, I could see the toll that the last week had taken on him—bags under his eyes, chin unshaven, worry lines around his mouth. He looked me up and down, then shook his head. "How do we get out of here?"

"Follow me."

Okay, so we weren't going to be best buds. That was fine with me. Who could blame the guy for being a jerk—handsome, rich, successful, and now hounded by the press. It would make being around him a lot easier if I didn't have to worry about lusting after his tight ass or wanting to kiss his pouty lips.

The gate agent led us through a locked door and into the bowels of the airport, depositing us at a side entrance where a black limousine waited. Randy Johnson climbed into the back and slammed the door behind him, leaving me to sit up front. The driver announced that Randy's luggage was already in the trunk, and we took off.

I saw Randy pull out a Blackberry and start punching keys, and I settled back for the ride to the Mandarin Oriental in Kahala. I knew the security at the property pretty well because my brother Haoa had done a lot of the landscaping. If I could convince Randy Johnson to stay in his room except for his time on the field, this would be an easy job.

No such luck. "I'm going to hit the hotel pool for a while, then take a nap," he said, leaning forward. "Get me a dinner reservation at Roy's for nine. After that I want to go to a place called Surf Boyz." Surf Boyz was Honolulu's newest, hottest gay bar, a multi-level place with three dance floors and five bars. It would be hell to keep track of him. "Who knows, maybe I'll get lucky."

I called a guy I knew, who'd dated a waiter at Roy's for a while, and got Randy the reservation he wanted. Then I called the Mandarin Oriental and asked for a VIP check in. The clerk gave me Randy's room number and arranged for someone to meet the limo and escort us there.

Randy's suite had an ocean view, and while he stalked into the bedroom to change I stood admiring the surf, wanting to be out on my board more every minute. He was worse than my friend Terri's seven–year–old, Danny. I was going to be a glorified baby–sitter, and worse, the chief of police would instantly hear of anything I did wrong. It was clearly a no–win situation.

"What the hell is this shit?"

Randy stalked out of the bedroom, buck–naked, brandishing a bottle of Longboard Lager.

"Beer," I said. "Maybe you've heard of it?"

Oops. Probably shouldn't mouth off to a guy who had the ability to get me fired with a single phone call.

"I only drink Corona. I want a six–pack here, now. And don't forget the lime."

He turned to stalk back into the bedroom, giving me a prime view of that gorgeous ass, two round white globes dusted with a few pale blonde hairs. "I'm your bodyguard, not your secretary. You want room service to bring you a beer, pick up the phone."

He turned to stare at me, and I saw his dick had begun to stiffen. Hmm, being an asshole made him hard. Interesting.

I smiled blandly, and I could see he wanted to say something, but instead he turned and went back into the bedroom, returning a moment later in a skimpy Speedo and a pair of complimentary hotel flip–flops. "Let's move," he said, heading toward the door of the suite.

As Randy swam laps, I sat under an umbrella, trying to look inconspicuous in my work khakis and polo shirt, my Glock in a holster attached to my belt. When Randy flopped on a chaise lounge a couple of giggling teen-aged girls asked for his autograph, which he was gracious about providing. Only one older man muttered "Faggot" under his breath—but I wasn't sure if the gibe was intended for me or Randy.

We went back up to the suite after an hour or so, and while Randy napped, I called Lieutenant Sampson to map out the strategy for the next few days. "The hotel's providing you with a room across the hall from Johnson," he said. "I'll send a uniform over to relieve you for a few hours so you can get yourself organized."

By the time Randy woke at eight that night, I'd gone home and thrown together enough clothes and other gear to get me through his visit. When he came out, stretching and yawning, naked once again, I was sitting in the living room of the suite reading a mystery novel by Mark Richard Zubro, one of his series about a Chicago high school teacher and his baseball player boyfriend.

"I hope you won't be uncomfortable in a gay club," Randy said, smirking, and I realized that he didn't know I was gay. It was a surprise; since I'd come out so spectacularly, it seemed that everybody who cared knew that I was the "gay cop." So that's why he'd been so antagonistic, I thought.

"I'm fine with a range of sexual orientations," I said.

His dick was limp again, though impressive in its length and girth, nestled in a blond bush. His six–pack abs rippled as he walked. I noticed he was carrying another Longboard Lager, and this one had been opened. As I watched, he took a long pull from it. "It isn't bad," he admitted, seeing my gaze. "For a local brew."

"Glad you like it."

I'd secured a table by the window for him at Roy's, and I held back as the maitre d' escorted him there. I figured I could sit at the bar and keep an eye on him. "Come on," he said, when he reached the table. "I hate to eat alone."

I sat down across from him. In the flickering candlelight, he looked even more impossibly handsome. The shadows highlighted his cheekbones, the strong line of his jaw. His blue eyes caught the light and glittered.

Outside the velvety darkness glittered with occasional pinpricks of light. A gentle breeze blew in the scent of jacaranda blossoms. It was the most romantic of settings. If only I'd been there with a boyfriend rather than a handsome jerk.

"What's your name again—Como?" he asked, after we'd ordered.

"Kimo." I spelled it for him. "Hawaiian for James. A pretty common name in the islands."

"More than I needed to know."

Fine. We were quiet for a few minutes, and then our drinks arrived—a dirty martini for him, a Coke for me. "You don't drink?" he asked.

"Not on duty."

He nodded. After a minute he said, "Listen, I'm sorry for being a prick. It's been a tough couple of weeks."

"I can imagine."

He frowned. Little did he know.

I steered the conversation to baseball. How he'd played in his most recent game, what he thought of the Racers, and so on. We ate, we talked. Every now and then I'd steal a glance at his handsome face in profile, and almost unconsciously lick my lips in hopes that I might be able to kiss his. Dumb hope, though once when his leg accidentally brushed against mine I got hard, fast. Then he shifted again without seeming to have noticed.

It was exquisite torture, sitting across from a handsome, sexy man at a romantic restaurant, knowing nothing was going to happen between us. His light blue button–down shirt was open at the collar, exposing a triangle of lightly tanned flesh and the barest hint of blonde chest hair. The flickering candlelight cast occasional shadows over his face, highlighting the strong line of his jaw, the angle of a cheekbone.

The longer dinner wore on, the more in lust I fell. Randy became every baseball hero I'd worshipped as a kid, every handsome man I'd spotted across a crowded room and longed to touch. By the time we finished a pair of slices of chocolate mousse cake studded with macadamia nuts and set in a pool of coconut puree, I was feeling a serious case of blue balls approaching.

He paid the bill with an American Express black card, and when we stood up I had to turn my back to him to arrange my throbbing hard–on so that it wouldn't be obvious to every person we passed on the way out. I'd already notified the manager of Surf Boyz that Randy was coming, and we were ushered right in to the VIP area, gathering a lot of attention as we passed.

He had another dirty martini, then announced that he wanted to dance. I followed him to the floor, figuring to stand in the shadows. But on the way, guys kept calling out to me. "Hey, Kimo. Looking good, Kimo." I spotted my friend Gunter, who came up and gave me a big kiss.

"I'm working," I shouted over the music. I nodded toward Randy Johnson.

"A suspect?"

"A baseball player."

Meanwhile, Randy was standing around looking lost. For once, no one was paying attention to him, and he didn't like it. In the dark club, it was hard to see how handsome he was, and the gay men of Waikīkī didn't seem to be big baseball fans.

As I was talking to Gunter, Randy stalked over and said, "I want to dance."

"Go ahead."

"With you."

I looked at Gunter and shrugged, then followed Randy to the dance floor.

The guy had some moves on him. His hips swiveled while the top of his body gently rocked and his legs executed a complicated choreography. He grabbed my hand, pulled me close, then swung me out. I struggled to keep up with him, tingling every time his hand touched mine.

Fortunately I had to focus on dancing, or I think I'd have come in my pants the third or fourth time I felt his hand on the small of my back, then stray down to briefly caress my butt.

After an hour he pulled my head close to his. "Gotta take a leak." He started toward the bathroom, then stopped when he saw I wasn't following him.

"You're not coming?" he yelled.

"You need me to help?"

He wagged his eyebrows. What the hell, I was supposed to keep an eye on him.

I followed him into the men's room and took the urinal next to his. We both pulled our dicks out and started to pee noisily. I'd already seen the size of his trouser snake, so I kept my eyes on the wall, but I could feel his gaze straying down toward my crotch. Almost unconsciously I pressed my pants back, letting my dick hang out as far as it would go.

We both finished at the same time, and zipped up. As we turned to leave, though, he grabbed the back of my head with his hand and pulled my lips to his. I was startled at first, but it doesn't take me long to react to the feeling of a sexy guy's mouth on mine. His thick, pouty lips pressed against mine, tasting of olives, and his tongue pushed past my teeth as if he was trying to swallow me whole.

He smelled like soap and sweat and a spicy, lime–tinged cologne. He kept one hand behind my head, while the other reached around to encircle my upper waist. Our upper bodies pressed against each other, and I wrapped my arms around his Oxford–cloth–covered back and pressed my crotch against his. I was so overcome with lust I forgot where I was, until an old queen pushed past us on his way to the urinal and said, "Get a room."

"I'm ready to go back to the hotel," Randy said, as we washed our hands. Our eyes met in the mirror, his sparkling blue in the overhead light. A deep hunger rose in my stomach and I wasn't sure I could hold out that long.

I called the limo driver, and he met us outside. This time, when I held the door open for Randy, he said, "Aren't you getting in?" and moved across the back seat.

What the hell, I thought. And I was getting paid for this gig?

I hopped into the back seat with him, and as soon as I had the door closed he had his hand on my crotch and his mouth on mine. We made out furiously, pulling each other's shirts open and massaging each other's crotch. I'd been with a bunch of guys by that time in my life, but it was rare to find one whose passion matched my own. Randy's lust seemed to drive my own to new heights.

"Why didn't you tell me you were gay?" he said, when we stopped to take a breath.

I flopped back against the seat of the limo, catching my breath and waiting for my heart to return to its normal rhythm. "I thought you'd be able to tell."

"I can sure as hell tell now," he said, leaning over to bite my lower lip. He swung over me, planting one knee on either side of me, and I could feel his hard dick jammed against my stomach. My own strained up toward the sexy ass that hovered over it. I thought we might melt into a pool of lust right there on the limo seat.

We were both a disheveled mess by the time we pulled up at the hotel. I squirmed away from him and said, "Button your shirt," closing mine up before I opened the door. "You don't know who's out there with a camera."

"What the hell do I care?"

"I care. You think this is what the chief of police had in mind when he asked me to take care of you?"

"I know what I have in mind, as soon as we get upstairs."

I glared at him, and he buttoned his shirt and smoothed his hair. I got out of the limo first, pushing my stiff dick aside so it wouldn't tent my pants. Then I held the door for him and followed him at a discreet distance through the lobby.

I loved the way he sauntered, a pure jock posture, as if he knew that everyone in the lobby was admiring his strut, knew how successful he was, how much money he made.

Once we got inside his suite, though, there was no longer any distance between us. He grabbed me in a big bear hug, and wrapped his hands around my ass, pulling me toward him. We mashed our lips together and kissed, both our hearts racing as we connected. I was overwhelmed again by his spicy lime cologne, the feel of his shirt beneath my fingers, the warmth of his skin where we touched.

His five o'clock shadow rubbed against my cheek as I kissed the line of his jaw. I felt his hard–on jammed against me as I unbuttoned his shirt and began kissing and licking my way to his nipples, first one, then the other. "Man, you're driving me wild," he said, as he shucked his shirt and massaged the sides of my head.

I pulled off my shirt and unbuckled, unzipped and dropped my pants to the floor as he did the same. Fortunately I was wearing deck shoes without socks so I could kick them off, but Randy was wearing sneakers and thick white tube socks, and his pants hung up on his shoes.

I kneeled to the floor in my boxers, passing his crotch, encased in white briefs, along the way. He tried to pull them down but I grabbed his hand. "Wait," I said. He fell backwards on the sofa, stretching his right foot out to me.

I untied his right sneaker and pulled it off, then began massaging his foot through his sock. He groaned softly. Then I pulled the sock off and started to kiss and suck on each of his toes. Big toe first, rough and callused, hard as a stubby dick. Then each toe in sequence. He squirmed and moaned, urging me to his dick instead, but I took my time. When I'd finished sucking the little toe of his right foot, I applied myself to his left, repeating the process.

Then I slid his pants off and lifted my head to his crotch. His dick was rock–hard, tenting the white cotton fabric, and there was a round wet spot at the head where he was leaking precum.

I licked my tongue up the length of his shaft through the fabric, and he shivered and moaned. Then, without removing his briefs, I started sucking him. After only a moment or two I felt his body stiffen and then he ejaculated behind the fabric that separated us.

"Man, that was awesome," he said, relaxing his body against the cushions.

My own dick was hard, tenting my boxers and leaking precum against a pattern of palm trees and hula dancers.

I peeled Randy's cum–soaked shorts down then, put my hand into the cream, and then rubbed it up from his crotch toward his chest. He groaned. "Dude, you are so hot."

"This is only the beginning." I peeled his shorts down and dropped my boxers. Then I turned Randy so he was lying on his back on the sofa, and lay down on top of him, rubbing my body against his, my dick against his thigh, the cum on his chest migrating to mine.

I felt myself coming and leaned down to kiss him as my body stiffened, closing my eyes as my tongue found his and my body erupted in passion. I slumped against him, sucking on his lower lip, and he rubbed my back with the hand that had earned him $12 million. I could see he was worth it.

We lay like that for a while, until I pulled off and our bodies stuck together, cum and sweat mingling with body hair. "Yuck," he said. "We need to hit the shower." He pushed me off him and stood up. I slumped back on the sofa.

"You coming?"

"Been there, done that," I said, grinning.

"I'm a professional athlete," he said. "I never shower alone."

I couldn't resist the wicked smile on his face, so I dragged my sorry ass off the sofa and followed him into the lavish marble bathroom.

If anything, Randy's reflection in the full–length mirror across from the shower was even sexier, knowing that I'd made him sweat, that it was my cum mixed with his caking the wiry blond hairs of his bush together. He turned the water on full blast, unwrapped a bar of fancy lavender soap, and beckoned me to join him. I was happy to oblige.

We alternated soaping each other's bodies, and I got to explore every single muscle group in Randy's finely toned body. Man, it didn't get much better than that. Wild sex with a world-class athlete, then an invigorating hot shower, the scent of lavender rising around us as we rubbed our soapy bodies together.

Randy dropped the soap. "Oops," he said. "You'd better pick that up."

When I bent over, he stuck his finger up my ass. "You know what they say about us faggots. Don't drop your soap in the locker room."

I wondered how many times he had heard that phrase since he'd come out of the closet, and I wanted to be his protector, to beat the shit out of any guy who dared make a nasty crack at the man who could make me feel so good.

I stood back up, and his finger slipped out of my ass. But he made up for it by sticking his tongue in my mouth. We kissed under the cascading hot water until it had washed away every trace of soap. Randy stuck his close-cropped blonde head back under the tap for a minute, then said, "I'm ready for bed. How about you?"

"With you, stud?" I said, worried for a minute that I was sounding like someone in a bad porn movie. "In a heartbeat. Just let me wash my hair. I think you must have massaged your cum into it."

He stepped out of the shower and grabbed a towel. "I'll be waiting for you." Through the clear glass door of the shower I watched him towel off, and only turned to the shampoo after he'd left the room, naked as usual.

When I got to the bed, though, he was sacked out, fast asleep and snoring lightly.

I looked around for my clothes. I probably should go across the hall to my own room, I thought. But how many chances would I get to share a bed with a handsome, sexy baseball player? Not many, in this life. So I slipped into the bed next to Randy, and he threw a leg over me and pulled me close.

I woke up alone, to rosy fingers of light creeping in through the sliding glass doors that framed the ocean view. I looked around for a minute—the 400–thread count sheets, the cloud–soft pillows, the elegant furniture and gorgeous painting of Diamond Head on the wall. It took me a minute to realize that the night before hadn't been just an amazing dream.

Randy was in the living room of the suite, his head toward the balcony, doing pushups. "You work out?" he asked.

I flopped down on the floor next to him, then joined his rhythm. I didn't know how many pushups he'd done, but I stopped at thirty and watched him do another twenty after that. Then he rolled over and started doing sit–ups.

"Don't just sit there—make yourself useful. Sit on my feet."

I did as I was told, plopping my naked ass onto his ankles and feet. He clasped his hands behind his head and began his sit–ups, those glorious abs rippling. With every movement, his dick began to stiffen, until he was fully hard, but nothing stopped his rhythm. I counted for him, and when he got to fifty his dick finally subsided. When he got to one hundred, he quit.

"Someplace on this property where we can run?" he asked. I slipped off his feet and he sat up, massaging his calves.

"I'm sure."

"You have gear with you?"

"I think so. Across the hall."

"Get it and meet me back here."

Just outside the hotel's front door, we stretched out, then Randy took off down the driveway, me in hot pursuit. We loped around the hotel grounds for a while, then took off down

Diamond Head Drive for what had to be at least three miles before he turned back.

I'm in pretty good shape, but he was killing me. I wished I had my radio so I could call for backup. It wouldn't look good if the chief found out Randy'd been out on the road by himself. He took pity on me, though, and slowed the pace for the last mile back to the hotel.

"I have to be at the stadium at ten for practice," he said, when we got back to the hotel.

"Man, what do you do on days when you don't have practice?" I asked.

"This kind of perfection doesn't come easily," he said, grinning.

He promised to stay out of trouble for the next hour or so, and I got to take a nice, long soak in a hot tub, trying to ease all those muscles I'd strained between the night before and that morning.

In the limo on the way to Les Murakami Stadium, he said, "Sorry about crashing last night." He looked out the window. "I haven't been sleeping all that well since I made the big move." Without looking at me, he took my hand and squeezed it. "Thanks. I needed the rest."

I squeezed back.

I sat up in the stands and watched as the Kings practiced. UH security kept the media out, and it was a glorious day, sunshine, blue skies, and temps in the low 70s. I wished I could have had my dad and my brothers next to me, watching what was going on down on the field. They'd have loved it.

The first exhibition game was the next day, so Randy and the rest of the players were under strict instructions not to get out and raise any hell. In the limo back to the hotel, he said to me, "You know a quiet place we can get some dinner?"

I suggested a Japanese restaurant perched on a cliff on the windward side of the island. He gave the limo driver the evening off and I drove us up there in my truck, relishing the chance to be just a pair of guys out on a romantic date.

We shared platters of sushi, drank just a bit of sake, and spent a long time talking. I told him about my coming–out experience, and he told me some of the responses he'd been getting. Our feet danced with each other under the table, and occasionally we even clasped hands. If there'd been even a chance that our romance could blossom, it would have been perfect. But I knew Randy was leaving as soon as the last ball was hit, and that gave the evening a bittersweet tinge—even though with luck we would spend most of the next week together.

That night, I followed him up to his suite, but he stopped outside the door. "Listen, I have this superstition," he said. "Ever since high school."

"No sex before the big game?"

He nodded. "Are you cool with that?"

I kissed his cheek. "Absolutely. You only play every other day, right?"

"And every other night, we play," he said. "Sleep well, handsome."

I did. I joined Randy for a brief workout the next morning, and then delivered him to the stadium. I'd given my ticket for that game to Ray, who joined my dad and brothers in the stands, and I watched the game from the owner's box with Jeffrey Kitamura, the chief of police, the owners of the Kings and the Racers, and a bunch of other dignitaries, staying in the background as much as possible.

At the end of the third inning, Jeffrey Kitamura's cell phone rang. Irritated, he picked it up and barked at the caller. Halfway through the call, he put the phone aside and whispered something to the owner of the Kings, then nodded. To the phone, he said, "Pull him out of the game. I'm not taking any chances."

He got up and walked to the back of the private box with the owner of the Kings and the chief, who caught my eye and nodded for me to join them. "There's been a phone threat," the chief said in an undertone as we walked. "They've decided to pull Randy off the field. I want you to meet him down in the locker room and keep him there until the game's over."

"He's not going to be happy about that."

"I think we'd all rather have him unhappy than dead," Kitamura said. "Go."

I went. There was a uniform outside the locker room, who said he'd be guarding the door to make sure no one got in until the game was over. I walked inside to find Randy pounding the door of a locker with his million–dollar fist.

"Whoa, whoa," I said, grabbing his arm. He hit me instead, a solid punch to the gut.

I swung his arm around and pinned it against his back, leaning my face against his neck. "I know you're pissed off. But if you hurt yourself, you're out of the game, and the assholes have won."

He started to shake, and I realized he was crying. I turned him around and kissed him. "Don't cry, baby. You've got to be strong."

"I'm tired, Kimo. I'm ready to give up."

"You can't. You don't have to. Lean on me."

He wrapped his arms around my back and hugged me fiercely, and we kissed some more, our tongues dueling with each other. I felt myself getting hard as our bodies pressed together.

I reached up under his uniform jersey and pulled it off, then began kissing and licking my way across his chest. I had him pinned against a locker with my hands, and I felt his chest rising and falling in a steady rhythm.

I untied his pants and let them slide to the floor. He was wearing a jock with a cup, which I found incredibly sexy. "I want to fuck you, Kimo," he said. "I want to fuck you so bad."

"Fortunately, I was a boy scout when I was a kid," I said, pulling my wallet out of my pocket. I kept a condom in the back. "Always prepared."

While he pulled the jock off to the side and unwrapped the condom, I pulled my pants and boxers down and leaned against an inclined sit–up board. Randy squatted behind me, spit into my asshole, then slicked his index finger up in his mouth and began to finger–fuck me.

"Yeah, you've got a tight asshole," he said. "You're going to love me filling you up with my big bat."

I squirmed under his digital assault. We were in the locker room, for god's sake, and I was about to be fucked by a handsome, sexy ball player. Could it get any better than that?

Then he stuck his dick up my ass. It hurt for a minute, but once he found the sweet spot and started fucking me I realized, yeah, it could get better, and it just had. He was pulling on my shoulders, moving my body back and forth as his hips pistoned his dick into me. I wanted to yell out with pleasure but I worried that any excess noise might cause the uniform outside the door to burst in on us.

His blond pubes tickled my ass as his slippery dick slid in and out of me. He left one hand on my shoulder and reached around with the other to jerk me off. It wasn't long before we were both whimpering and catching our breath and then ejaculating madly. He pulled his dick out of me and flipped me over, so I was laying on my back on the inclined board, and lowered himself over me.

We kissed deeply, our bodies pressed against each other, sweat and cum mingling. "You are some hot fuck," Randy said.

"Back at you, stud. They don't call you Randy for nothing."

He laughed loudly. "Man, that felt good. I haven't laughed in a long time."

I pushed him off me. "Come on, let's hit the shower," I said. "And this time, stud, if you drop the soap, you're the one who'd better watch out."

They caught the jerk who'd been threatening Randy that night, and the rest of the exhibition series went off without a hitch. And as promised, when Randy didn't play during the day, he and I played at night. I could see why he was paid as much as he was; he sure knew how to handle bats and balls.

I met Javier Moreno at the Rod and Reel Club one hot, muggy night in March. He was talking about MP3 files with another guy at the bar, and I'd just bought an iPod and wanted to learn about places I could download music online, so I jumped into the conversation when I could.

Oh, and he was really cute, too.

He was in his late twenties. Slim, like me, but he had a kind of Latin bearing, a smoothness to the way he moved his hips and torso, something I'll never master. I am part Hawaiian, part Japanese, and part haole, and I can do a little hula, but I could never move the way Javier did.

We hit it off, and his friend melted away. "I've got a ton of MP3s at my place," Javier said. "If you want to come over, you could pick out the ones you like and I'll burn a CD for you. Then you can upload them to your iPod."

"That would be awesome." He lived a few blocks away, in a high–rise between Fort deRussy and the Ala Wai Canal. On the way there, we traded bits of background. He was Cuban–American, raised in a place in north Jersey called Union City, and he had moved to Honolulu to get as far away from his family as possible. "They don't like *maricons*," he said. "But that's okay with me, because I don't like bigoted assholes."

"My family's cool. I'm lucky."

He was a computer programmer, but he didn't want to talk about his job. "Tell me about being a cop," he said. "Sexy."

"Lots of guys have a thing about uniforms," I said. "But to me, it's just an itchy piece of polyester that comes with a big thick belt and half a hardware store hanging off it—radio, nightstick, flashlight, holster. You name it, I've carried it at one time or another."

He fired up his computer, and I pulled a kitchen chair next to his desk chair. We looked through his MP3 files, and he copied them to a CD. While it was burning, we started to kiss. We made out for nearly an hour, long after the completed CD had slid out of his computer. We went so slowly I was afraid I'd get blue balls from the pressure building up inside me. But Javier insisted we had all night.

I felt like the luckiest guy in the world—I'd gone to the Rod and Reel Club just to get a beer and cool down after work, never imagining I'd meet a guy who was as hot as Adonis and as sexy as any porno actor. I'd been fooling around with a Chinese guy I met on line, who I called Mr. Hu, and though sex with him was hot, and addicting, someone new and horny was always good.

It was three a.m. when we were finished and I kissed Javier goodbye. My body was sweaty, lubed up, and aching in all the right places. Fortunately it was Saturday morning, and I didn't have to work again until Monday. I figured I'd have plenty of time to rest up before my next shift.

I spent Saturday sleeping and surfing, recharging my batteries, and when Javier called around eight to see if I wanted to get together again, I figured if he was up for something so was I.

We did talk, you know. In between bouts of sex, we lay there in bed, our bodies touching in a half dozen places, and traded stories. I thought, this is a guy I could really fall for. It seemed like he felt the same way.

He stayed at my apartment Saturday night. We fell asleep, spooned together, with the air conditioning on low and a thin sheet covering both of us. We indulged ourselves in one more round of sweaty sex on Sunday morning, then showered and went to brunch together. I was carb loading, replacing all those spent calories with banana French toast with macadamia nut syrup and a tall glass of fresh–squeezed orange juice.

"You are one sexy dude," I said to him, as we sat back over the debris of brunch. He'd sprinkled his scrambled eggs with lots of Tabasco sauce, and a pool of red liquid was all that remained on his plate. It seemed like we were matched in all our appetite for music, food, sex—whatever.

"Right now I'm one tired dude. You wore me out this weekend, Kimo. I haven't met a guy who could keep up with me for a long time."

"I never knew I could go on for so long 'til I met you. Most of the guys I've met, it's over before you get your heart rate up."

"You won't have that problem with me. But I've got to get home and get some real sleep. I've got a tough week ahead of me at work."

He scribbled his email address on the back of his business card. "I'm up late," he said. "What shift are you working this week?"

I had to think for a minute. My usual shift starts at seven-thirty and ends sometime in the afternoon, whenever the leads for whatever case I'm investigating run out. But a couple of the detectives on the second shift were going to be testifying on a big case, so I'd been moved up to a ten a.m. start, to cover for them. I told Javier, and he said, "Great. Maybe we can cyber late at night."

"Cyber?"

"Cyber sex," he said, grinning slyly. His foot rubbed against my calf, and despite how much it had been through in the last forty-eight hours, my dick got hard. He stood up and pulled some cash out of his wallet, which he dropped on the table. "See you on line, *mi cielo.*" He leaned down and kissed my cheek, his tongue wiping swiftly across my ear as he stood back up.

I looked that word up online when I finally got back to my apartment. My sky, he'd called me. I liked that.

Around ten o'clock that night I sent him an email. "U online?"

When I didn't get a message back by eleven, I went to sleep. I wanted to drive out to Makapu'u Point for some real surfing in the morning since I didn't have to be at work so early. The wind was up, an onshore breeze tossing the waves, and I stayed out there for two hours, rushing back home and then to the station.

I couldn't check my email until I got home that afternoon. There was no message from Javier, but I knew he'd said he was going to be busy that week. I left my computer turned on and connected to the Internet for a couple of hours that night, with my instant messaging program running in the background, but no message from Javier came through. No email either.

When there was still nothing by Tuesday night, I decided I needed Gunter's advice. I found him at the Rod and Reel Club, wearing a sleeveless muscle shirt that showed off his ropy biceps and the wavy tattoo that circled his right one. It's not his only tattoo; he has a dolphin on his left ankle and a radiant sun at the base of his spine. I've always teased him that he needs to add the words "Welcome! Come on in," under the sun.

"I want details," Gunter said, when I laid out the bare bones of the Javier story.

"I want advice."

"You give me details, I give you advice."

We took our beers over to a table in the corner, and I filled in the blanks. It was almost as fun retelling what we'd done as it was doing it. Almost, but not quite. "When you're finished with him, I want his number," Gunter said.

"Don't hold your breath. I might have found Mr. Right."

Gunter frowned. "You found a really hot lay."

The sick feeling I'd been getting since Javier refused to answer my emails grew. "You think that's all it was?"

"Why else hasn't he called you or emailed you?"

"He's busy."

"Kimo, I get busy, too. But if I've got a guy I want to keep I make the time to call him."

I shook my head. "We had such a connection. I refuse to believe that I read him so wrong."

Gunter shrugged. "You'll know in another day or two."

"Maybe not 'til the weekend," I said defensively.

"Maybe not."

Wednesday afternoon I broke down and called Javier's office number. My heart was racing and I felt like a stalker. His voice mail picked up and I heard his gentle Spanish accent. "This is Javier. I can't take your call right now. Please leave me a message."

I didn't. I sent him another email instead and tried to accept I'd been wrong.

But my cop instincts kicked in, confusing me. What if something had happened to him? I knew very well that bad things happen all the time, even to the most innocent people. And Javier, who picked me up at the Rod and Reel Club and took me home based only on his first impression, might have gotten in trouble more readily than most.

Thursday morning Ray and I were at our desks when he looked up and said, "Is something bugging you, Kimo?"

"What makes you ask?"

"You've picked up that same piece of paper three times, stared at it like it was written in Chinese, and then put it down again."

I had worked with Ray for nine months by then, and I'd come to trust him and his instincts. He'd been forthcoming with details about his personal life—the difficult adjustment he and Julie were making from Philly to Honolulu, their tight finances, his frustration that she was always working when he wanted to relax and have fun.

I hadn't been so open myself. A lot of the cops on the force weren't pleased about having a gay man working with them, and I'd learned to keep a low profile. When I mentioned going to the movies, or eating out, it was always with "a friend."

But it was time for me to open up. "Did you ever go out with somebody, and you thought she was really into you, and it turns out you were totally wrong?"

He laughed out loud. "Before Julie? All the time, man." Then he sombered. "That what's got you down? Some guy playing with your head?"

I looked around. There was no one in our immediate area, but voices carry and people are always snooping. After all, that's what we do as homicide cops—we snoop. It's hard to turn that off.

"You want to take a drive?" I asked. "Maybe we can swing by Ala Moana Center, see if the pickpockets are out."

There'd been a problem at the mall, one of the busiest and most profitable in the U.S., and our department was supposed to be on special alert looking for crooks preying on tourists. "Sounds like a plan," he said.

We didn't say anything more until we were in my truck, heading towards the mall. "I met this guy."

"Congratulations. I've been worrying about you. You need to find yourself a man, girlfriend."

I burst out laughing. "You been watching *Queer Eye* reruns?"

"Hey, I'm trying to learn the language."

"Don't worry, I speak straight fluently." I gave Ray a brief, G–rated rundown of what had happened between Javier and me.

"Sounds like you connected."

"I thought so. But he hasn't called me or emailed me since Sunday."

"And you think he's blowing you off."

"Either that, or something happened to him. I mean, if he was just putting on an act and I didn't see through it…."

"I know. Makes you feel like shit." He pulled out his cell phone. "Give me the guy's number."

"What are you going to do?"

"The number?"

I pulled Javier's card out of my wallet. Ray dialed, and listened for a minute. "Voice mail." He dialed information and got the company's main number. "Javier Moreno, please." He listened. "Do you expect him in today?" Another pause. "Oh, okay. Thank you."

He hung up the phone. "Javier has not been in the office all week, and the receptionist's worried."

"Shit."

"Looks like your instincts might be right. Let's skip the mall and head for Javier's apartment."

"I don't want to seem like some kind of stalker. I emailed him a couple of times, I called his office and his apartment."

"If the guy's family's back in Jersey, like you said, no roommate, there's nobody to report him missing except the office, and I think if I'd told the receptionist I was a cop she'd have said something."

I parked my truck in the drop–off zone in front of Javier's building. The neighborhood was a tough one, a cluster of cheap high–rises, convenience stores and industrial buildings. There was a high crime rate, mostly sex and drug–related. I couldn't stop images of Javier from running through my mind—him getting gay–bashed, or picking up the wrong guy, or trying to buy drugs from some shady character on the corner.

"What do you know about this guy?" Ray asked, as we got out of the truck.

"Nothing more than I told you. We talked, but mostly we fucked."

As soon as the words were out of my mouth, I regretted them. I didn't want Ray to get any mental pictures. But he laughed and said, "Been there, done that."

"Not exactly like I did."

"Buddy, it's all the same in the end." We rode the elevator up to Javier's apartment, on the twelfth floor, and as soon as we got close to the apartment I knew something was very wrong.

"He cooking something very stinky," a Japanese lady said, coming down the hallway toward us, and motioning toward Ray's apartment. "I gonna report him to manager."

Ray showed her his ID. "You don't have to bother, ma'am," he said. "We're on the case now. How long have you noticed that smell?"

"Start yesterday." She wrinkled her nose. "He nice guy, but always lots of mens going in and out."

I hoped she didn't recognize me. "You know anyone who has a key to his apartment?" I asked.

"Manager."

It didn't seem worth knocking; Javier Moreno wasn't going to be in any condition to open the door. Ray and I went back to the elevator. "You okay?" he asked.

I thought about it. "Not sure."

"This old high school buddy of mine, back in Philly," he said, as the elevator arrived and we stepped on. "Got himself in trouble—you know the drill. My second year on patrol, I got a call to an address I thought I recognized, back in my old neighborhood. Garage door was open, so we looked inside—and there he was, on the floor, his brains blown out. I stumbled over to the grass, barfed my guts out."

I could feel I was distancing myself from Javier as the elevator fell to the ground. "I'll be okay," I said, because I knew I had to be.

We got the manager to let us in the apartment, holding some tissues over our noses and trying to breathe through our mouths. Javier was in the bedroom, sprawled face down on the sheets where he and I had fucked a few days before. He was naked, and his legs were spread. Next to the bed was a syringe without a needle, a tiny drop of water at the end of the plunger.

"Oh, man," Ray said.

We called the medical examiner's office, and reported in to our dispatcher. We turned the air conditioning up on high, and opened the windows. Neither of us wanted to stay in the bedroom, so we waited in the small living room. There were a few photos on a bookshelf—Javier at his high school graduation, with a couple of friends back in Jersey, a few vacation shots on the family islands. A computer against one wall, programming books piled haphazardly around it.

"I'm assuming the rules are the same in Honolulu as they are in Philly," Ray said. "Department frowns on you investigating the murder of a guy you fucked."

I'd been through this problem before, when I was undercover on the North Shore and a guy I'd had sex with had been killed. At the time, I was the only detective Lieutenant Sampson could trust, and he had no choice but to keep me on the case. But here, I'd be pulled off as soon as I made a statement. And inevitably, word would get around the department, and there would be rumors and gossip and people saying that a gay guy shouldn't be a cop at all.

"Looks to me like a booty bump," Ray continued. "Strictly off the record, did you guys ever…"

I shook my head. There are lots of ways to get crystal meth into the body; one of them, used among gay men, is the booty bump. Meth crystals are poured into a syringe without a needle on the end. Then water is dripped into the syringe to dissolve the crystal. You squirt it up your own ass, or have your partner do it, and in ten to fifteen seconds you're feeling the high. I'd never tried it, but we'd learned about it in drug interdiction cases. "We did a lot of stuff, but no drugs."

"Once the crime scene techs get here, are they going to find your prints?"

I nodded. Ray looked at me. I could see he was considering things in his head. Finally, he said, "I don't see any reason to put the full extent of your relationship with this guy in the file. At least not now. You met him at a bar, you talked about trading MP3s, and when you couldn't get in touch with him, you thought something was wrong. You gave me his number, and I called his office to track him down. The receptionist said he hadn't showed up for work, so you and I decided to check out his apartment."

If I'd had any doubts about Ray Donne before that, they were gone. He trusted me. We weren't going to lie; we were just going to present selected facts. As detectives, we used our judgment like that every day, deciding whose story to believe, which facts to consider and how to interpret them.

By the time the crime scene techs arrived, the air was a little better in the apartment. We set them to the computer area in the living room first, so we could log in ourselves and explore. While they were in the bedroom, jockeying with the ME to collect what they needed, Ray turned on Javier's computer. "I think it's best if I do this," he said.

"I understand." I hovered over his shoulder, though. Windows booted up, and Ray double–clicked on the Microsoft Outlook shortcut. "No password," he said, as the program opened. "Beauty."

"The shoemaker's children always go barefoot," I said.

"Excuse me?"

"It's a saying. When you do something for a living, often you ignore the simplest things in your own life. Like a programmer not securing his email with a password."

The most recent message in the list was dated on Sunday, around eight o'clock, showing us that was the last time he'd downloaded his email. Because I hadn't emailed him until after that, there were no messages from me. A few messages down on the list, a title read "U Free Tonight?"

"Click on that one," I said, pointing.

Jojo28@alohamail.com had written to let Javier know he had some premium coke and a hard dick. "Let's look at the sent mail," I said.

Ray switched folders and found the response Javier had sent, which read, "Bump me, dude! My hole is waiting for u."

Ray right–clicked on the address and brought up Javier's address book listing for Jojo28. Javier kept good records; Jojo's full name was Jose Santilla, and Javier had a cell number for him.

Back at the station, we ran Jose Santilla through the system and found he had a rap sheet for prostitution and drug possession. My buddy Thanh Nguyen in the fingerprint lab matched Santilla's prints to those found on the syringe from Javier's bed. By two o'clock we had a booking photo of Santilla and a warrant for his arrest.

Though Santilla was twenty-nine, from his photograph he was a scrawny guy who looked no older than nineteen. He had no fixed address, but from his rap sheet we could tell he usually hung out in the triangle at the end of Waikīkī, around the area where Javier had lived.

Lieutenant Sampson raised an eyebrow when we presented the story of how we'd come to find Javier's body, but didn't say anything more, and didn't tell me I had to leave the case to Ray.

As we drove toward Waikīkī, Ray asked, "How're you taking all this, Kimo?"

I wasn't happy; I didn't like my personal life entering the station, and I didn't like massaging the truth when it came to my own behavior. But I shrugged and said "I'm taking it."

I slowed down as we crossed the Ala Wai Canal and started scanning the sidewalks. We spotted Jose Santilla, in a tank top and skimpy shorts, lurking against a building near the corner of Niu Street and Ala Wai Boulevard. I pulled the truck over and Ray and I got out.

"How you doing, Jojo?" Ray asked.

Santilla twitched his nose, like a nervous rabbit with a drug habit, and sniffed. "What's it to you?" he asked.

Ray leaned his hand on the wall next to Jojo. "You know, I've got a sixth sense when it comes to the kind of kinky stuff people are into. I look at you, and I think booty bump. How about it, Jojo? That turn you on?"

Jojo took off down Ala Wai Boulevard. Ray and I raced after him, and Ray took him down just before Kuamoʻo Street. "What made you run, Jojo?" Ray asked. He pointed at a glassine bag sticking out of Jojo's waistband. "You got something there you don't want the police to see?"

He turned out to be holding a felony quantity of crystal meth, and his eyes were wide and bloodshot. I thought I'd be angry with him—he'd killed my hot date—but all I felt was sorry for the guy.

We took him downtown, processed him, and put him into the system. There was enough evidence against him to put him in jail for a long time, but I didn't feel particularly good. On my way home, I stopped past the Rod and Reel Club.

Gunter was there, relaxing after his shift as a security guard at a pricey building in a much nicer part of Waikīkī than the one where Javier Moreno had lived. I told him what had happened.

He shook his head. "Like Nancy Reagan always said. Just say no to drugs."

"I was right, you know. Javier and I hit it off. He wasn't just dodging me."

"Kimo," Gunter said. "You had great sex with the guy. That doesn't mean he was going to marry you."

"I know. But we would have had some more sex, I'm sure."

"And would that have been enough for you?"

I shifted uncomfortably on my barstool. "You know what I want, Gunter."

"You want to meet a guy and fall in love at first sight, then pledge to spend the rest of your lives holding hands behind a white picket fence."

"Something like that."

"I hope you find it, Kimo." Then he smiled devilishly. "But I hope you have a lot of hot sex while you're looking."

NEIL PLAKCY is the author of *Mahu, Mahu Surfer, Mahu Fire, Mahu Vice,* and *Mahu Men,* about openly gay Honolulu homicide detective Kimo Kanapa'aka. His other books are *Three Wrong Turns in the Desert, Dancing with the Tide* (2010) and *GayLife.com.* He edited *Paws & Reflect: A Special Bond Between Man and Dog* and the gay erotic anthologies *Hard Hats, Surfer Boys* and *Skater Boys* (2010). His website is www.mahubooks.com.

THE TREVOR PROJECT

The Trevor Project operates the only nationwide, around-the-clock crisis and suicide prevention helpline for lesbian, gay, bisexual, transgender and questioning youth. Every day, The Trevor Project saves lives though its free and confidential helpline, its website and its educational services. If you or a friend are feeling lost or alone call The Trevor Helpline. If you or a friend are feeling lost, alone, confused or in crisis, please call The Trevor Helpline. You'll be able to speak confidentially with a trained counselor 24/7.

The Trevor Helpline: 866-488-7386

On the Web: http://www.thetrevorproject.org/

THE GAY MEN'S DOMESTIC VIOLENCE PROJECT

Founded in 1994, The Gay Men's Domestic Violence Project is a grassroots, non-profit organization founded by a gay male survivor of domestic violence and developed through the strength, contributions and participation of the community. The Gay Men's Domestic Violence Project supports victims and survivors through education, advocacy and direct services. Understanding that the serious public health issue of domestic violence is not gender specific, we serve men in relationships with men, regardless of how they identify, and stand ready to assist them in navigating through abusive relationships.

GMDVP Helpline: 800.832.1901

On the Web: http://gmdvp.org/

THE GAY & LESBIAN ALLIANCE AGAINST DEFAMATION /
GLAAD EN ESPAÑOL

The Gay & Lesbian Alliance Against Defamation (GLAAD) is dedicated to promoting and ensuring fair, accurate and inclusive representation of people and events in the media as a means of eliminating homophobia and discrimination based on gender identity and sexual orientation.

On the Web: http://www.glaad.org/

GLAAD en español:

http://www.glaad.org/espanol/bienvenido.php

SERVICEMEMBERS LEGAL DEFENSE NETWORK

Servicemembers Legal Defense Network is a nonpartisan, nonprofit, legal services, watchdog and policy organization dedicated to ending discrimination against and harassment of military personnel affected by "Don't Ask, Don't Tell" (DADT). The SLDN provides free, confidential legal services to all those impacted by DADT and related discrimination. Since 1993, its inhouse legal team has responded to more than 9,000 requests for assistance. In Congress, it leads the fight to repeal DADT and replace it with a law that ensures equal treatment for every servicemember, regardless of sexual orientation. In the courts, it works to challenge the constitutionality of DADT.

SLDN
PO Box 65301
Washington DC 20035-5301
On the Web: http://sldn.org/

Call: (202) 328-3244
or (202) 328-FAIR
e-mail: sldn@sldn.org

THE GLBT NATIONAL HELP CENTER

The GLBT National Help Center is a nonprofit, tax-exempt organization that is dedicated to meeting the needs of the gay, lesbian, bisexual and transgender community and those questioning their sexual orientation and gender identity. It is an outgrowth of the Gay & Lesbian National Hotline, which began in 1996 and now is a primary program of The GLBT National Help Center. It offers several different programs including two national hotlines that help members of the GLBT community talk about the important issues that they are facing in their lives. It helps end the isolation that many people feel, by providing a safe environment on the phone or via the internet to discuss issues that people can't talk about anywhere else. The GLBT National Help Center also helps other organizations build the infrastructure they need to provide strong support to our community at the local level.

National Hotline: 1-888-THE-GLNH (1-888-843-4564)
National Youth Talkline 1-800-246-PRIDE (1-800-246-7743)
On the Web: http://www.glnh.org/
e-mail: info@glbtnationalhelpcenter.org

If you're a GLBT and questioning student heading off to university, should know that there are resources on campus for you. Here's just a sample:

US Local GLBT college campus organizations
        http://dv-8.com/resources/us/local/campus.html
GLBT Scholarship Resources
        http://tinyurl.com/6fx9v6
Syracuse University
        http://lgbt.syr.edu/
Texas A&M
        http://glbt.tamu.edu/
Tulane University
        http://www.oma.tulane.edu/LGBT/Default.htm
University of Alaska
        http://www.uaf.edu/agla/
University of California, Davis
        http://lgbtrc.ucdavis.edu/
University of California, San Francisco
        http://lgbt.ucsf.edu/
University of Colorado
        http://www.colorado.edu/glbtrc/
University of Florida
        http://www.dso.ufl.edu/multicultural/lgbt/
University of Hawai'i, Mānoa
        http://manoa.hawaii.edu/lgbt/
University of Utah
        http://www.sa.utah.edu/lgbt/
University of Virginia
        http://www.virginia.edu/deanofstudents/lgbt/
Vanderbilt University
        http://www.vanderbilt.edu/lgbtqi/

Stimulate yourself.
READ.
www.manloveromance.com
THE HOTTEST M/M EROTIC AUTHORS & WEBSITES ON THE NET

Breinigsville, PA USA
21 December 2010
251874BV00001B/9/P